PROTECTION & SECURITY
PASS
SERVICES

I0732806

PRAISE FOR FREYA BARKER

Freya Barker writes a mean romance, I tell you! A REAL romance, with real characters and real conflict.

~Author M. Lynne Cunning

I've said it before and I'll say it again and again, Freya Barker is one of the BEST storytellers out there.

~Turning Pages At MidnightBook Blog

God, Freya Barker gets me every time I read one of her books. She's a master at creating a beautiful story that you lose yourself in the moment you start reading.

~Britt Red Hatter Book Blog

Freya Barker has woven a delicate balance of honest emotions and well-formed characters into a tale that is as unique as it is gripping.

~Ginger Scott, bestselling young and new adult author and Goodreads Choice Awards finalist

Such a truly beautiful story! The writing is gorgeous, the scenery is beautiful...

~Author Tia Louise

From Dust by Freya Barker is one of those special books. One of those whose plotline and characters remain with you for days after you finished it.

~Jeri's Book Attic

No amount of words could describe how this story made me feel, I think this is one I will remember forever, absolutely freaking awesome is not even close to how I felt about it.

~Lilian's Book Blog

Still Air was insightful, eye-opening, and I paused numerous times to think about my relationships with my own children. Anytime a book can evoke a myriad of emotions while teaching life lessons you'll continue to carry with you, it's a 5-star read.

~ Bestselling Author CP Smith

In my opinion, there is nothing better than a Freya Barker book. With her final installment in her Portland, ME series, Still Air, she does not disappoint. From start to finish I was completely captivated by Pam, Dino, and the entire Portland family.

~ Author RB Hilliard

The one thing you can always be sure of with Freya's writing is that it will pull on ALL of your emotions; it's expressive, meaningful, sarcastic, so very true to life, real, hard-hitting and heartbreaking at times and, as is the case with this series especially, the story is at points raw, painful and occasionally fugly BUT it is also sweet, hopeful, uplifting, humorous and heart-warming.

~ Book Loving Pixies

ALSO BY FREYA BARKER

ON CALL SERIES

BURNING FOR AUTUMN
COVERING OLLIE

ROCK POINT SERIES

KEEPING 6
CABIN 12
HWY 550
10-CODE

NORTHERN LIGHTS COLLECTION

A CHANGE OF TIDE
A CHANGE OF VIEW
A CHANGE OF PACE

SNAPSHOT SERIES

SHUTTER SPEED
FREEZE FRAME
IDEAL IMAGE

PORTLAND, ME, NOVELS

FROM DUST
CRUEL WATER
THROUGH FIRE
STILL AIR

LuLLaY
(a Christmas novella)

CEDAR TREE SERIES

SLIM TO NONE
HUNDRED TO ONE
AGAINST ME
CLEAN LINES
UPPER HAND
LIKE ARROWS
HEAD START

FREYA BARKER

HIT & RUN

PASS Series

ISBN: 978-1-988733-40-1

Cover Design: RE&D - Margreet Asselbergs

Editing: Karen Hrdlicka

Proofing: Joanne Thompson

Interior Design: CP Smith

ACKNOWLEDGMENTS

Time to show my love and appreciation to the usual suspects;
My agent, Stephanie Phillips of SBR Media, who was the driving force behind me writing Hit&Run.

My editor, Karen Hrdlicka, and alpha reader and proofreader, Joanne Thompson, who as always held my hand.

My publicists, Debra Presley and Drue Hoffman of Buoni Amici Press, who start working on promotion and marketing months in advance.

My amazing formatter, CP Smith, who turns my ratty manuscripts into little pieces of art.

My awesome beta team who share their welcome opinions and offer suggestions.

The fabulous blogs and early reviewers who help get the word about my books to you.

And of course you, my readers, who are my motivation, my drive, and my gratification.

A mountain of gratitude to you all.

Lots of love!

CHAPTER 1

"YOU LOOK LIKE you could do with a trip to the spa and a tub of concealer."

I glare at who I thought was my best friend, as he takes in my appearance with a snicker. Granted, if I look half as rough as I feel, after battling this yucky cold all week, he may have a point. But he doesn't have to rub it in.

"You're mean," I grumble, dragging two large garbage bags through the lobby to the front desk where he is laughing at me.

"Just telling it as it is, girlfriend," he drawls, doing that side to side snake thing with his head. "Keeping it real."

I snort at that, taking in his carefully waxed eyebrows and newly extended eyelashes. Grant Peabody—an incongruently pompous name that doesn't fit the massive black man—is as artificial as they come. Real? My ass.

Shaking my head at his deep chuckle, I choose not

to take the bait, and instead redirect the conversation to the buzz that has been filling the hotel the past few weeks.

"So? Have you met him yet?"

The *him* I'm referring to is the outrageously sexy, daytime-gone-big-screen actor, Kyle Steele, who along with his entourage, has taken over the top two floors of the Spring Ridge Suites. They are filming a movie in and around Grand Junction and picked our hotel for their base. Of course that comes with some annoyances. Like having our personnel parking lot reallocated for their use, while we are relegated to the public parking lot, or the horny fans digging through the towels and sheets in the laundry room in the basement at all hours of the night. Not to mention the trays upon trays of room service leftovers shoved outside almost every door on the top two floors.

Even so, the thrill of having bona fide film people—crew, producers, directors, and best of all, actors—roaming our hotel, is admittedly kind of fun. Especially after discovering I share my immature crush on the star actor with my friend, Grant. Ever since admitting that to each other, he and I have a running bet on who's going to meet him first. Since both of us work the nightshift, we've struck out so far. Hell, one of the reasons I give the hotel gym such a thorough scrubbing every night is because I harbor fantasies of Kyle Steele walking in for a midnight run on the treadmill. So far, no luck on that, clearly, because who would willingly exercise in the middle of the night? From what I hear from the hotel grapevine, the guy is an asshole in reality. Still, it's my fantasy and I haven't given up hope yet.

"I did," Grant says smugly.

"You did not!" I lean over the counter to punch his solid shoulder, only to shake out my fist from the painful impact.

"He walked up to me, smiled—oh God, you should see his smile, it's to die for—and held out his hand for me to shake. I touched him, Rosie, and it was electric."

My mouth falls open in shock, but Grant clearly can't keep up the ruse because he starts laughing, and I almost make the mistake of hitting him again. Instead I growl, bend down, and pick up my garbage bags.

"Just kidding, Rosebud. All I did was catch a glimpse of him heading into the bar."

If asked, I will deny with my dying breath that I actually performed an internal fist pump hearing that. Catching glimpses is not *meeting* someone, which means I still have my fantasy. It's the little things that give my life some color, even if it is a childish bet.

"Not nice, Grant. Not nice," I admonish him before heading for the back door.

These past eight months, since moving back to Grand Junction, haven't been a cakewalk. Looking after a mother with Alzheimer's that's progressed to a point where she can't take care of herself anymore is a challenge. Especially when you weren't on the best of terms to begin with. I hate to admit it, but her rapid descent into dementia is almost a blessing. Most of the time she can't remember who I am, which means she also can't remember how much of a disappointment I've been to her. Something she used to remind me of any time I fulfilled my daughterly duties and checked in on her.

After my father died too young from a massive heart attack when I was twenty, I tried hard to fill the hole he left behind in her life, but whatever I did was never enough. How could it be, when I was the reason he died in the first place? At least that's what Mom liked to point out to me at every turn. Eventually, I gave up, but it was still seven years of listening to her tell me how my father would be turning in his grave if he knew I never took the Colorado Mesa University scholarship, before I packed up what little I had accumulated and hit the road. I never wanted to go to school locally, I had my mind set on NYU, which is what our last argument had been about. It took me seven years to rediscover my determination, and follow my own path, and set out for New York. That was fifteen years ago, and sadly, I never made it farther than Denver.

So yeah, I don't miss Mom's scathing tongue, but

I hate seeing the confusion in her eyes those moments when a random memory surfaces, dragging her back to a reality she no longer recognizes.

When I received a phone call from one of Mom's neighbors eight months ago, letting me know she'd gone to check on Mom and found her in the tub sitting in ice-cold water because she couldn't remember how to get out, I knew it was time to step in. My mother had warded off any kind of involvement on my part over the years, and other than checking in on her from time to time by phone, I'd respected those boundaries. Until now.

Clearly she was no longer able to look after herself and it was time to put the hurt behind me and come home. I'm ashamed to say I had no idea how bad things had gotten. Not just healthwise, but financially as well.

It was surprisingly easy to let go of my life in Denver. Sad, really, after setting out all those years ago with big plans. I sold the small condo I didn't love anyway, gave my two weeks' notice for a job I hadn't particularly enjoyed doing, and I said goodbye to a man I would never have, despite his promises.

Before I knew it, I'd moved back, living in a double-wide trailer with my mother.

"Let me take those bags," Grant offers, as I struggle to open the side door with my hands full.

"If you can just get the door. I'm heading out anyway. I have a hot shower and a soft bed waiting for me."

"I have a hot guy and a hard ride waiting for me," he counters.

"Nobody likes a bragger," I admonish him, but I can't help smile when I see the massive grin splitting his face.

For two weeks, ever since those movie people settled into the hotel, he's been eyeing one of the cameramen. A nice guy: mid-to-late twenties, with a blond shock of hair, pretty blue eyes, and a shy smile. While he's been eyeing blondie, I've done my best to catch a glimpse of one of the security guys I've see a few times. Dark, rough, and dangerous; the proverbial bad boy and very different from Grant's fresh-faced pretty boy. How my somewhat threateningly large, black friend managed to charm the much younger kid, I have no idea, but apparently they went out for 'drinks' the other night.

I, on the other hand, have no such luck and Mr. Dark and Dangerous has stayed well on the sidelines of my social life. Truthfully, I never really had much of one, even when I was still living in Denver, but these days I'm a bona fide spinster at only forty-two. I can't even remember the last time I rode anything hard, let alone a hot guy. Who has the time? Between working nightshifts in housekeeping at the Spring Ridge Suites and days looking after my mother, the only interaction with the opposite sex I have is with my buddy, Grant, the very gay night clerk manning the hotel's front desk. Not exactly conducive to any kind of social existence, not to mention sex life.

Grant holds open the door, so I can wrestle through toting the industrial-sized garbage bags, but holds me back by the arm at the last minute.

"We still on for lunch on Tuesday?"

Grant and I mostly work the same shift on the same days. Mondays and Tuesdays are our weekends, and for the past six months or so, we've taken my mother to lunch at the Golden Corral every week. Such is the sum of my weekly excitement.

"You bring the wet wipes," I joke in confirmation.

The reason we choose the Golden Corral is because being a family restaurant, its clientele is very forgiving. They're used to food flinging, drooling, and spitting kids, so my mother, who often resorts to the same antics these days, doesn't stand out like a sore thumb. We tried other places, but having to apologize constantly wreaks havoc on the appetite. The staff at the Golden Corral is familiar with us and shows our odd trio to the same table in the far corner—where we are out of the way and can do little harm—every Tuesday.

The outside air is crisp for the season. It's only just after four in the morning, and unlike most people, I go into work when it's still light out, and head home in the dark of night. Come winter, it'll be dark on both ends of my shift, making my days even longer and more tedious.

I breathe in deep, ignoring the pungent odor coming from the dumpsters at the edge of the parking lot. One of these days, when I can get Hillary—the nurse who looks after Mom overnight—to stay a few extra hours, I'd love to go for a hike in McInnis Canyon Conservation Area. It's been at least fifteen, maybe even twenty, years since I've been up there. When I lived in Denver, I used to head out into the mountains regularly to hike one of the many trails, it's the one form of exercise I truly enjoy. These days the only exercise my body gets is at work from scrubbing toilets, or at home from lifting my mother. Neither of which includes the fresh air I crave so much.

The containers are enclosed with fencing and the gate is locked with a keyless numeric padlock. I punch in the code and hear the noisy scramble of a few of the resident raccoons, when I pull the gate open. It's not unusual to open one of the containers to have a pair of eyes staring up at you. I'm too short to lift the lid though, and have to climb onto the frame at the bottom of the fence to reach.

I'm just lifting the heavy cover when a loud crash startles me, along with the rev of an engine. From my vantage point, I can look over the enclosure to see down the alley on the other side of the road. An expensive-looking car is backing away from a pile of garbage stacked next to a dumpster, in the back of one of the restaurants on the next block. I don't think too much of it and return my attention to the two bags I hauled out here, throwing the first one over the side of the bin. Another look in the direction of the car shows it moving erratically down the far alley, almost veering into another trash receptacle, before it crosses right into Third Avenue. Luckily, at this time of the morning, there is no traffic.

The lid of the container is getting heavy, so I quickly toss in the last bag and close it. I step out to shut the gate, and barely miss getting hit by the black luxury sports car heading straight for me. My front is plastered against the fencing as I turn my head and watch the car go by and pull into the small parking lot beyond, which has been sectioned off for the film crew.

It was fast, and the glass was tinted, but I'm pretty sure I recognized the guy behind the wheel. It's hard not to when we were just talking about him. Anger gets rid of any remaining hopes or fantasies I might have had, and I'm left shaking and upset. Despite the fact I'd love to give the self-righteous prick a piece of my mind, it might well cost me my job, so instead I turn resolutely in the opposite direction where my 2001, ugly-ass, wood-paneled and rusted-out PT Cruiser is parked in the public lot.

My hot bath and soft bed are waiting.

JAKE

"Hutch, did you find him?"

I grind my teeth at my boss's voice.

Fuck.

Should've known better than to check with Dimi if he'd seen the asshole leave. First thing he did was probably call his brother. I get this is a make or break contract for PASS, the security company I work for, but I didn't exactly sign on to hold the hand of a spoiled, arrogant prick intent on self-destruction. Three tours in Iraq didn't exactly prepare me for babysitting duty.

Sadly, Kyle Steele is not only an actor, but he's also co-producer and therefore someone to keep happy. That means I constantly have to handle the man with kid gloves, when I really just want to rip him a new one. He seems intent on making my job difficult, which in turn makes my boss very nervous. I'd wrongfully assumed the trouble might come from groupies and rabid fans, following their favorite actor around, but the bigger threat to the production is its own damn star.

PASS stands for Protection And Security Services, a company owned by Yanis Mazur, older of the two Mazur brothers. I grew up with these guys, was best friends with Dimas, the younger of the two, and even enlisted with him when we were barely eighteen. Dimi was injured during our second tour in Iraq and lost his left leg below the knee. Something Yanis to this day holds me responsible for. I can't really blame him, after all, I was a bit of a self-destructive asshole myself at the time, and I had no qualms dragging my friend along with me. Dimi would never have signed up for that second tour if not for me.

I ended up signing on for a third and did my best to alleviate my guilt by volunteering for the riskiest goddamn missions, but as irony would have it, I walked away unscathed from each and every one of them. Not a fucking scratch. Back stateside, I'd had a hard time adjusting and drifted for a while, made a decent living as muscle for hire, until Dimi tracked me down. He read me the riot act, and I let him talk me into joining his brother's security company.

PASS mostly handles short-term contracts and individual assignments. Often referrals from GFI—Gus Flemming Investigations—but after that company moved their headquarters to Cedar Tree a few years ago, our less-established business had suffered.

This contract with Guild Film Productions means long-term work for every single PASS operative. A considerable benefit is this job will add to the company's credibility; solidify the PASS name in the business, which is why Yanis is on my case and why I'm trying hard not to lose my shit on the asshole I am assigned to.

"Not yet. Working on it. We should sit his ass down when I get my hands on him. Maybe call in Drexler?" I suggest, referring to Phil Drexler, who is the big dog at Guild and might be able to lean hard on his prize pony.

"Track him down first," Yanis barks. "Not about to admit to Drexler we can't keep their pretty boy leashed. Call me when you have him."

Sure, let me get right fucking on that.

First place I checked when I found Kyle gone was the hotel bar, but it closed at two and the bartender had already left. The night clerk, a big black dude, remembered seeing Kyle enter the bar sometime around one, but couldn't recall seeing him leave. A quick check of the parking lot showed his black Lexus LC gone. That's when I touched base with Dimi, who mans the hotel surveillance room, working with in-house security. He hadn't seen him leave either.

My frustration only growing after having Yanis dress me down, I tuck my phone in my pocket, check the suite one more time, and then head down, taking the stairs. Just as I step into the lobby, one of the maids—the tired-looking redhead I've seen around—gets off the elevator, carrying two garbage bags, and heads straight for the front desk. I watch for a moment as she chats up the night clerk, before I slip out to the parking lot.

It's after fucking four o'clock in the morning, I've barely slept, and I've already run out of patience. Starting my truck, I pull out of the lot and turn down Third Street, toward the railroad.

The newly updated hotel is right in the middle of historic downtown Grand Junction, with a small back parking lot reserved for the production. The film crew picked the Spring Ridge Suites in Grand Junction to stay at while they focus on some inside scenes after two weeks of filming outside. The movie they're shooting is called *Basics*, some post-apocalyptic survivalist tale, most of which is being filmed in the

McInnis Canyon National Conservation Area. For the inside work, they rented an old warehouse, just at the base of Third Street, with use of the rail yards behind it as well. That's where I'm heading.

The rundown building is owned by a developer, who by all accounts, is waiting for the appropriate permits before turning the place into high-end lofts. He saw dollar signs when Guild Film Productions showed interest in the place, and since construction was held up for the time being, he wasted no time signing on the dotted line of the short-term—and very lucrative—rental contract.

The place looks deserted. No cars, no lights. I drive around the back to the railroad yard, which looks to be abandoned as well. No luxury cars and no activity at all.

"Yeah," I answer my phone when it rings. It's Dimi.

"Your detail just stumbled into the lobby. Dude's wasted. Where are you?"

"Heading back. Keep your eye on him."

"Ten-four."

It takes me two minutes to get back to the hotel parking lot, where I easily locate Steele's Lexus. It's almost parked fucking sideways, across two accessible parking spots. *Figures.* From my vantage point, it almost looks like he rammed the bumper into the production trailer parked in the next spot. I park the truck and walk over to check it out.

The Lexus isn't touching the trailer, but the front

end looks damaged. Nothing on the trailer, though, so I don't think that's what was hit. *Fuck.* I don't exactly have a good feeling about this.

***

"Exhausted…can't talk…"

I roll my eyes at the theatrics of the grown-ass man rolling on the bed. Exhausted—my ass. Drunk out of his mind is more like it. It takes everything out of me not to wake him up with my fist in his face. I don't have time to play games.

"Keep your goddamn eyes open, or I swear I'll dunk your ass in an ice bath. I need to know where you were and why there is damage to the front end of your car. Were you in an accident?"

"F–fever titty-bar. F–fuck me, that Brandi could pull the dollar bills from my fingers with her pussy lips. Ne'er seen anything like it," he snickers, slurring his words.

"What about the car?" I prompt him.

"Dunno."

That's the last word I manage to drag out of him before he passes out cold. I roll him on his side, just in case he pukes during the night—it wouldn't do to have my charge end up choking on vomit—and back out of the room, making a note to check the Fever Gentlemen's Club on the west side of town.

I'm not getting paid enough.

CHAPTER 2

ROSIE

"*I*'M NOT HUNGRY."

I'm on my knees, trying to pull my mother's support stockings back up after she, once again, stripped them down her swollen legs. A dance we engage in all too often. Just like the back-and-forth we do every time we have to leave the house. Of all the things Mom might have forgotten; who I am, day of the week, or even her own name at times, she never forgets how to be stubborn.

"Grant is waiting for us, Mom," I try, hoping today she'll remember who Grant is, but the blank look in her eyes tells me she doesn't have a clue.

Luckily, Grant is a master at charming my mother. When I finally get her dressed, out the door, and over to the restaurant, he's there waiting with his disarming smile and endless patience. My mother shrinks back when she sees his large, looming body, an involuntary response to a nonexistent threat. Grant doesn't fault her for that, which endears him even more to me. He instead ignores the fact she clearly doesn't recognize him today and gently coaxes her to her chair, while updating her on this week's headlines from the gossip rags.

My mother and Grant share a passion for movies and for the *National Enquirer*.

"Come sit by me, Connie," Grant coos, never letting go of my mother's small, bony hand in his massive paw. The man is exceedingly gentle for his size. "Did you hear they're remaking *Murder On The Orient Express*? The lineup of actors is unbelievable…" I listen to him prattle on, slowly engaging Mom, for which I'm grateful.

Most days I feel like I'm carrying the weight of the world on my shoulders, the sense that I can never take my eyes off the ball or my precariously balanced life collapses. The only time I feel true relief is during our standing lunch date at the Golden Corral with Grant.

I catch his wink over Mom's head. He knows.

Mom, like a lot of folks suffering from Alzheimer's, more frequently will mentally revert back decades, easily remembering people, events, thoughts, feelings from her youth, but is at times unable to recall her own daughter's name. That's tough, when, despite the less than stellar relationship I had with her, she's all I have. Except now I have Grant too.

I never was very good at making friends. I'm not sure why that is. Maybe because I tend to live inside my head? I guess I'm outwardly quiet, even though inside my head it's never silent. I sometimes simply forget to say things out loud. It makes me seem demure, or boring, even when I'm not. Not really.

Grant never appeared to notice my relative silence to his nonstop banter. From the moment we met, he was determined for us to become friends, even though we are the most mismatched pair there ever was. His size, his bubbling personality, his deep ebony skin, and his ready smile stands in stark contrast to my short, stocky body, red hair—complete with pale skin and freckles—and my pensive nature. You'd think I'd have the cheerful smile and he'd be the brooder of the two. Not so.

It didn't take Grant much time to drag me out of my shell, at least with him. In the almost eight months I've known him, he has fast become the best friend I've ever had. This is why I can sit back and let my mind empty, while he looks after my mother, and therefore me. I trust him.

"…When are you going to make an honest woman of her?"

My head whips around as my mother's words drag me out of my daydreams. I can tell from the sharp look in her eyes that she's present in the moment. Her awareness comes and goes, with the pendulum swinging more and more toward the going.

"Mom! We're just friends." I glare at Grant who can't keep a straight face.

"You wound me," he quips, dramatically grabbing for his chest.

"See?" Mom jumps in. "You're forty-two years old, overweight, without any education to speak of, and the only work you can find is cleaning toilets. You should consider yourself lucky."

I close my eyes tightly, reining in the equal feelings of anger and inadequacy my ruthlessly sane mother invokes. It doesn't help every word she uttered is the truth. Perhaps not all of it, the fact I didn't get to college doesn't mean I'm uneducated, and my job in housekeeping is not the only one I can find, but it's the only one that allows me to look after her during the day. But I don't say that out loud. Why would I? By the time I'm done defending myself, my mother will have disappeared again, lost in the maze of her memories. The only reason her words still have the ability to wound me is because those rare moments of brutal lucidity in her otherwise permanently clouded mind surprise me.

"Au contraire, ma belle," Grant addresses her, interjecting on my behalf with his rich Cajun heritage shining through. "I should be so lucky. Your daughter is smart, funny, and stunning, but she's a girl and I like boys." He smiles at Mom, but I can tell she's already lost the thread.

"See you tomorrow night?" he says, closing the car door after having buckled my mother into the passenger seat. My shifts start at eight, he doesn't work until nine, but I make it a habit to stop by the front desk on my break.

"You will."

With a wink and a wave, he turns and I get behind the wheel, my mind already on getting Mom down for her nap and finishing up the loads of laundry before the workweek starts again.

⌒

"Hey."

I look up from the pile of laundry I'm folding on the kitchen table when Hillary walks in.

Hillary Glenwood is my savior. I met her the day I returned to Grand Junction and walked into the emergency room at St. Mary's Medical Center, where they had taken my mother after she was found by the neighbor. The young woman calmly directed me to the ward where they'd kept her for observation, since she was hypothermic and clearly very confused. She'd checked up on us when her shift was over and found me overwhelmed and quietly crying by Mom's bedside. With Mom fast asleep, Hillary had resolutely walked me to the cafeteria where she made me eat the first meal I'd had all day.

She helped me get a handle on what to expect in terms of Mom's needs and her care. There'd been so much I didn't know, but Hillary didn't give me time to feel guilty. In the days that followed, she helped me connect with the right people to discuss my mother's care. When it became clear Mom needed someone around twenty-four hours a day, she made me an offer I couldn't refuse. For half of what I would have to pay for daytime help, Hillary would stay with Mom overnight, five nights of the week. She needed the additional income to finish paying off student loans. It worked for everyone.

"Hey," I respond, smiling.

"How was your weekend?" She sets her bag on the kitchen counter and turns to face me.

"Relatively uneventful. She was good enough on Monday to play a game of cards, after we finished her exercises, and yesterday at lunch with Grant, she had a moment of clarity, but other than that she's been quiet. Sleeping a lot."

"Have you seen any improvement in her tremors?" Hillary asks. Just two weeks ago, she was started on a new medication that's supposed to minimize her disabling tremors.

"Not really," I grudgingly admit. "She insisted on drinking tea from a mug, but even with my help, ended up wearing most of it, so we reverted back to her sippy cup."

"I'm sorry," she commiserates, but I wave her off.

"Meh, such is reality. On a more exciting note," I tease her, smirking. "How was your date with Dr. McDreamy? Or was it McSteamy? I can't seem to keep them straight." Hillary rolls her eyes, but I can see the smile pulling on her mouth. That's a good thing, I'm guessing.

"Well, during dinner he started off as McDreamy…" she drawls, fanning herself with her hand as she drops down in the chair across from me,

"…but he totally morphed into McSteamy after he drove me home."

"Way to go, Hill," I encourage, leaning over and slapping her a high five.

I'm happy for her, after a few, short, failed relationships and a string of disastrous dates, Hillary deserves to find a good guy. One who appreciates her. At thirty-two, she's ten years younger, but a lot more discerning and aware of her self-worth than I was. Or am. She doesn't need a man; she wants one. There's a huge difference.

I thought I needed one and let myself fall for the first handsome smile and sparkling eyes that came along. Even if it was in the form of my boss: my very married boss.

Don't judge me. I had no idea. I was twenty-seven and just out on my own for the first time. An innocent with dreams to study psychology at NYU. My first stop had been Denver, when my car irrevocably broke down, and my meager savings were quickly decimated by lodging and food. I'd walked into a temp agency, working as a receptionist that afternoon, and fell for my new boss within the week. There were no pictures in his office, no indications of a life outside of work, and I was too naïve to look beyond the boyish charm and exciting flirting he drew me in with. I almost left when I discovered he had a family: a wife and two kids. He swore he only stayed in the marriage because of the kids, that there was nothing left between his wife and him. He promised me I was the only one he loved, and I bought it. Hook, line, and sinker. Not something I'm particularly proud of.

I can admit now that I was willingly gullible. It's amazing what a few flattering words and some well-timed attention can do for an insecure and fragile ego.

Excuses, all of them. The truth is it was easier to be weak and stuck in a reality of someone else's making, than it was—is—to stand on your own without a safety net and risk discovering you are not even a fraction of the person you imagine yourself to be in your mind. So I stayed, eventually learning all the empty promises were just that; nothing would change.

The call from Dora Shipman, Mom's neighbor, had been a bucket of ice water, a healthy dose of reality.

"He says he'll take me to his cabin near Moab one of these weekends."

Hillary's voice drags me from my thoughts and I smile, listening to her wax poetic about her tall, blond Adonis, ignoring the pang of jealousy at the hopeful glow on her cheeks.

"Make sure you check him out first, okay?" I caution her. A date or even a one-night stand is one thing, but the promise of a weekend away deserves closer scrutiny. Safety first.

"Of course." She rolls her eyes, and I suddenly feel a hundred years old.

"I'm happy for you." I smile and give her shoulder a squeeze when I stand up and move past her to put away the laundry.

It's time to get ready for work.

JAKE

"You don't need to hold my hand, you know?"

It's been a rough fucking couple of days already, and the last thing I need at this point is his prima donna attitude.

"Just get in the elevator, Steele."

"I just don't get why I can't drive myself to the warehouse."

I swing around and plant the flat of my hand in the middle of his chest.

"Then let me refresh your memory. You got wasted Sunday night in a fucking strip club, flinging your name around when the bartender tried to take your keys from you. You ended up driving while under the influence and somehow, somewhere, you ran into something. Your damn car is in the shop, and I wouldn't trust you with a tricycle at this point, so suck it the fuck up."

"You can't talk to me that way," he blusters, getting in my face, his cheeks flushed in anger. "I could fire you."

I don't flinch, even as the spittle flies from his lips. I just stare him down, unblinking, until he eventually starts fidgeting. That's when I respond. "For the record, you can't fire me since your name isn't on our contract. That would be Phil Drexler, so if you have a problem with the way I do my job, take it up with him."

Without another word, I turn and step into the elevator, a distinctly more demure Kyle following me. Good. I would've tossed his ass in there otherwise. When Dimas called a few minutes ago to tell me to get Steele the fuck out of the hotel and to the warehouse, I didn't stop to ask questions. I'll get the answers eventually.

It was just two days ago the idiot was still sleeping off his bender in his room, while I met up with Yanis in the small coffee shop in the hotel lobby to give him an update.

"Where was he?" Yanis asked, before my ass even hit the chair across from him.

"Fever. That place off the 70 on the west side? According to the bartender—who, by the way, was not too impressed with the early morning interruption— Steele came in just before two in the morning, already half in the bag, and made short work of getting in the rest of the way. The guy tried and failed to convince Steele to take a cab. He said, normally he'd have called the cops on him, but Steele threatened the club with a lawsuit. Not wanting to get in trouble with his boss, the guy let him go."

"Is he gonna keep his trap shut? Can we suppress this without alerting Drexler?"

"That depends."

I explained about the damage to the Lexus and that Steele had no recollection of what he may have hit. I informed him that, since before the sun came up, the car was at the mechanic we occasionally use when we need discretion. Other than Dimi watching the monitors, no one had seen Steele come back into the hotel. According to the security monitors, the night clerk had been in the bathroom at the time.

"We may appear to be in the clear, but there are a shit-ton of variables that are unknown or unaccounted for—like the busted fucking front end of his car—so we best not get too comfortable. Not yet."

Yanis agreed to hold off alerting the big honchos at Guild Film Productions until I had some more information.

"Update me the minute you have something."

Later that afternoon, I questioned Kyle again, after pouring a gallon of coffee down his gullet, and he remembered hitting a dumpster. That was a relief, and rather than rustling the bushes, drawing more attention, I opted to lay low and keep my ear to the ground. My charge however, had other ideas.

I was in the surveillance room, talking with Dimi, when I spotted one of the baristas from the coffee shop sneaking out of Steele's suite, still buttoning up her goddamn shirt. So much for studying lines. Dimi kept me from charging upstairs for an ugly showdown with the stupid son of a bitch. Instead we intercepted the young girl, escorted her to the monitoring room, and proceeded to scare the living shit out of her. Dimi checked her phone for incriminating pictures or messages, while I had her sign a non-disclosure form and sent her on her way with a pile of cash, enough to pay off her student loans. I stayed out of Steele's way the rest of yesterday.

I fucking hate this assignment.

The moment the elevator hits the lobby and we get out, I can feel a charge in the air. Something is going on. Not that there is anything visible, but the hair on the back of my neck stands on end. My eyes scan the lobby, but other than a few people at the front desk going about their business, there is nothing obvious.

Yet as soon as we step out the service door in the back and turn to the parking lot, I see it. Flashing lights from at least six police and first responder vehicles down the alley on the other side of Third Street. An officer is cordoning off access and exit to the alley with yellow tape and looks this way. I pretend not to notice, but Steele is gawking, so I yank on his arm and march him to my truck.

"What's going on?" he wants to know, and I shake my head sharply by way of response. I'm focused on getting us out of here as instructed.

Instead of driving out to Third Street, like I normally would, I turn down the narrow alley that takes me to Main Street. There I turn west, avoiding

Third Street altogether, as I take an alternate route to the warehouse. I don't know what the fuck is going on, but I know it's not good.

Dimas is already waiting outside and motions for us to follow him to a service door around the side of the building.

"What's going on?" Kyle asks again, but before I have a chance to shut him up, Dimi has him up against a wall, a forearm cutting off his air.

"That was you, wasn't it?" he spits in Steele's terrified face.

"Dimi…" I try to get his attention, but he is on a roll.

"You self-centered fuck! You don't care how much havoc you wreak as long as you get what you want—am I right?"

"Dimi," I call out a little firmer, putting a restraining hand on his shoulder, but still he won't let go. Steele's eyes are bulging out of his face.

"Fuck. Dimas!" I finally yell, wrapping my arms around him from behind and wrestling him off the guy, who collapses, gasping for air.

"What the fuck is going on?" Yanis storms into the empty storage space and casts one look at Steele's crumpled form before turning his focus on us. "Anyone?" he bellows.

It takes his brother only two minutes to fill us in, and then all three of us turn our glares on the man on the floor.

"We need to be sharp," Yanis finally announces.

"Get hotel surveillance video from one to five early Monday morning, ASAP," he starts barking out orders. "And go over it frame-by-frame. Tag anyone you spot by time and location, and call the office the minute you've got something so Radar can pull as much background info he can get his hands on. I'll get Bree to put out her feelers with our contacts in the police department. We need to know where they are at all times. No time to waste."

I don't bother answering and neither does Dimi. This is what Yanis is good at, damage control and delegating. We all have our roles within PASS, Dimi and I are more hands on than, for instance, Radar or Bree, who spend most of their time in the office. Radar is a former hacker, now our resident techie, and Bree has a background in social work and focuses on behavioral analysis and liaising with authorities when needed.

I lift my chin in acknowledgment and with one last pointed look, Yanis heads for the door, where he turns around, his hand on the knob.

"You—" he barks at Steele, who in the meantime has scrambled to his feet, his face white as a sheet. "You're coming with me. I'll let you explain to Drexler how you managed to put a sixty-five million dollar project at risk."

"I remember seeing her." I point at the screen where

Dimi just spotted the redhead dragging her garbage bags to the front desk.

"Rosie Perkins, forty-two," Dimi says, scrolling through the personnel files. "Assigned to housekeeping and on nightshift per request, according to her file. Hasn't been here quite a year, and from what I can see in the note, doesn't have a blemish to her name."

"Rosie short for something?"

Dimi turns his head slowly away from the screen and eyes me with one eyebrow raised. "Come again?"

"Rosie—is that her full name? Not Rosanne, or Rosalind, or something like that?"

"It just says Rosie. Why?"

I shrug, not quite sure myself why that seems important, but something about the woman nags at me.

"She was chatting with the front desk clerk that night. I talked to him when I was trying to find Steele, but I never checked with her. I probably should."

"She's off Mondays and Tuesdays. Her next shift starts at eight tonight," he informs me.

"Good. I'll catch her when she gets here."

CHAPTER 3

JAKE

"Hey."

Her eyes grow big in her small face, as she swings around at my voice, and presses her back into that ugly as shit rust bucket she drives. When I approach, her hand comes up and slaps against her chest, right where the skin shows over her V-neck shirt. My eyes are automatically drawn to the dusting of freckles over her generous cleavage. It takes effort to lift my gaze up to meet the fear swimming in hers. She casts a quick glance around the quiet parking lot before finally coming back to me.

"Yes?"

Her voice is soft, like her body, and a little breathless. If I wasn't watching as she tries to disappear into the ratty wood paneling on her piece of shit car, I could've sworn she was trying to seduce me with that near-whisper.

I'm well aware of the intimidating presence I have. I actually work at my dark, forbidding exterior.

At just shy of six feet, it's important to maintain my bulk with exercise. I don't really smile, generally have little reason, and have what Bree jokingly calls, a *resting asshole face*. With my mostly black clothes and gravelly voice, I usually capitalize on the badass vibe I give off, but I don't even know if she's seen anything. I'm not getting any satisfaction seeing this woman cower in front of me, and scaring her may be premature.

So I wrestle my face into what I hope is a passable smile and soften my voice.

"Didn't mean to startle you," I assure her, reaching out and touching her lightly on the shoulder, before quickly pulling my hand back, flexing my fingers.

ROSIE

Holy crap.

He spooked me, calling out like that.

Especially after seeing the heavy police presence on Third Street. I have no idea what's going on, but it makes me uneasy.

I'm always aware of my surroundings, especially at night. A habit I brought back with me from the big city, where such vigilance was merited. I have to admit, spinning around to see the dangerous-looking security guy I've occasionally ogled approaching, turned the initial cold stab of fear into something a bit warmer.

My heart is still beating in my throat, but right

now almost as much in excitement as in fear. The man is hot, in capital letters. His voice is rough, but quiet, and my mind instantly associates it with a lazy morning in bed. I can feel myself blush at the wildly inappropriate leap my imagination takes. Sadly these are the thoughts of a woman with no life to speak of. The mind is where all the fun stuff happens, because it isn't happening anywhere else.

His words are intended to soothe, as is his touch, but the brief brush of his fingers on my shoulders has the effect of a cattle prod. It sets off a charge that seems to spread along my skin in a hot tingle.

Yowza.

"I just got here myself, and heard about what happened. Came back out to have a look when I saw you." He tilts his head to one side, and I'm so focused on his face, it's all I can do not to mirror his move. "You work the nightshift, right? Name's Jake—my team provides security for the movie people, I've seen you around."

I nod stupidly, still a bit flustered that I'm standing here talking to him. Well, technically he's talking to me, since my mouth doesn't seem to be working.

"I do, and I know. I'm Rosie," I manage—barely—sounding more like a phone sex operator than a middle-aged spinster on a dry spell the size of the Mojave Desert. I clear my throat and try for a more natural tone. "You mentioned something happened?"

"Yeah, behind one of the restaurants on the next block." I notice he doesn't specify what and is looking at me closely as he continues. "They say it probably happened in the last couple of days. It wasn't discovered until this morning when someone took the garbage out."

My skin goes clammy as my mind travels back to an incident I'd all but forgotten over the weekend.

"Discovered what exactly?" I cringe at the note of anxiety in my voice, and quickly try to hide it with a smile.

"Homeless guy. Found him dead beside the dumpster. Crushed."

There is no hiding my shocked intake of breath. My thoughts start spinning. The sound of a crash. An engine revving. The familiar face behind the wheel, belonging to a man who used to make my heart beat faster, but has lost all his appeal since he almost ran me over.

"My God," I whisper, my hand covering my mouth.

"Shit, I'm sorry," Jake apologizes, his hand once again reaching out, giving my shoulder a squeeze before dropping it back to his side. This time his touch helps to anchor me when it feels like the ground is shifting under my feet. "Really," he continues, "I didn't mean to be insensitive."

"No, no," I jump in; masking the panic I feel encroaching me. "It's just so horrifying, and sad. Crushed?"

He nods somberly. "Pretty horrific scene from what I hear. I just came out here to see if I could find out anything more."

I wrap my arms around myself protectively, trying to ward off the shakes that want to take over. I'm eager to go inside where I can hide out in the laundry room and gather my thoughts.

"Afraid I can't help you there." I force an apologetic smile. "I should go in or I'll be late for my shift."

"Of course," he acknowledges and steps out of the way when I start moving around him. But I can feel his eyes on my back all the way inside.

—

"The cops are probably gonna want to talk to you too."

Grant steals another bite from my half-eaten sandwich. He's welcome to it. I have no appetite, but tried to force myself to eat a little anyway.

I never mentioned Monday morning's incident to anybody. Had my hands full of daily life with Mom. I probably would've gotten around to telling Grant, but now I'm not so sure I should. Something tells me to be real careful about sharing any information—with anyone.

Especially since I'm not even quite sure what I've heard or seen. Hell, I don't want to be responsible for ruining someone's career by jumping to conclusions. What a mess.

"When did they talk to you?" I ask nervously.

"Were waiting for me when I got in. I guess they have an approximate time pinned down. They have a witness who heard a crash in the early morning hours on Monday. They're checking with anyone who was on the nightshift. Not only here, I just got off the phone with Marvin. He's the concierge at the Hampton Inn across the road, and the brother of a tall lean hunk of brown sugar I used to date. He says the cops are there, questioning their staff as well."

"They have a witness?" I repeat the one piece of information I'm stuck on.

"Apparently." Grant shrugs as he takes another bite, before mumbling through a full mouth, "Marvin's wife is a police dispatcher. He gets all the dirt."

If there is someone else, a witness to the incident, it takes some of the pressure off me. I've been struggling about what to do, and this may leave me off the hook.

Don't get me wrong, I want to do the right thing, but I'm not quite sure what that is. I have my mother to take into consideration, since everything I do relates directly to her. I'm well aware it's cowardly to stick my head in the sand and pretend I don't know anything, but the only way I can create some order, in the chaos that is my life, is by tightly controlling any parts I can. There are already too many erratically moving pieces. The moment I open my mouth about the incident Monday in the parking lot, it'll be like throwing myself off a cliff into raging waters. I just know it.

"Ms. Perkins?" I start at the voice behind me. "Officer Bergland with the Grand Junction PD. I have a few questions for you."

JAKE

"She knows."

Dimi's head twists away from the monitor.

My eyes are still focused on the lobby, where we just watched Rosie almost jump out of her sneakers, when the officer approached her. On the screen, I see the officer gesture to the small office behind the front desk, and Rosie rubbing the palms of her hands on her jeans as she precedes him inside.

"You sure?" Dimi wants to know, probably sensing my hesitation.

A student, renting a studio apartment over the pizza place facing the north side of the alley, came forward with information. We checked it out to see if it would be damaging to our client. Yanis had been able to find out that other than hearing the crash, the sound of a car engine, and the approximate time of night, she wasn't able to give any more information. On its own not necessarily a threat, but if someone can place Steele out and about during that time, it would become problematic. We have the bartender at the club taken care of, the night clerk never saw Steele leave the hotel bar, so that leaves only the skittish redhead with the big green eyes. *Fuck.* Part of me hoped that matters would be taken out of our hands when word of a witness came down. I really don't want to lean on Ms. Rosie Perkins, but it may be unavoidable if we have any hope of keeping our client out of this.

Personally, I don't give a flying fuck if that entitled asswipe goes down. In fact, I'd happily report the bastard myself, if not for what it would mean to the future of PASS and all my colleagues. Not to mention what it means for the future of this movie and all the people whose livelihood depends on it.

I never realized how many people are involved in a major production like this. The rich and famous are only a small percentage, compared to the many small cogs that keep the machine moving and are dependent on its survival. For someone who for years disregarded morals and ethics, I feel surprisingly conflicted.

The worst part is, I had some time tonight to go over the extensive background file on Rosie Perkins, Radar was able to pull together in a handful of hours. Life has not exactly been kind to the woman, and it's about to get even worse.

Sonofabitch.

"She knows," I repeat, turning my eyes to my friend. "But I don't think she's telling."

"Why?"

I shake my head, taking a moment to sort my thoughts. "She would've said something when I talked to her outside." I quickly raise my hand to cut Dimi off. I know he's going to grill me, but I feel strongly about this. "If that's not enough, the one person she would've told right away, would be him." I point at the monitor where the night clerk is still chewing on the remains of a sandwich, apparently not too concerned with his friend who is being questioned by police. "If she told him anything, his eyes would be glued to that damn door." I give Dimi a chance to check the screen, before I finish, "And finally, she rubbed her palms on her legs, which means she's nervous. People don't get nervous about telling the truth, they're nervous about lying."

The last comment earns me a nod.

"Point taken, but how do we—" he starts asking before I cut him off.

"I'll make sure. Let me handle Rosie Perkins."

ROSIE

I suck at lying. Was never any good at it.

I'm generally good at reading body language, though, and this officer's body screams ambivalence.

Sticking as close as possible to the truth seemed the way to go, but when he asks me once again if I saw or heard anything when I dumped the garbage and got in my car on Monday morning, I'm starting to doubt.

Before I have a chance to panic at the thought I may now have committed a crime by giving a false statement to the police, Officer Bergland snaps shut his notebook and stands. I leap up in relief and wipe my sweaty palms on my jeans again.

"Guess that's all I need, for now. We may have some follow-up questions at a later time," he announces, appearing slightly annoyed when I just nod with my lips pressed tightly together. He reaches out his hand and I automatically reach out my own. "I've got your information and will be in touch."

His tone, and the fact he's still holding onto me, suddenly gives off an uncomfortable vibe and I quickly retrieve my hand. Suppressing a shiver, I watch his eyes take a slow gander of my attributes before raising an eyebrow at me. He turns and walks out the door, leaving me feeling in need of a shower. *Ugh.*

I wave at Grant, who is busy with a guest, when I enter the lobby. I'll have to fill him in later; work won't wait.

The gym is deserted when I haul my cleaning cart down the hall, on the way to clean the women's locker room. No one seems to be working out, or in the adjoining pool, which closes at midnight, only ten minutes away. The gym stays open all the time.

It doesn't take me long to clean the locker rooms, and when I head over to do the gym, I hear splashing coming from the pool area. A quick glance at my watch shows a few minutes past twelve. Odd—normally security would have locked it up. Maybe they have their hands full with the police presence. Not my place to enforce the rules, but I can give a gentle reminder. After all, I have to get in there to clean, and I'd prefer to do that without someone looking over my shoulder.

"Excuse me," I call out, sticking my head around the door. A dark head pops out of the water, using a hand to wipe the strands from a familiar face. A very handsome face, which days ago would've had me giddy with excitement, but now has me swallow hard. "The pool is closed, you can't be in here," I finish in a much more subdued tone.

"I don't think we've met before." The charming smile, directed at me as Kyle Steele makes his way over to my side of the pool, reminds me of the Cheshire cat: big and toothy, slightly foreboding. "Do you know who I am?"

If I weren't turned off on the guy already, that last question would've surely done the trick. Who asks that? *Conceited ass.* My unease is quickly replaced by anger.

"I'm afraid this area is off-limits, Mr. Steele," I enforce, letting him know that yes, I know who the hell he is, but I don't care.

"Surely you can make an exception? I've had a hard day and the water helps me relax." I watch in amazement as he actually bats his eyelashes at me. It has no effect on me, other than to elicit a snort, which seems to confuse him.

"Afraid not. I need to clean this area."

Clearly not used to taking no for an answer, the man makes his way to the edge of the pool and hauls himself up on the edge, making sure every single muscle on his body ripples with the effort. A body that should absolutely be illegal, it's so pretty.

Picture perfect, with the water sluicing down from his chiseled chest and abs.

It occurs to me how absolutely unfair it is that a man only seven or so years younger than me, can make me feel old enough to be his damn mother. And isn't it sad I finally find myself in the middle of one of my favorite fantasy scenarios, and yet am wishing I could be anywhere else? Especially when he slowly stalks toward me.

"Why don't you join me instead?" he coos, holding out his hand. His voice is hypnotic and for a brief flash I'm tempted, before reality hits with brute force and I take a step back, bumping into something solid.

"Steele," a voice sounds behind me, as two large warm hands land on my shoulders. "You're needed upstairs in your suite. Let Rosie do her job."

Kyle Steele's eyes narrow on the man behind me and his face changes into something a lot uglier; but he seems to listen, snatching his towel off the chair on the side of the pool. Jake, whose voice I instantly recognized, removes his hands and shifts to partially shield me as Kyle stomps by. That doesn't stop the star from bending down to my eye level, and with childlike defiance to his security detail, proceeding to flirt with me.

"I'm sure you know how to find my suite after your work is done."

I can immediately sense a dark energy pour from the other man shielding me, but before he has a chance to react, I quickly respond, "I'll pass, thank you, Mr. Steele."

"You sure? You don't know what you're missing." His cocky smirk sickens me as he grabs his less than stellar package and suggestively fondles himself in front of me. That's apparently enough for Jake, who grabs his arm and starts hauling him out of the pool area. Kyle is taller than Jake by a few inches, but although he is nicely muscled, he's no match for the sheer force of the solid security guy.

"You okay?" Jake walks in a little while later, when I'm wiping fingerprints off the mirror in the gym.

"Fine."

He moves in close, scrutinizing my face like he's trying to gauge my truthfulness.

"Sorry about that," he says, taking a step back when I nervously spray more Windex on the mirror, but he doesn't leave. Instead he folds his arms over his chest and leans against the rack with weights of all shapes and sizes—watching me. I try to focus on wiping the streaks from the glass, but it's difficult when I feel his eyes boring into my back.

"I'm really okay." Flustered, I finally snap and swing around to face him. His expression is impassive, but his eyes intense. "No need to worry," I add for good measure, and because I don't know how else to get him to stop staring.

"You felt it," he states, unfolding his arms as he straightens up and takes a step closer.

There isn't a question in my mind what he is referring to, since I've not just felt it once in the parking lot, but again when he interrupted my little showdown with Mr. Steele, but I'll be damned if I admit it. So I do what any woman who recognizes she is well out of her playground would do, I pretend to be clueless.

"Sorry, I'm not quite sure what you're referring to, but I should probably get this done." I suck at lying. I hate that I suck at lying, because now his formerly impassive face breaks open in a wide grin. It transforms that taciturn expression into something stunning, which only serves to make me feel even more out of my league.

"What time are you done?"

I shake my head; it's like he didn't even hear my denial and I don't know what else I can say, so I don't say anything. That doesn't stop him either.

"I'll find out," he says, turning toward the door, and it looks like he's finally going to leave me be. But just as he gets to the door, he adds, swinging his head around, "We'll grab breakfast."

My mouth drops open, and by the time I have my firm denial formulated, he's long gone.

CHAPTER 4

JAKE

"SHOULDN'T YOU BE in bed?"

I expected her to try and make a run for it, which is why I tried keeping my eye on the lobby monitor. I also expected a reaction when I caught up with her—but I didn't expect the strong reaction my body had at her words.

After I left her in the gym, I went straight to the surveillance room where Dimi was waiting with a concerned look on his face.

"You like her." He barged right in, making it sound like an accusation. "I knew it," he added with smug satisfaction.

"She's a job."

"Bullshit. I'm not blind and I'm not stupid."

"It doesn't matter, whether I do or don't is irrelevant. I'm doing my job; I'm handling Rosie

Perkins.”

“Hope so,” Dimi mumbled, as he turned back to the monitors, pissing me off even more. “Maybe I should take over.”

“Like hell you will,” I barked, to which Dimi only raised an eyebrow, but he didn’t say a word.

Not until hours later, when I’d dozed off with my head on the desk, and Dimi alerted me to our subject grabbing her coat and purse from the staff room, ten minutes before the end of her shift.

“Looks like she’s making a run for it.”

By the time he finished his sentence, I was already ripping open the door to the stairs, which I took two steps at a time. I caught up with her at the rear door, her friend watching with a bemused look on his face from behind the front desk.

“Is that a statement or an invitation?” I respond to her comment, and watch as her eyes go big when I continue, “because if it’s the first, the fact that I’m standing here should be obvious—and if it’s the second, the fact that I’m standing here should also be obvious.”

In the background, I can hear Grant bark out a laugh, but apparently Rosie does not think it’s funny. Fuck. Maybe Dimi is right and I should hand this over to him.

“We have a date,” I forge on, because like hell I’ll

hand her off to Dimi.

"I don't recall…" She tries shaking her head adamantly, before her buddy cuts her off.

"Go on, you crazy bitch," he calls out, waving his hand in the air. "Last week you were whining because I was getting it on with Olaf, and you haven't had action since a Bush held office. Least you can do is give it a try."

I swallow down a chuckle when her pale face goes beet red and she throws a glare in her friend's direction. "You are out of my will," she bites off, which only serves to make him laugh louder.

"No skin off my nose, Rosebud—you ain't got nothing worth having. Yet," he adds, raising an eyebrow and checking me over top to bottom. My turn to squirm a little, and I quickly grab the still seething Rosie by the arm and steer her out the door. She follows me willingly until we get to my truck, and then she stops in her tracks.

"I can't go with you," she sputters. "I don't date and I have to get home."

"Fine, but you've got to eat though, right?"

"I'll grab something at home, I usually do."

"Today you'll let me buy you breakfast at the all-night diner a few blocks down. I'll drop you back here to that rust bucket you drive, and you can be home within the hour." I don't wait for a response, but hit the release on the locks, and lift her into the truck before she even realizes what's happening.

By the time she does, we're already halfway there,

and she huffs loudly before turning her face to me.

"You're bossy."

ROSIE

Again with that grin.

It's like ten years drop off his face when he shows his teeth. Nice teeth at that. Strong, mostly straight, with a slight overlap of one of his incisors. An imperfection that makes the overall appeal even stronger. Damn him.

If I hadn't seen him all over the hotel, and knew he was legit, I would never have let myself be handled the way I let him push me around. I have to admit though, that small but sharp edge of danger, combined with the charge I get from his touch, is very seductive. This is why, when we get to our destination, I willingly let him lift me down from the cab of the truck, only so I can feel that tingle his hands leave behind.

With his hand on my elbow, he leads me through the door into the old diner. The original fifties interior is old but squeaky-clean and familiar. I remember coming here a few times with my parents when I was a child, and maybe once or twice as a teenager with some friends from school.

"Menus are on the table. Anywhere will do." A tired-looking man in a white apron waves his hand at the empty restaurant from behind the counter. "I'll get some fresh coffee going," he adds, already putting his words in motion as he scoops fresh grounds in the industrial-sized machine.

"Pick a table," Jake offers and I walk over to one in the far corner, away from the window. When I sit down and grab a menu, he sits down on the other side of the table, his eyes watching me.

"Why?" I finally ask when the silence starts drowning out the sputtering of the coffee machine. It frustrates me that I can't read his face and have no idea what is going on in his head, so I repeat, "Why? You basically manhandle me to come here and I don't get it."

"How come you haven't dated since the Bush administration?" he returns, completely ignoring my question and reminding me to murder Grant, first chance I get.

"I've been busy." I demonstratively turn to the aproned gentleman walking up with the fresh pot of coffee, and flip over the upside down mug sitting on the table in front of me. I watch Jake do the same from the corner of my eye, but his attention still appears focused on me. He hasn't even touched his menu yet.

"What can I get you?" the man asks, fishing a stubby pencil from behind his ear and a ratty notebook from his apron.

"Just some scrambled eggs and toast, please."

"I'll have the workman's special," Jake orders. "Eggs over hard and oatmeal instead of toast."

I peek at the menu and my eyes almost roll out of my head when I see the quantity of food his order includes: three eggs, a short stack of pancakes, three kinds of meat, home fries, and toast. Except he clearly prefers oatmeal.

"That would feed a family of six," I blurt out when our server disappears into the kitchen. Apparently he's our cook as well.

"It may need to last me the day," he explains, shrugging. "In my line of work there are no set times for meals, so you tend to fill up when you have a chance."

I nod my understanding while I doctor my coffee. Jake drinks his black, apparently, but I need my milk and sugar. Especially since it appears I'll be forfeiting my sleep this morning; I could use the energy boost. Maybe I can catch a few winks this afternoon if I can get Mom down for a nap, although that's been more of a hit-and-miss lately, with emphasis on the miss.

"So what are you really doing up at four in the morning?" I try again, still trying to figure out what exactly is going on. Jake apparently is no fool; his grin indicates he knows exactly what I'm fishing for.

"Having breakfast with a beautiful woman."

I roll my eyes at that, which elicits a chuckle from him. Beautiful, my foot. I've been scrubbing floors and bathrooms all night, my hair is flying all over the place, I've grown garbage bags under my eyes and I probably reek of Pine-Sol.

"Laying it on a bit thick, are we?"

"Not really," he responds, the impassive mask on his face back in place, which makes him impossible to read. "I wouldn't be up at four in the morning otherwise." His eyes are intense and I finally lower mine, not quite knowing what to do with the heat I see there. "I'm not sure I could do what you do, though. Do overnight shifts all the time?" he continues in a lighter tone. "The rare time I have to go through the night, I need a few days of sleep to make up for it. I don't know how you do it."

"You really do get used to it. Eventually." I shrug, peeking up at him, relieved when I no longer see the smolder in his eyes. "It took me a month to get my sleep pattern reorganized."

"Have you always been on nights?"

"God no, just the past eight months, since I moved back here."

"Where did you live before?"

"Denver." I glance at the kitchen, hoping for our food to appear. Feeling a little like a bug under a microscope with all the questions. I really don't want to talk about Denver. "My mom's health started deteriorating and I came back home to look after her."

"And you do that during the day, while you work the night shift," he concludes correctly, an odd tone to his voice.

"I have someone stay with her during the night. It works for us."

"You get off at four, drive home and catch whatever sleep you can before she wakes up?"

"Pretty much. Sometimes she'll nap in the afternoon and I join her," I admit.

"So the last thing you need is something disrupting

your morning routine, and here I am, doing just that," he says, attempting to look contrite, but failing miserably.

"Yes, you are," I agree, smiling. "And, if I might point out, you still haven't explained why."

He is quiet for a moment, as he scans my face with those dark eyes. "I think I answered that question already." His voice rumbles deeply and I feel goosebumps rise on my arms. Then he leans forward, his elbows on the table, and reaches out, covering my folded hands with one of his. "But so there's no mistaking; I'm attracted to you, I'm curious about you, and I'm trying very hard to stay on this side of the table."

The last is said on a growl I can feel in my bones. What does one say to that?

"Oh."

That was the extent of my remaining vocabulary as I feel the blood rush to my head, while my intelligence drains to my toes. I'm so lost in the dark depths of his eyes, I don't even notice our waiter returning with the food, until Jake lets go of my hands and sits back in his seat.

"Workman's special and scrambled with toast. Can I get you a refill on your coffee?"

JAKE

Perfect timing.

One more second and I'm not sure I would've

been able to stick to my side of the table. Not with her mouth still forming the *oh* she whispered.

Son of a bitch. Way to keep my head in the game. I shift slightly in my seat, trying to adjust myself without using a hand, without any luck.

"Be right back," I tell her as I quickly get up from the table. "Don't let it get cold." I point to her plate before heading to the restrooms. There I make the necessary adjustments, wash my hands and splash some cold water on my face, before leaning my head against the mirror over the sink. This is going to be messy, one way or another. Normally I wouldn't think twice about misrepresenting myself to a target, if it means getting the job done, but this is different. The *job* is protecting a spoiled asshole from facing his responsibilities, and the target is an innocent, hardworking woman, who doesn't deserve to be at the core of this mess.

By the time I get back to the table, I'm glad to see she didn't wait and is eating. Without delay, I dive into my breakfast and we eat our meal in reasonably comfortable silence. I'm not sure if it is my profession, or my unhealthy interest in Rosie, that has me notice every little detail about her. The way she uses her knife to slide her food on the fork, instead of stabbing at it like most do. How she dabs her mouth with her napkin before taking a sip of her coffee. And how she constantly has to tuck the one strand of hair that doesn't seem to want to stay in place behind her ear, while shooting me a quick glance from the corner of her eyes. I notice it all.

Rosie is still working on her last piece of toast when I signal for the bill. She immediately drops it to her plate and dives under the table to grab her purse.

"Here," she says, pulling out a couple of bills.

"I've got it," I assure her.

"I can pay for my own breakfast," she insists.

"Good to know, but you're not paying for this one. Put that away."

It's cute, the way she pouts in silence, all the way to the truck and to the hotel lot where her car is parked. I barely have the truck to a stop when she already has the door open. I just manage to reach in front of her and slam it back shut, but she wrestles me for the handle.

"Stop." She freezes in her seat and I twist, leaning into her, my face just inches from hers. "I'm guessing you're tired and you're used to looking after yourself, but I don't want to see your wallet come out when you're with me." She snorts and rolls her eyes at that, while attempting to stifle a yawn, and I bite my lip not to react. She's funny, and tries hard to avoid looking at me. "Rosie—look at me." I wait until she finally meets my eyes. "I'm gonna need your phone."

"Why?"

"Just give me your phone."

She digs through her purse and reluctantly hands me her cell, which I quickly program with my number. I call my phone from hers, so I have her number, before handing it back to her.

"Call or text me when you get home, so I know you're safe."

"I think I can get myself home, I've—"

"Humor me," I interrupt, cutting off her objections. She surprises me by quietly nodding her acknowledgment. Her eyes scan my face and her mouth pulls up a bit at the corner.

"Thank you." I can barely hear the words, but I can see them clear as day on her lips. Lips I've been staring at all morning.

I'm clearly not thinking when I breach the few inches that separate us, and give in to my urge to cover those lips with mine. Silky, plump, and when I sneak a taste with the tip of my tongue, slightly sweet from the jam on her toast. A soft puff leaves her lips when I pull back a little.

"Call me," I repeat.

———

"She's a job, huh?" Dimi gloats when I walk into the control room after seeing Rosie off. Rather than engage, I ignore him.

"Any movement from the suite?" I ask, scanning the monitors for movement.

"All quiet. You probably have time to get home and catch a couple of hours."

I check my watch; five fifteen, and filming doesn't start until nine.

"Yeah, but I'll crash here."

PASS has a couple of adjoining rooms for operatives to take breaks, store equipment, hold team meetings, or catch a few z's.

"Thanks for bringing me breakfast," Dimi complains as I walk out the door.

"Get your own," I tell him without slowing down.

"Asshole!" His voice follows me to the elevator and I chuckle as I get on.

One of the PASS rooms is empty and only kicking off my boots and taking off my holster, I roll into bed. I'm already half asleep when my phone buzzes in my pocket.

"Yeah," I answer groggily.

"Oh. I'm sorry. I…I mean, you…you told me to call."

"Rosie." I'm suddenly wide-awake. "You got home okay?"

"I did. Thanks again for breakfast. Go back to sleep."

I don't get a chance to answer because she's already hung up. She's got a great voice, but it's even better over the phone. Slightly raspy and sexy as fuck. Suddenly my jeans feel a little too tight and I'm very awake, at least my body is.

A hot shower and a quick hand job later, I roll back in bed, falling asleep in seconds—pretending her pretty lips and bright eyes on the pillow beside me.

ROSIE

I tuck my phone back in my purse and get out of the car, a smile on my face.

The moment I open the door, however, the smile fades. I hear Mom before I see her, calling out for my father. Something she does from time to time when she wakes up and feels disoriented. Hillary is trying to keep Mom in bed, but I can see she's struggling.

"I'm sorry I'm late," I direct at Hillary, as I move into the room. "Mom? Can you help me brush my hair?" I grab the brush from her nightstand and hold it up for her to see. When she doesn't respond, I grab one of her hands, batting at poor Hillary, and press the brush in her palm. "Can you brush my hair, Mom?" I try again, and this time she stops struggling and her eyes search around until she spots me. Hillary slips off the bed, as I smoothly take her place, like a well-orchestrated dance we've executed many times before. Mom's other hand comes up and reaches for my hair so I turn around and let her do her thing.

"Go back to bed for a bit," I whisper to Hillary who nods and shuffles off.

We discovered it quite by accident, a while ago, when Hillary suggested brushing Mom's hair to relax her. I barely got one stroke in and Mom had snatched the brush from my hand and started brushing mine instead. It's an odd experience, reminiscent of a time before she became disappointed and bitter, and ultimately forgot who I was.

Although physically relaxing, it often leaves me feeling emotionally raw. Something I would've liked to avoid this morning, since I already feel a bit wobbly on my emotional feet. By the time Mom is relaxed enough for me to take the brush from her hand and tuck her in, I'm crying.

I head straight for my room, barely managing to strip down before I dive under the covers. And with my face still wet with tears, and the sweet concern of a dark, confusing man rooting in my mind, I finally fall asleep.

CHAPTER 5

JAKE

"SO WHAT'S THE deal with the maid?"

I struggle to keep my temper in check when Yanis directs his attention to me.

We're in the small kitchen on the second floor of the warehouse. A space used as a break room by our guys, but doubles as a meeting room. Today is an indoor film day, which means we have a team meeting. When they shoot outside, it's all hands on deck for security, but guarding the film crew inside doesn't require as much manpower.

Of course, the main topic of discussion is the police probe into the hit-and-run, which apparently is half-assed at best. At least hearing Bree talk about it. She's the one who's been keeping feelers on the investigation through her connections with the GJPD. It would appear the poor homeless sap, who was left dead in the alley, takes up less blotter space than a council member's garage door graffitied by vandals. Which is good news for us, I guess. Although I find myself wishing the incident wasn't so damn easy to cover up. Then whatever Rosie did or didn't see would become irrelevant. Now she's a loose end Yanis keeps picking at.

"Under control," I bite off, staring at the floor, forcing my irritation down. I'm not happy with the focus on her.

"What does that mean, exactly?"

"She keeps to herself. Her circle is small and she has no social life to speak of. If she was planning to say anything, she would've done so already, but she won't. She'll keep whatever she heard or saw to herself."

"How can you be sure?" Yanis prods. "Doesn't she know you're part of the security detail?"

"Because I'm planning to keep a close eye. Besides, she had reason and opportunity to talk when that sleazeball propositioned her last night in the pool, but even then she didn't say a word." I look up at my boss and find his gaze on me, assessing me. I'm still pissed at Steele after having to drag him to his suite and read him the riot act—again.

"Very well, but just so you know, our client has some concerns, and is willing to put some money on the table if need be," he finally states.

"Drexler was told about her?"

"Hutch, Drexler is the one signing the checks. You know what's on the line here. Of course he was told," Dimi interjects for his brother. From the corner of my eye, I see Bree shifting restlessly at the spike in tension in the air, and I catch the subtle shake of her head as she motions for me not to push it. Hell, it wouldn't be the first time if I did.

"Fine," I give in, turning to Yanis. "Tell Drexler your man has it under control, and he can keep his money in his pocket, but his own star is the one to worry about."

"Fair enough," he concedes. "I will reiterate that with Phil, as long as you can assure me that if there is even the smallest doubt this woman might become an issue, you won't hesitate to use money, or whatever else, you need to convince her to stay quiet."

I can't bring myself to respond to that, since I'm grinding my teeth so hard I'm afraid I'll chip one, I nod sharply instead.

"Dude," Dimi says later, when we're grabbing a quick slice of pizza before the production calls a wrap for the day. "Why do you keep poking the bear?"

"You're talking about your brother?" I ask, mouth full of pizza. Dimas nods affirmatively. "Not about poking anything," I explain. "But don't you ever wonder what happened to fighting the bad guys? Because that's as simple as it used to be; the bad guys were the enemy. Now?" I shove a frustrated hand in my hair and tug a few times. "Fuck, man—we're upside down—shielding a bad guy and threatening an innocent woman. What the fuck? Doesn't that bother you?"

I look over at Dimas, who tosses the slice he was eating on his plate and wipes his hands on a napkin.

"Yeah, it bothers me," he finally replies. "Which is why I'm not the one making those kinds of decisions. I can't do what Yanis does, always keeping an eye on the big picture, seeing the gray between the black and the white. Sometimes innocents pay the price for the benefit of all. Always have—always will. Only difference is we see it now. But don't think for a second it doesn't plague him, because it does, and you questioning him every step doesn't make it easier— for anyone."

I let that simmer for a bit while he picks up his slice again and finishes it off.

"Her life is not a cakewalk." I'm not sure why I tell him that, he's seen the background check, but a reminder felt appropriate. Dimi claps a hand on my shoulder in response, tosses a few bills on the table, and then walks out the door.

ROSIE

"Are you gonna tell me, or do I have to drag it out of you?"

Grant has been hounding me all night and I've successfully avoided him, until now. He has me cornered in the supply room off the hotel lobby, which I snuck into to grab some more toilet paper. He must've been lying in wait.

"Are those my only options?" I counter, trying to scoot around him, but he won't let me through the door. "Grant, I've got work to do."

"All the more reason to rip the Band-Aid off and tell Grant all about breakfast with *dark and broody* this morning." I'm tempted to bite at the index finger he waves in my face. I hate when he resorts to speaking in the third person.

"Well," I start, managing to squeeze by his massive form and stack the toilet rolls on my cart. "I ordered scrambled eggs and toast. It was actually quite tasty. I had no idea that diner was open all night. Did you know that?" I ramble purposely as I push my cart to the elevator, knowing full well Grant can't venture too far from the lobby.

"You're being a tease," he pouts when I push the elevator button.

"And you're being nosy," I fire back. "But just so you know, we talked a little, we ate a little. Actually; I ate a little, he ate the contents of a well-stocked, industrial-sized refrigerator."

"Ooh, a voracious appetite. Me likey." Grant grins big and claps his hands like a kid in a candy store. "And what did you talk about?"

"Me, mostly," I admit, going over this morning's events in my head, realizing how much I gave away and how little I learned. "I may well have shared a tad too freely." It could explain why he'd been sleeping already when I called. I probably bored him to tears with my tales of woe, but if that were Band case, the kiss confuses me. I'm pretty sure that actually happened, although I'm not going to tell Grant that. I'd never hear the end of it.

"Nonsense," he says. "Getting you to talk is like pulling teeth. I'm surprised you did any sharing, let alone too much. I highly doubt it. Besides, men like that kind of stuff," he adds, and I can't help snicker. "What?"

"You mean *you* like that kind of stuff. Hate to break it to you, but you're not like regular men." I try to be sensitive but I needn't have worried. This is Grant we're talking about; he'll take anything as a compliment.

"Bet your luscious ass I'm not," he declares. "I'm my own brand of extra-special."

I'm still snickering when the elevator doors slide open and I roll my cart inside.

"Later, Grant." I turn to face him as the doors close.

"Later, Rosebud."

The smile is still on my face when I get off on the second floor where the gym is located. It fades quickly, though, when I see someone has turned the lights off in the hallway. Irritated and a little apprehensive, I slide my hand along the wall to where I know the light switch to be. I flick it, but nothing happens. I try again, with the same result.

Pulling my cart close, I rummage through the small basket on the top shelf where I know I have a flashlight. I let out a sigh of relief when I find it and it turns on, no problem. With the narrow beam of light, I find my way over to the other side of the hallway by the locker rooms, where a second switch controls the lights on that side of the hallway.

That one doesn't work either. None of the sconces lining the walls light up. The ceiling fixture inside the locker room does, though, and I prop the door open so its light filters into the hallway.

Normally this is a job for maintenance, but I just talked to Alex maybe fifteen minutes ago and he was on his way up to check on a plugged toilet. I don't want to wait around for him to make his way down. I'll first have a look myself.

I'm too short to reach the bulbs in the sconces, but when I shove my cart against the wall underneath, I can climb it like a ladder. Now I can easily stick my hand in, but I'm surprised to find the bulb gone. I find the same in the second sconce, and when I check the other two, the bulbs are missing as well.

An uneasy feeling gnaws at my stomach as I climb down. By the faint light coming from the locker room, I dig through the shelves of my cart for spare bulbs, looking over my shoulder every so often. Of course I have none, it's Murphy's Law. I recall leaving some in the small storage closet in the pool room, where we keep mops and chlorine tablets for the pool. It seemed easier since the lights on this floor tend to be on all night and burn out faster. The disappearing bulbs are something new.

Armed with my flashlight and keys, I make my way around the pool, trying not to slip on the still wet floor. Someone must've been swimming late for it to still be wet. The pool closed maybe forty-five minutes ago. The lock opens easily and I shine my flashlight inside. Three boxes of bulbs are stacked on the small shelf above the brooms and I'll have to reach to take one down. Slipping the flashlight in my pocket, I brace the wall to steady me, and perching on tiptoes, I stretch my other arm up, scratching the tips of my fingers on the box of bulbs, trying to grab hold. I almost have the box teetering on the edge, when I feel myself yanked back and flying through the air before hitting the hard, wet surface of the water, a heavy weight pushing me down.

I struggle to stay close to the surface, fighting my instincts to scream and take in a lungful of water, but whatever, or whoever, is on top of me holding me down, is too strong. I don't give up. I never stop fighting until darkness starts filling in my senses, pulling me under.

JAKE

"Thought you went home?"

Bree looks up with an eyebrow raised when I walk into the control room. My eyes scan the twelve monitors in front of her, most of which are focused on the main floor, lobby, entrance, and parking lot. To access the upper floors from the main floor, you need a key card to operate the elevator, or to enter the stairwell. Every so often, whoever is manning the screens will flip through the different feeds to check the other floors, but the prime focal point remains the entrance and exit points of the hotel.

"I crashed here," I explain. "Steele was holed up with his agent in his suite, so it just seemed easier to crash here. Did you see the guy leave?"

"I did," Bree confirms, flipping through a notebook in front of her. "Left at ten fifty-three." She turns back to face me. "So why are you here in the middle of the night, wide-awake?"

I shrug and pull up a chair. "I crashed around eight. Four hours will do me most nights."

"Not me. I need a good eight hours or I'm cranky as shit."

"I don't get cranky." I try not to laugh at the disgruntled snort that remark earns me.

"Because cranky is the only way you come," she fires off. I like Bree, she doesn't take shit from anyone. The only complaint I have is she seems to have a sixth sense for bullshit. "Now I like shooting the shit as much as the next guy, but why don't you tell me why you're really here? You're worried about her."

Shouldn't surprise me that she's calling my bluff. I'm well aware she knows me better than I'm comfortable with, so I don't even bother denying. "Find her for me?"

"She was in the lobby just before you walked in. Talking with her buddy. I think she went up. Let me check." She clicks a few different feeds on the main screen when I see her lean closer. "What the hell?"

I hear her mutter and my eyes follow hers to the monitor on the far left showing the second floor hallway, which looks much darker than usual. You can just see light from the open door of the men's locker room. Rosie's abandoned cart is sitting at an awkward angle in the middle of the corridor, but there's no sign of her.

"Check the feeds from the gym and the pool." All I see is a black screen when she pulls them up. Something is most definitely wrong. "Keep looking," I order her as I grab a radio and haul ass to the stairwell.

I barge through the doors on two and am momentarily disoriented by the much darker hallway. Focusing on the sparse light at the other end, I find my way to the gym, drawing my gun from the holster as I go. My eyes are still adjusting, and I can barely make out the equipment when I cautiously move in, but there's no one here. With my back to the wall, my weapon in hand, I slowly ease my way to the door leading to the pool, when I hear the slam of a door on the far side.

There's only one way into the pool, but there is a second door that leads out to the rooftop patio and hot tub. From there you can double back into the hallway on the other side of the elevators.

I push away from the wall and run along the pool to the door at then end, when something catches my eye in the water and stops me in my tracks. Initially it looks like fabric, billowing under the surface, but then I recognize the color. The rich copper tones of Rosie's hair.

I don't even think, I drop the gun and the radio to

the pool deck, and dive right in, reaching for her.

Her body is dead weight as I drag her to the surface. Instinct takes over as I pull her on the edge, place her on her back, and begin blowing air into her lungs. Almost immediately she starts convulsing. I roll her to her side while she retches to expel the water from her lungs.

"Jesus, Rosie," I mumble, wiping the hair from her face as she sputters and coughs. She blinks a few times and opens her eyes. I know the instant her confused gaze lands on me, because she starts scrambling away from me. "Easy," I try, but I doubt she hears me.

The crackle of the radio draws my attention and I hear Bree's voice calling my name.

"You've got me," I answer, after snatching the radio off the floor without taking my eyes of Rosie, who's cowering against the wall.

"Goddammit, Hutch. All I saw on the monitor was you diving into the water, but I never saw you come up. Is she okay?"

"Call an ambulance," I bark, watching her eye me until I mention an ambulance, then she sharply shakes her head no.

"No ambulance."

"Hold off on that for a sec, Bree." I slowly approach Rosie, who no longer looks scared, but appears determined, despite the tears coursing down her cheeks.

"No ambulance," she says again, firmer this time.

"You need to be looked at."

"Hillary, my mom's nurse, she can check me out. Please…" It just takes me a second to decide.

"Forget the ambulance, Bree. I'm taking her home. Have Grant Peabody grab her belongings and meet us at the door to the alley. Keep a close eye on the monitors and back up all the feeds from eleven o'clock until now. I also need you to close off access to the second floor. I'll contact Dimi and will update you in a bit." Professional that she is—Bree doesn't waste time asking questions—she follows instructions.

I pass a rack with bath towels and robes, and grab a few. She lets me wrap her in one of the robes, but makes me turn around while she strips off her sopping wet pants and shoes. I use a few towels to dry myself off as best I can, before turning back to Rosie, who looks ready to keel over. She lets out a little yelp when I bend down, lift her up in my arms, and walk her to the elevators—my feet sloshing in my boots with every step.

"What are—"

"I'm taking you home, and getting you looked at. That's all you need to worry about right now."

"But—"

"You gotta let me do my job, Rosie. I'll get you an answer, but first I have to do my job." She doesn't utter any more protests, and allows her body to relax in my arms, which makes carrying her a damn lot easier.

Peabody is already waiting by the back door,

alarm on his face when he sees me carrying his friend.

"I'm fine," she quickly says, struggling to be let down, which I grudgingly give in to. "I slipped, hit my head, and fell in the pool. Jake fished me out."

I'm surprised at the ready lies flying from her mouth, but it makes things a lot less complicated. I quickly take over.

"Thanks for grabbing her stuff," I follow up; well aware of the suspicious glances the large man throws me. I'm sure I could take him, but with his bulk and size, it would be a challenge. "I'm getting her looked at right away. Can you cover for her here?"

"Thanks Grant, I owe you one," she murmurs, reaching her hand to touch his arm. "I'll call you later, okay?"

He nods, and hands her a purse and a lunch bag, which she clutches to her chest when I swing her back up in my arms.

"I'll get the door," Grant offers, holding it open for us. He moves to the side when I step outside, but bends his head toward Rosie, forcing me to slow. He kisses her on the forehead, and then I hear him whisper, "I'll have to remember that play. Nice catch, girlfriend." I can feel her body go rigid and keep walking before she can voice a protest.

Grant's deep chuckle follows us all the way to the parking lot.

CHAPTER 6

I WATCH FROM the doorway as Hillary tries to squeeze her car by Jake's massive truck, taking up most of the driveway.

She'd been alarmed when I got home in the middle of the night, a strange man in tow, but believed the same story I'd fed Grant. It's true what they say; the only way to get away with a lie is to stay as close as possible to the truth.

After she looked me over—Jake's orders—I managed to convince her to go home and catch a few more hours of sleep.

I close the door and walk into the kitchen to find Jake on the phone, giving someone directions to my house. I busy myself putting on a pot of coffee, but the moment he ends the call, I'm all over him.

"I hope you're going to fill me in on what's going on."

Jake doesn't seem impressed with my stern tone, leaning back in the kitchen chair, and folding his hands behind his head, as he calmly looks at me. For extra emphasis, I put my hands on my hips, but all that does is bring his eyes down to that level, and it's mostly bravado on my part anyway. The smirk on his face reminds me I'm wearing a pair of leggings Hillary had grabbed me from my dresser. Leggings I bought exclusively for use around the house, never to be seen in public, since they boast flying piggies. Apparently they amuse the otherwise brooding security guy.

"Look," I try again. "There's a reason you whisked me out of the hotel, right after someone attacked me, instead of…oh, I don't know…calling the police?" As the shock wears off and my mind clears, I'm starting to think this whole sequence of events is off. Too many things don't make sense, and some I prefer not to contemplate. For instance, my initial thought when I saw Jake lean over me on the side of the pool; I was half convinced it was him who tossed me in to begin with, but that thought was debunked when I heard him talking on the radio.

I haven't been able to shake the possibility this has something to do with what I witnessed in the alley last weekend. That perhaps, somehow, somebody knows I was there and is afraid I'll say something. I can't think of any other reason someone might want to hurt me.

"I offered to call an ambulance," Jake points out, dragging me from my thoughts. "You're the one who didn't want one, so I assumed you wanted to keep this under wraps. You already told me you never saw a face, only that whoever jumped you was significantly bigger. Not that that's a surprise, you're tiny."

"*Hardly*," I mumble, but he must have some bionic hearing or something, because he stares me down with an eyebrow raised.

Okay, so he's got a point. I was pretty adamant about not wanting an ambulance there, but that was more about insurance than anything else. A trip to the ER would've come with a claim against the measly medical insurance I have through work, along with a thousand dollar deductible I can't afford. That insurance, plus the small emergency savings account I'm building, is to cover Mom if something happens. Her old age pension pays for Hillary and most of my income goes to living expenses, food, and medication. What little is left gets tucked away for emergencies.

"So what now?" I want to know.

"Someone from my team is on his way here, his name is Dimas. He's gonna need whatever information you can give him. Whoever attacked you did not come in off the street. It's someone who is staying there."

"A guest? That doesn't even make sense. Why attack me?"

"That's what we're going to try and find out," he promises.

Suddenly he gets up and walks to the door, opening it to whom, I assume, is this Dimas he mentioned. I didn't hear a knock, no car doors slamming, but clearly something alerted Jake.

The two men make for an interesting contrast.

Although Jake appears a bit shorter than his friend, they both have significant bulk. Where Jake is all dark and shadows, Dimas is the opposite. Dirty blond hair, an open face, and a bright smile that is impossible to resist. He walks toward me with his hand outstretched and I notice a slight limp to his gait.

"Hi," I mumble, when he reaches me and grabs my hand tightly in his big paw.

"Love the pigs," he returns by way of greeting.

"Dimi," Jake growls in warning.

Meaningful looks are exchanged, the significance of which I'm not privy to, so I dislodge my hand and go about getting us set up with coffee.

"So tell me what happened from the moment you got off the elevator," Dimas asks. when I sit down across from him.

For the next half hour or so, I am poked and prodded for every minute detail, from the missing bulbs to the size of the person forcing me to the bottom of the pool. Did I hear anything? Did my attacker say anything? Could I detect any particular scent? Could I think of any reason why someone might want to harm me? Keeping secrets is hard work, and by the time the blond man gets up to leave, my head is spinning, I'm ready to cry, and I'm tired and shaky.

"Why don't you try to get some sleep?" Jake says, looking at me with concern darkening his gray eyes.

"Are you leaving too?" I realize how needy those words sound the moment they're out of my mouth.

"Nope. Just seeing Dimi out. I'll be right outside."

I wait until I hear the click of the door, and then I gather up the coffee cups, giving them a quick wash and stacking them back in the cupboard. That's one thing you learn fast, living in small quarters; cleaning up behind you. All it takes is a few plates and cups to make the small kitchen feel cluttered and messy. Life is messy enough, so whatever order I can create to allow me some semblance of control is welcome.

With the kitchen straightened, I slip into my bathroom to brush my teeth. Mom's larger bathroom is on the other end of the trailer home, tucked between her bedroom and the spare, where Hillary sleeps. My quarters are to the right of the front door, separated from Mom's side by the small living room and kitchen. There's just enough room for a small couch and a couple of chairs in the living area, and the kitchen boasts a small dining table and chairs.

Usually, when Hillary is not here, I leave my bedroom door open so I can hear Mom. I've learned to sleep with one ear and one eye open, over the past months. Especially after waking up one morning to the smoke alarm going off, when Mom was trying to cook breakfast in a moment of clarity, to then promptly forget the frying pan she'd set on the stove. Luckily there was no damage, but it definitely made me more alert.

Without thinking I leave my door ajar, crawl into bed and curl on my side. The moment my head hits my pillow; I can feel fatigue drag me under. I willingly let myself, until I'm suddenly back in the dark pool, being held down until I had no choice but to give in to the darkness claiming me. My eyes pop open, and I flip on the light on my nightstand and roll on my back, willing myself into the present.

I still lie like that when sometime later, the front door opens and Jake steps inside, immediately turning his head to glance into my bedroom.

"I thought you'd be sleeping," he says, closing the front door behind him and leaning his shoulder against it, his eyes on mine.

"I tried."

I watch as he closes the distance to my bed. Sitting on the edge, his face wearing its customary impassive expression, he reaches out, brushing a few stray hairs off my forehead.

"Try again."

His voice is at a near whisper, but the deep rumble still manages to reach my bones. His eyes hold mine captive, as he softly strokes the callused pad of his thumb in soothing patterns on my cheek. It doesn't take long for my eyelids to drop, and with the comfort of his gentle touch, I let myself drift off.

JAKE

"You're right," Dimi says when we get to his car. "She knows." He turns, leans back against the fender, and crosses his arms over his chest. "And she won't tell."

"Excuse me?"

The ice-cold chill, running from the top of my

scalp all the way down my spine, at his words is reflected in the tone of my voice. He notices and looks confused.

"Her," he clarifies, jerking his thumb in the direction of the front door. "I'm saying, the fact she isn't sharing after an experience like this is pretty conclusive evidence she won't say a word."

"How convenient," I grit out between clenched teeth, my hands in tight fists by my side. It's all I can do not to take my best friend down. "Your idea or was this your big brother's doing?"

"What?"

"Where were you tonight, Dimas?"

I watch him squint his eyes before they widen in understanding.

"You cocksucker!" he bites off as he plants his palms in my chest, shoving me back a few steps. "You think I set that girl up? You think I'd attack some innocent woman to silence her? What the fuck is wrong with you?"

My suspicions dissipate as quickly as they'd surfaced at the look of disbelief on Dimi's face.

"Look," I start, my hands up and palms out. "That was fucked up, I'm sorry. I know better."

"I fucking thought you did," he huffs, running both his hands through his hair. "Jesus, man."

"Whoever did this was smart, disabling lights and cameras. They knew Rosie's schedule and planned this out carefully. An inside job," I explain my train of thought. "Your brother didn't want to believe me when

I said she wouldn't talk. He's the one who suggested securing her silence by whatever means necessary. Not to mention the massive price tag attached to this security contract."

"All right, all right," Dimi stops me. "I get the train of thought, but if you weren't at least partially thinking with your dick when it comes to this woman, you would have realized no matter what the payoff, Yanis wouldn't physically harm an innocent person. Not for any amount of money."

"Then what the hell would be the motivation to harm her? She had fucking blue lips, Dimi. That wasn't a warning, it was an attempt at murder made to look like an accident."

He nods in agreement, and both of us fall silent, taking in deep breaths and letting heart rates settle.

"Money is always the best motivation. So if it wasn't you, me, or Yanis," Dimi adds pointedly. "Then it's likely someone else associated with the movie."

This time it's my turn to nod in agreement. "See what you can find on the second floor. I had Bree seal it off, but we can't leave it like that for long. We don't want anyone getting wind of this, if this came out it would draw too much attention. We don't need cops asking more questions."

"You staying here?"

"Both to protect her and to protect our client," I tell him, even though the first is fast outweighing the second for me.

I watch Dimi drive off before returning to the

trailer. Pushing through the door, a soft light to my right draws my attention. I can make out Rosie's form under the blankets; her bright eyes wide open and turned to me.

"Hey...Rosie."

I gently shake her shoulder, hating to wake her already.

It's barely been three hours since she finally fell asleep. I was tempted to crawl in bed with her, and touch her to see if her skin was as soft all over, but I resisted. Instead, I crashed on the couch for a bit before the texts started coming in from Dimas. I'd been sitting at the kitchen table, having a coffee from the fresh pot I made, and working on my phone, when a very frail and very confused woman came walking out of one of the other bedrooms. I presumed that was Rosie's mother, who looked to have had an accident, judging from the wet nightgown tangled around her legs.

Christ.

"Your mom is awake."

That appears to do it. Like a Jack-in-the-box, she sits up straight in bed and furiously blinks the sleep from her eyes. There's a crease running down the side of her face from the pillow, and her eyes and lips are swollen with sleep. She looks cute as fuck.

"I'm up. I'm up," she mumbles, as she swings

her legs over the side and shoves me out of the way as she beelines it to the bathroom. To give her some privacy, I walk back into the living room, when I see her mother cracking eggs in a bowl. Judging by the pile of eggshells on the counter, she's gone through half a dozen already.

"Why don't you let me do that?" I offer, guiding her firmly to one of the kitchen chairs. "Do you like your eggs scrambled?"

"Maxwell likes them scrambled, so that's how we make them."

"Maxwell was my dad," Rosie says, walking in and going straight to her mother. "Morning, Mom, how about we have a quick shower? Get some dry clothes on you?" Continuously chatting, she helps her mother up and into the bathroom, quickly poking her head out the door. "Sorry, I won't be long. Feel free to grab yourself whatever you like." Before I can answer she's gone again.

Twenty minutes later, a much drier and fresher Mrs. Perkins shuffles into the kitchen, Rosie right behind her, her arms full of laundry and wrapped in only a towel. My eyes automatically scan down her curvy body, down to her narrow ankles and tiny feet.

"Good thing she can cook."

I look up at Mrs. Perkins and see she has a scowl focused on her daughter, who looks quite embarrassed.

"Sorry?"

She turns her much clearer eyes to me, a sly little smirk tugging at her mouth.

"Well, she doesn't have much else to offer," the woman says, cackling heartily at her own words.

"Mom, please," Rosie whispers before scooting past me, avoiding any eye contact.

"Aren't you a piece of work?" I turn back to her mom to give her my unbridled opinion, but whoever had been spouting that vitriol was replaced with the placid, slightly confused-looking woman I met earlier.

I wonder if that poisoned tongue was what had Rosie finally run to Denver. It would make her move back home to look after her ailing mother even more of a sacrifice than it already was.

I was so young when my parents died; I only have a few vague memories of them. So I may not be an expert on the subject of parenting, but I'm pretty damn sure it's not normal for a mother to belittle her child like that.

When she returns a few minutes later, dressed, and with her wet hair hanging in a braid over her shoulder, she looks and acts like nothing happened. I give her that—for now. There'll be a time and place to tell her what I think about her mother's words, I'll make sure of that.

"I hate to ask," Rosie says, after a predominantly silent breakfast. "I have to take Mom to her appointment at eleven. Do you think you could drop us off at the hotel so I can grab my car?"

"I'll just take you to your appointment."

"What about work? Don't you have a job to get back to?"

I don't tell her that sticking close to her is my job. Except the focus has shifted from making sure nothing touches Kyle Steele, to making sure no one touches Rosie. My fucking loyalties are stretched all over the fucking place. Brain versus heart has never really been a dilemma I've had to struggle with, but I'll be damned if I'm not struggling now.

"Nah, no worries. Dimas has things covered back at the hotel, so I'll stick around for a bit. We'll play things by ear for today."

What I don't mention is that my buddy will be making sure the whole team is up-to-date, and additional security measures are put in place, since we now have one additional person to keep not only quiet, but also safe. Things are getting complicated.

"Just so you know, it's her standing monthly appointment at the salon," Rosie clarifies, a hint of a smile on her face.

Well, shit. I can handle a doctor's office, but I'm pretty sure it says somewhere in my job description, hanging out in a hair salon goes is against the rules. If not, it should.

"Right," I grind out to Rosie's apparent amusement, even though she tries to hide the grin on her face behind her hand. "I'll just wait in the car."

CHAPTER 7

ROSIE

"Dammit, girl, you shoulda called me. Would've loved to have been a fly on the wall."

Grant shakes his head while he steals another fry off my plate.

We're in the small office behind the front desk, eating the burgers and fries Grant's new squeeze dropped off for us. I already gave my hamburger to Grant after one bite, but had been looking forward to the salty fries.

"Don't touch," I admonish him, slapping at his hand.

"Delicious, right?" he says, chewing happily on my food. "It's from that new organic place down Main. Olaf took me there a few nights ago. He knows I love their elk burger." As far as I'm concerned they can keep their elk—yuck—but apparently it's a big hit with Grant. From the blissed out look on his face, it's clear my friend is absolutely smitten—and not just with the burger—which is kind of sweet to see.

I just finished telling him about Mom's hair appointment today, and the stir she caused when she walked in on the arm of a very surly and intimidating bear of a man. Poor Jake made a big mistake when he gallantly offered his arm to my mother as we left home. She immediately took a shine to him and refused to get out of the car in front of the salon, unless it was on his arm. The resulting commotion inside was enough to put a satisfied smile on Mom's face and a deeply disgruntled scowl on Jake's. For the entire hour and a half we were there, I had to keep my hand over my mouth so I wouldn't bust out laughing.

I'd expected resistance when I got ready for work this afternoon, but other than, "Are you sure you're up for it?" Jake voiced no objections. That didn't mean I didn't feel some apprehension myself, something Jake seemed to pick up on, but he assured me I'd have eyes on me at all times. I'm not sure how I feel about *that*, exactly—I find myself constantly checking my surroundings for cameras or actual people—but I'll admit it beats being scared.

"I'd better get going," I announce, grabbing my now empty paper plate and tossing it in the garbage.

"Be careful, please. We don't need a repeat of last night," Grant reminds me. Not that I needed reminding, he doesn't even know the half of it.

Despite Jake's assurances, I'm still a bit nervous hitting the elevator button for the second floor. If those doors open and I see anything out of the ordinary, I'm out of there, I don't care how many eyes are supposed to be on me.

Flinching a little, I take a step back when the elevator stops and the doors slide open. The hallway looks the way it should, with every lamp burning, which is encouraging. I give myself a firm shake, before determinedly pushing my cart toward the locker rooms at the far end of the hall.

"Hey."

I jump about a foot off the floor, and I may have yelped, in the second it takes me to recognize the voice coming from behind me.

"Jesus, shit!" I curse, bending over with my hands on my knees, trying to catch my breath.

"Saw you go up the elevator and thought I'd hang around while you do this floor," Jake says, putting a hand in the middle of my back. "Took the stairs. Sorry I startled you."

"It's all good," I lie, forcing my heart rate to a normal level as I slowly straighten up, not wanting to lose his reassuring touch between my shoulder blades.

"You know you lie for shit, right?" he chuckles, sadly removing his hand and shooting me a wink, before he turns to lead the way to the locker rooms.

It takes a minute for his words to register. Is that true? Am I that transparent? If that's the case, it would mean he knows I lied about last Sunday as well. Is that what he's referring to? I couldn't tell from his expression. Cautiously I follow him to the men's room, which he quickly checks while I wait outside.

"I'll wait," he says, gesturing for me to enter.

He does the same for the ladies' room and the gym, but when we get to the pool, he doesn't let me go in alone, he walks in with me and stands guard while I clean. My stomach is cramping and I feel a little queasy, but I'm not sure if it was the elk burger or nerves, being in here again.

Other than my first few nights on the job, I've never had anyone watch me while I'm working. It's a little unnerving. I'm not sure whether I'd feel this acutely aware of myself under anyone's scrutiny, or if it's just Jake's dark gray eyes zoomed in on my every move that make me feel a little unstable.

Safe but shaken: that about sums up how I feel about Jake. He's an enigma to me. A different guy from the Jake I had sitting across from me at the diner a few days ago; who kissed me when he dropped me off at my car. And he wasn't the same guy who was all business just last night, except perhaps when he stayed with me until I fell asleep. Today I've seen at least three different versions of Jake, this last one being silently observant, and I honestly don't know what to make of him.

Except he makes me feel safe.

"Thanks," I mutter as I pass him back out to the elevators.

"Hang on one sec," he says, as he grabs me by the arm, taking me by surprise. It's not like we've exchanged more than two words to each other since he caught up with me in the hallway earlier. The ding of the arriving elevator seems to throw him for a second, but the next thing I know I'm hustled inside along with my cart. Once the doors close, and we start moving, he produces a key and fits it in the lock underneath the floor numbers on the panel. With a simple turn, the elevator comes to a stuttering stop.

"What the hell?"

"Just one more sec," he says, holding his finger up as he pulls a cell phone from his pocket with his other hand and dials a number. "Bree? It's me in the north elevator. Just checking something out. I'll have it going in a minute." Without waiting for an answer, he tucks the phone back into his pocket, slips his hands on either side of my head—his fingers tangling in the loose strands hanging down from my ponytail—and slams his mouth on mine.

I'm shocked and at first frozen, trying to wrap my head around what's happening, but then my mind quiets and my body comes alive. My mouth opens to his probing tongue and my hands sneak around his waist where my fingers anchor in the fabric of his black T-shirt, pressing into the muscles of his back underneath.

It could be seconds or hours; I lose all sense of time, only aware of the hunger of his mouth, his warm masculine scent, and the electrical charge that seems to spark through my body.

I'm not sure who pulls back first, but we end up foreheads touching, both struggling to catch our breath.

"*Holy shit*," he finally mutters, lifting his head to

look me in the face. "Kissing you is like touching a live wire." I would launch an immediate objection to that comparison, but I still can't get words to form, which gives him a chance to add, "It fucking blows every circuit."

That's much better. I can't stop the smug little smile that joins the deep blush on my face. Jake doesn't smile, he scowls down on me, right before he turns the key on the panel, and the elevator starts moving.

"I'll follow you home after your shift," he orders. "Don't walk out of the building on your own."

Before I have a chance to react to that, the doors slide open and he slips by the cart, disappearing down the hall without another word.

No wonder I can't figure him out, the man can't seem to make up his own damn mind.

JAKE

"What was that all about?"

I'm half-expecting Bree's question when I walk into the surveillance room.

"Nothing," I answer curtly, before radically changing the subject. "If you can keep an eye on her, I'm gonna grab a couple of hours. Do we have a bed free?"

"Probably. Yanis was in here earlier when you called, he's gotta pick up Drexler from the airport early tomorrow morning. I think he's in 316, so that means 314 is empty."

With a lift of my chin, but lead in my boots, I hightail it out of there before she pins me down with more questions. I do hear her throaty chuckle as the door shuts behind me.

This is how I know I fucked up. I should never have gone there again, but those loose tendrils dancing around her face and that little pink tongue sticking out between her lips as she was working eventually got to me. And fuck me if she didn't feel and taste like a dream.

I'm done with that now, though. Too distracting, and not just for me. When you find yourself breaking rules and lying to colleagues just to steal a taste of a sweet mouth, you know you're in trouble. Hoping my indiscretion escaped Yanis, when Bree and Dimi already seem to have my number, is a waste of time. That's the problem with a team, its strength is defined by the weakest link—and right now—I'm the fucking weak link.

Just a few hours ago, I sat across from my boss in an impromptu meeting with both Mazur brothers, going over what little Dimas had been able to find on the second floor. Other than half a print on a can of black spray paint, in a trashcan by door to the outside patio, and a partial palm on the doorknob, there wasn't much else. Not a lot for us to work with, and PASS doesn't have the resources for a proper investigation the police department has. Protection and security is more our gig.

"What if it was Steele?" I suggested, giving voice to an idea that had been bouncing around my mind. "She rejected him the night before—he was pissed off—maybe he decided to teach her a lesson."

Dimas admitted the thought had entered his mind, but Yanis seemed a bit more skeptical. He ended up busting my balls about handing off the Steele detail to his brother today, and then questioned the level of my interest in Rosie, which I told him was nothing more than professional. I lied.

Already being suspicious, I'm sure he has a pretty clear picture of what went down in that elevator just now. Not like he was my best friend before, so I really screwed the pooch on this one.

I try to be quiet when I get to the room, closing the door carefully, not even bothering to turn on the light or take off my boots when I lie down on the bed. Even so, my head barely hits the pillow when the connecting door between the two rooms opens and Yanis pokes his head through.

"I'm fucking exhausted so it's probably not a smart idea to get into this, but it's high fucking time you and me talk, one-on-one, tomorrow after my sit down with Drexler. Make sure you stay close." Without waiting for a response, he slams the door shut with a bang.

So much for a few hours of shut-eye.

"Ready?"

Rosie has her back to me, talking to Peabody, who's standing behind the desk, but both heads turn in my direction when I walk up. She simply nods; avoiding eye contact, but her friend has no such problem. He meets my eyes straight on, and is not afraid to show he is pissed off. I can take a good guess what they were discussing just now.

"You know, I was all for this before," Grant says, waving a finger from me to Rosie and back. "But that's when I thought you were going to be a straight-up guy and not a fucking tease."

"Grant…" she pleads, clearly flustered.

Rather than getting into a discussion when all he's doing is telling the truth, I put my hand in the small of her back and steer her toward the exit.

"Later, Peabody," I throw over my shoulder right before we walk outside, a very quiet Rosie beside me.

When we get to her place, she pulls into the driveway and I park at the end. I watch as she gets out and starts walking to the trailer, making a split-second decision.

"Do you have a minute?" I call out. She stops and looks at me. "Please?" I walk around the truck, open the passenger door for her, and then get back in behind the wheel.

"Jesus, that was embarrassing," she mumbles under her breath once she's seated in my truck, before looking at me. "I'm sorry, I—"

"Don't," I stop her. "You're friend has a point,

which is why we need to talk." I know I'm taking a risk, one Yanis would not be pleased with, but Rosie deserves to know.

"No need," she quickly interjects her hands raised defensively. "Clearly, I have no idea—"

"Do you think it might have been Steele?" I interrupt her and hear the sharp intake of breath at my question, telling me the idea is not new to her.

"Why would you say that?"

"For one, because only twenty-four hours before, in that same pool, the guy propositioned you and you turned him down. And you and I both know he could have more reason than that."

As if I'd hit her, at those last words Rosie snaps her head away from me, pulls her shoulders up to her ears, and wraps her arms around herself protectively.

"Rosie, look at me." I reach out and with my hand cupping her face; I slowly turn her toward me. I fucking hate seeing the fear in her eyes when she does as I ask. "I know you saw him that morning, and although he claims not to remember anything, we can't be sure he didn't see you too."

"Get away from me," she hisses, slapping my hand away from her face and scrambling for the door handle.

"It's a complicated situation, but I'm doing my best to look after you."

"Complicated?" she echoes, a hysterical pitch to her voice. "Looks pretty simple to me. Money talks, right? Famous actor gets himself in a pickle, and he pays you to protect his interests. Looking after me, my ass. You're here to make sure I keep quiet."

She finally finds the handle and scrambles out of the truck, but I'm not far behind. I catch her in the driveway and back her up against her car, bracing my arms on either side of her, and bending my head down to hers. To anyone looking, it might appear we're in the middle of a lovers' spat, when in reality I'm using my body to restrict her movement.

"Hear me out. I know this is fucked up, believe me. If it were up to me, I'd take you to the police station myself, so you could report what you saw. But this is not just about me, or you for that matter." I notice she's stopped struggling, and hope that means she's listening, I forge on. "It's about the hundreds of people, both crew and support staff, employees of local businesses, including your hotel, whose livelihoods would be impacted."

"How?" I just barely hear her question, but it gives me hope.

"Steele is not just the headliner of this movie, he's also a co-producer—he goes down, it's likely he'll take the entire project down with him. His name is what drew in the funds for this movie. He falls, it'll all come down, like dominoes."

I lift my head carefully and look down at her. Tears have gathered in her eyes, but she blinks them away.

"A man is dead. It's not fair." Her voice wavers. "This is a lot."

"I know."

"You played me."

"At first, but—"

The ringing of my phone interrupts me, and when I reach to answer it, Rosie frees herself from my hold. I watch her open the door to the trailer and slip inside.

"Yep."

"Where the fuck are you?" Yanis barks without introducing himself.

"I'll be there in ten."

I hang up and spend my drive back to the hotel trying to come up with a way out of this mess—without success.

CHAPTER 8

JAKE

"DREXLER IS IN a meeting with the director as we speak. He wants to switch up the schedule."

By the time I got back to the Spring Ridge, it was just coming up on six this morning, and Yanis already had everyone assembled in room 314.

"Switching up, how?" Bree, who looks a little rough after working through the night, asks.

"By moving the outdoor shoots scheduled for the end of the month at McInnis Conservation Area up to Monday, and leaving all remaining indoor scenes for last," Yanis fills her in.

"Maybe the more important question is why?"

Every eye in the room turns to me.

"Take a wild guess," Yanis offers, his face a stoic mask.

"He wants to get away from the heat."

"More accurately, he wants Steele away from the heat—especially after I filled him in on this last incident—but yes, the objective is to get away and let things cool down," he acknowledges.

"Right, so here's the way it'll go down," Dimas jumps in, taking over for his brother as he outlines everyone's assignments for the trip back to McInnis.

I'm surprised to find I'm no longer assigned to Steele, probably a good idea. In fact, I'm not scheduled to head back to McInnis with the rest of them at all. Am I being fired?

Dimas picks up on my confusion and walks over to me, while everyone files out of the room.

"Talk to my brother," he says, and walks out as well, leaving me to face Yanis.

"I fucked up," I admit grudgingly. I'm fully expecting to get my walking papers, so I may as well toss the cards on the table.

"Yes, you did."

"This situation is fucked up."

"Yes, it is," he agrees. "And more so because, for some goddamn reason, you pick this fucking time to get distracted, and let this fucking broad turn your head. What the fuck, Hutch? You're always so fucking disciplined and unmoving—always the reliable one—I've never seen you like this."

Confused, I do what I do best, I attack.

"What are you talking about? Reliable? You've been on my case since Dimi brought me on. Just waiting for a reason to send me packing."

"You're an idiot," he spits out. "Do you honestly think you'd be working for me, in the first place, if I didn't trust you? If I didn't think you were an asset?" He paces the floor, shaking his head, before he stops in front of me and pokes a finger in my chest. "You've carried that chip on your shoulder, and that guilt in your heart, like a goddamn badge of honor long enough. I asked Dimi to drag your ass out of whatever hole you were digging for yourself, and bring you home. You were out of control after he got his leg blown off, letting that guilt eat you alive. It was bad enough to have one brother come home on a stretcher, I wasn't about to sit by and wait for another to be brought back in a goddamn bag."

Stunned and slack-mouthed, I watch as Yanis swings around and plows a fist through the wall. In the silence that follows, all I hear is his heavy breathing as he keeps his back turned.

"I can't have you up in McInnis when your focus is elsewhere. I need someone to stay behind, coordinate transport of people and supplies, liaise with authorities…"

"Isn't that Bree's job?"

He turns to face me on a deep sigh.

"Bree is taking over your detail. You're taking over hers. That's the way it is for now. Think of it this way; it gives you a chance to keep an eye on your Ms. Perkins."

"I don't need…" I start protesting but I don't get very far. Yanis lifts a hand to stop me.

"What you need is to get your head out of your ass and quit being a martyr. You're so intent on paying for transgressions that don't exist, you can't see a shot at a good thing when it slaps you in the face." He rubs his hands over his face before clapping a hand on my shoulder and giving me a firm shake. "Look, I don't know if this girl is the one, but for fuck's sake, don't blow it off before you have a chance to find out."

I try to grasp at thoughts, but can't seem to focus on just one, let alone form any coherent words at this point.

"You're like a fucking brother to me," Yanis says in a much softer voice, as he reaches for the door. "And a royal pain in my ass."

ROSIE

"Do you have a minute?"

I'm in the men's restroom off the lobby, restocking paper hand towels when Jake walks in. It's not the first time I've seen him tonight, I was just more successful avoiding him earlier. He's got me cornered now, blocking the doorway.

"I'd rather not talk to you." I turn my back and continue filling the dispensers.

"That's fine," he rumbles in the deep voice that sends a little shiver down my back. *Damn him.* "You don't have to, I'll do the talking." I hear him let out a deep sigh when I don't respond. "I thought you should know the entire production is heading back out to McInnis tomorrow, for a couple of weeks of filming."

I can't stop myself from whipping around and

asking, "Are you?"

Jake shakes his head, hiding a grin as he checks out the toes of his boots.

"Nah. I'm staying here. Keeping an eye on things." He slowly looks up and meets my eyes. "On you."

All day I've been struggling with what he told me this morning. Feeling used, shocked, angry—but also finding understanding for some of his reasoning. Everything is not black and white in this world, I should understand that better than most, I lived in that gray area for many years.

I might be able to appreciate his motivations, but I can't get over his methods. The fact he took one look at me, and came to the conclusion I was an easy target to manipulate, stings like a motherfucker. Christ, was I really that weak? That stupid? I'd promised myself, after allowing a man to string me along and use me for over a decade, I would never let that happen again. And here I am.

So he can turn on the charm with those dark brooding eyes, and that deliciously gruff voice, but I'm no longer going to fall for it.

"Sounds good," I bite off, immediately dismissing him as I grab my cart and force him to step aside. Without looking at him, I walk out and head toward the ladies' room. My next stop.

Work provides a welcome distraction and any lingering frustration is taken out on the remainder of the public bathrooms. They sparkle. Maybe I should've saved some of that energy for the bathrooms at home, they could do with a good cleaning too, but it's usually the last thing I think about when I'm home. Maybe when I'm off tomorrow.

During my break, I patiently listen to Grant lament about his boyfriend leaving town with the rest of the film crew, and I'm embarrassed to admit I'm almost relieved when it's time to head up to do the second floor. I'm not even thinking about it until I push my cart out of the elevator, and almost run into a large body. It takes me a second to recognize him.

"He asked me to meet you here. He had some things to do."

I look at Dimas, slowly raising my eyebrow. Things to do, my foot.

"Thanks," I say curtly before starting down the hallway, but he quickly catches up and moves ahead.

Like Jake had done the night before, Dimas checks each space thoroughly before letting me inside. I realize they do it more for my peace of mind, than anything else, but it makes being here easier all the same. There isn't much conversation at all, and at some point, he actually starts helping; collecting garbage and dirty towels for me. The floor is done in no time.

"He's really a great guy—a good man," Dimas says while we're waiting for the elevator.

"I don't know what he told you," I start, but he doesn't give me a chance to finish.

"Nothing. That's not like him. But I have eyes; I've been up in the surveillance room all night, and

I've seen him trying to connect with you all over the hotel. I watched him go into the men's bathroom after you, and follow you out not two minutes later. I watched as he stood in the hallway, his eyes still on the ladies' room, long after you disappeared inside."

The ding of the elevator is a welcome sound, because this conversation is making me restless. The instant the elevator opens, I slip inside with my head down, but it's clear Dimas isn't done when he blocks the doors from closing.

"I don't doubt he did something to piss you off—the man wasn't graced with any social skills, so he'll probably do it again—but I know for a fact he's a good man."

I lift my head and glare at him. He holds my eyes for some very uncomfortable seconds, before removing his hand and letting the doors close.

Annoyed, frustrated, and even more confused, I make my way down to the hotel basement where the laundry facilities are. The large industrial-size machines run almost nonstop to keep up with the steady supply of dirty linens. I usually begin here, stacking my cart with clean sheets and towels before I start my shift. I end here too, to drop off the dirties I've collected.

I've just started a load with towels when the phone in my pocket buzzes. A look at the screen shows my home number, and I quickly check the time; two thirty. That can't be good.

"Hillary? What's wrong?"

"I'm sorry, Rosie. I swear she was sleeping before I turned in, but when I got up to use the bathroom, she wasn't in her bed and the front door was open. I looked around the block and I can't find her. Dora and Les Shipman from next door, along with the neighbors on their other side, are looking and I just came back to call you."

"How long?" I ask, already taking the stairway, two at a time, to the lobby.

"I can't know for sure, anywhere between forty-five minutes and two hours."

"Hang up, and call the police. I'm on my way."

I fly through the door and into the lobby, making a beeline for Grant, who sees me coming.

"What's wrong?"

"Mom's gone missing. I have to get home," I tell him, diving into the small office behind the front desk where I left my purse and keys.

"Hold on," he says, grabbing me by the shoulder when I try to rush by. "Let me call someone to go with you. You're shaking, I can't let you drive like this."

"Let me go, Grant. There's no time," I bite off, jerking out of his hold and bolting for the back door.

I hoof it to my car; click the key remote to unlock, to find the damn thing doesn't work. I try again, once more without success. When I go to unlock the door with the key, my key ring slips from my shaking hand and clatters to the pavement. My eyes blur with frustrated tears, as I drop down to my knees and use both hands to search. My fingers snag on the key ring and I scramble to my feet. Quickly, I unlock the door and jerk it open, sliding behind the wheel. I buckle up, start the engine, and turn on the lights by rote, when my door is yanked open and I about jump out of my skin.

"Move over."

I'm still so stunned; I blindly follow Jake's order and climb over the gearshift and into the passenger seat. In seconds, we're hustling down the road.

"What are you doing?"

"Saw you almost throw down with your buddy and rush downstairs. He tells me your mom's missing, and you shouldn't be driving. So I'm driving."

I open my mouth to protest, but then wisely shut it again. Mom is missing. I could use all the help I can get to find her.

"Hillary is calling the police," I say instead, wiping at the tears of frustration.

"Good." He throws me a quick glance before scanning the road in front of him. I'm not sure how fast we're going, but I don't think my Cruiser has ever hit these speeds. Not on city streets anyway. "Take my phone from my pocket," he instructs, lifting his right elbow to give me room. "I need you to speed dial three and put it on speakerphone."

I do as he asks, and in seconds, Dimas comes on the line.

"Rosie's mom's missing. I'm in the car with Rosie to look for her. Can you make sure GJPD has been notified? Her nurse, Hillary…"

"Glenwood," I fill in.

"…Glenwood, was supposed to call it in. Make sure dispatch knows Mrs. Perkins has Alzheimer's and is extremely confused. Wouldn't be a bad idea to have EMTs at the ready."

"Done."

The line goes dead before I even have a chance to say thank you, but it feels good to know things are being done.

"Thank you," I say to Jake instead, who quickly reaches over and gives my wringing hands a squeeze.

When we turn onto Centennial Road, we are right behind a police cruiser, and another one is just pulling into the driveway up ahead. Jake parks my Cruiser along the curb and I'm already getting out before he even turns off the engine.

"Ma'am, hold up," I hear one of the officers coming up the driveway call out when I run past on the front lawn, but I'm not listening. I'm aiming for the open door where I see Hillary waiting.

"Anything?"

"Sorry," Hillary apologizes, looking over my shoulder. I turn as well to see Jake walk up with the two officers.

I'm impatient to get out there and look, but Jake assures me we have a better chance of finding her fast if we do it in an organized fashion.

"Ms. Perkins, has your mother run off before?" one of the officers asks. I think he said his name is Conti.

"Run off? She's just confused, she has Alzheimer's; she forgets where she is. She's only wandered out of the house once before, but that was during the day and she ended up in the neighbor's yard three doors down. Never in the middle of the night." I don't even notice I'm wringing my hands again until Jake puts his on top, stilling my movement right away. I instinctively flip a hand, palm up, and let him slip his fingers between mine. He squeezes my hand to get my attention.

"Does she have any favorite spots she likes to go to? Places that might be familiar to her?"

His comforting voice and warm touch steadies me, and I focus on his question.

"The corner store—we sometimes walk to get milk, if it's a nice day. She likes the cemetery. Visiting my dad's grave."

One of the reasons Mom never wanted to move was because our lot backs up to the large cemetery she buried Dad in. She still wants him close.

"Have you checked there?" Officer Conti turns and asks Hillary, who shakes her head.

"The gates are locked between ten at night and seven in the morning. She wouldn't be able to get in."

"You'd be surprised," he tells her before turning to me. "Why don't you take me along the route you would normally use if you were to visit the cemetery? Ms. Glenwood can stay here with my colleague, in case she comes back."

I'm already up and out of the chair, eager to get

moving. To do *something*. But I don't let go of Jake's hand.

We walk south on Centennial and just where the sidewalk runs right alongside the fence, Jake spots something. He lets go of my hand and bends down beside the fence, picking something off the ground.

"Do you recognize this?" he asks, holding up a strip of fabric; the small, pink flowered pattern very familiar to me.

"Her nightgown," I whisper, my eyes already attempting to scan the cemetery beyond.

"She must've tried to climb over," Conti suggests.

"Succeeded is more like it," Jake counters, staring off into the darkness as well, before addressing me. "Is your dad's grave close?"

"It's farther to the south," I explain, pointing in the general direction, when something occurs to me, "but the pond is right behind that building."

"Pond?"

"She likes feeding the ducks."

Officer Conti starts talking into the radio clipped to his shoulder, but I ignore him, step up to the fence, and wrap my fingers through the chain links. It's not that high, between four and five feet. Determination can make things possible, and before anyone even notices, I'm up and half over.

"You can't just climb over," the young officer protests, startled. "I'm having dispatch contact someone to open the main gate."

"It's dark, the woman could be hurt, or worse,

she could have fallen into that pond." Jake swings himself over the fence like it's nothing, while I'm still trying to work out how to get down on the other side. His solution is to grab me under my arms and pluck me off, setting me safely on my feet. "You wait for someone to open that gate and it might just be too late. We're going."

With that, he grabs my hand again and pulls me along, weaving between the silent graves. Halfway to the pond, I hear whimpering and start running. We find her lying on her side on the path that runs from the building down to the water. Her torn nightgown like a beacon in the dark night.

"Maxwell," is all she whispers on a continuous loop, until the ambulance doors close her in a good twenty minutes later.

The moment they drive off, I lose it.

CHAPTER 9

JAKE

"*H*OW IS SHE?"

Dimas catches me just when I walk into the hotel.

"Broken hip. She'll probably need surgery."

"Damn, that's tough," he commiserates. "Rosie holding up okay?"

"She's got her mom's nurse there with her, and Peabody just showed up at the hospital. Figured I'd be more use here." I look around the busy lobby. With the big exodus of the movie people this morning, and the chaos it causes, security is a challenge. It's hard to keep track of who belongs and who doesn't with people constantly walking in and out. "How far are you?"

"Yanis went ahead with a few guys to secure the site at McInnis. Thankfully, he took Drexler with him, that's one headache less. But the other one is still in his suite, still drunk I'm guessing. Bree told me this morning that Drexler apparently gave him a good talking to last night. So good, one of the maids alerted security, the yelling was that loud."

I had been avoiding Steele—well, technically I'd been told to stay away from him—but I'd like a chat with him myself, before he leaves.

"Has he said anything? Steele?"

"About the accident or about Rosie?"

"Either one, or both, I guess."

Dimi looks around and grabs me by the arm, pulling me toward a quiet corner. "We've been told to back off," he whispers.

"By who?"

"Phil Drexler. He gave Yanis hell for questioning Steele. Not that the idiot said much, I think between his boss and the army of lawyers he has working for him, they'd already put a muzzle on him."

I can see why they would. It seems to be the preferred way of dealing with things in that industry; sweep it under the rug. It eats at me, by merit of our contract; we are complicit in that. From the frustrated scowl on Dimi's face, I'm not the only one.

"Drexler gone, you said? Then maybe I'll go make sure our big star doesn't miss his limo."

"Jesus, Hutch." Dimi shakes his head. "You put one finger on the guy, Yanis will have both our asses and we can kiss our contract goodbye."

"Not to worry, I'm just looking for a friendly chat."

The place is a pigsty.

I haven't been inside this suite for a few days, and it looks like a frat party went down here last night. Crumpled beer cans everywhere, a bottle of Jack—with maybe two fingers left in the bottom—sitting on the table, dirty clothes strewn over the furniture, and empty food containers on every surface. It smells like a fucking brewery.

As does the man sitting on the side of the bed, with his head in his hands, when I walk into the bedroom after banging loudly on the door.

"Tough night?" I ask, louder than I need to, just to see him flinch. The only answer I get is a groan.

Oh yeah, that boy is hurting. *Good.* He'll be hurting even more when I'm done with him.

"Here's the deal," I start, moving to stand in front of him, trying to ignore the sour stench of booze, body odor, and old puke wafting off him. "Take the time to really think about this while you're stuck in your goddamn trailer in the mountains; I have my eye on you. I've had my eye on you all along, and I have no compunction at all to use what I know to rip your career to shreds. And I'm not just talking about killing a man while driving fucking drunk. You're an entitled asshole, who thinks the world should worship his micro dick, and doesn't hesitate to resort to assault and attempted murder to get his way." The whole time I'm reading him the riot act, his head remains bent, until I mention attempted murder. Then his head shoots up, shock on his face.

"What? I never—"

"Don't," I butt in; cutting him off before I land my blow. "I have some interesting surveillance footage I confiscated but didn't destroy. Stuff the press will have a field day with, showing you in the hot tub, a couple of weeks back, with a pretty blond?" I get great satisfaction when I see realization settle on his face. "One step out of line from you, one misplaced word, and every major news outlet will anonymously receive a copy of that tape."

Without looking back, I walk out of the bedroom and out of the suite. I'd much rather have seen him forced to own up to his responsibilities, but this will have to do for now. He'll heel; he won't want those images of him drilling a *guy's* ass floating around.

Bree is just coming out of the elevator when I walk up, immediately casting a suspicious glance over my shoulder at the door of the suite.

"He's still breathing, if that's what you're worried about," I bite off, which earns me a punch in the shoulder.

"Playing with fire, Hutch," she admonishes me. "But I was actually hoping our golden boy had dragged his ass out of bed by now. I want to get going before too many crazy fans have a chance to gather. There's a few circling the parking lot already."

"He's up. You may want to get him to shower first, though. He fucking stinks."

"Wonderful," Bree grumbles, walking past me toward the door, where she stops. "By the way, I was at the office at the butt crack of dawn, making sure you have everything you need. There's a list with contacts and numbers I left with Radar, and you'll need to let the GJPD know we are pulling out today. I wasn't able to get hold of the guy in charge of the hit-and-run investigation, Bergland—he never returned my message—and we don't want him getting the wrong idea when he finds out for himself we've pulled up stakes."

"He wouldn't be wrong," I point out, earning me an eye-roll.

"Just don't forget."

"As soon as I get to the office," I promise.

It looks like the place cleared out while I was upstairs, because other than Dimas, who is doctoring up a coffee in the coffee shop, the lobby is virtually empty.

"Everyone head out?"

"All but pretty boy upstairs, but Bree's got him covered. The trailers are lined up in convoy along Third Street, I'm just grabbing a coffee for the road," he smirks.

"You have the whole production waiting on you?"

Dimi grins wide. "Yup. Tit for tat. They've done nothing but keep me waiting for the past month or so." He elbows me in the ribs in passing. "You better get moving too. They were loading the equipment on the trucks at the warehouse, last time I checked, but you'd better head over and make sure they're on their way in short order as well. Just give me a heads-up when they leave."

I watch him walk out the front doors, and get into the passenger side of a company Tahoe with the PASS logo on the side. One of our guys is behind the wheel, and he doesn't waste any time pulling away from the curb, a long line of limos and trailers following behind.

Fucking Dimi.

ROSIE

Waiting is torture.

They'd warned us surgery would be two hours, minimum, but it could be longer.

Well, it's been four hours and we haven't seen anyone.

Since we ended up at St. Mary's anyway, and apparently it was a busy morning in the emergency room, Hillary was pulled in to work. I guess it's still busy in the ER because I haven't seen her since. Luckily Grant showed up, so even after Jake left, I was not alone. Not that it matters much. Grant, tired from working the night shift and not feeling well, is curled up on the other love seat across from me in the small waiting room, snoring like a wild boar. I can't sleep. I've tried, but my mind won't let me rest.

Good thing I was somewhat prepared for emergencies, because when we got back to the trailer, all I had to do was grab the folder with all Mom's medical and insurance information. Jake insisted on driving me to the hospital, and Hillary said she'd follow as soon as she packed a few things for us.

I guess she'd drawn her own conclusions based on Jake's description of how we found Mom, and guessed, quite accurately, we'd be spending some significant time in the hospital. So she had grabbed some things for Mom, but also packed a change of clothes for me, along with a few toiletries I might need. The last thing she'd tossed in the duffel bag were a few bottles of water and some granola bars, one of which I'm munching on.

It's well past lunchtime, and the last thing I ate was around midnight: a handful of fries and a bite of that burger that churned in my stomach all night. Of course, the horrible coffee from the vending machine, outside the closed cafeteria this morning, didn't exactly help. The granola bar feels a little better in my stomach, although what would really be nice is a hot tea.

As if conjured from thin air, Jake walks into the waiting room, carrying a paper bag and a cardboard tray with four take-out cups bearing the logo of a coffee shop around the corner.

"Any news?" he asks, setting the tray and bag on the table.

"Still waiting." I have my feet up on the love seat and move to make room for him, but he sits down and simply lifts my feet on his lap.

"Stay," he orders. "I didn't know what you wanted, so I brought a couple of coffees, a hot chocolate, and a tea. I also snagged a few sandwiches because I wasn't sure if you'd eaten."

It takes me less than a second to find the tea and am pleased to spot a few containers of milk in the bag.

"Thank you," I mumble after having taken my first sip. That feels so good in my stomach.

I notice Jake watching me, one side of his mouth tilted up, and I realize I may have moaned out loud.

"What are you doing here? Aren't you supposed to be working?"

"Just came from the office, thought I'd check on you before I head home. Haven't been there in weeks, for all I know, it's no longer standing."

"You didn't have to go out of your way," I indicate, trying hard not to show I'm fishing for info. Judging from the flash of a smile on his face as he digs a sandwich from the bag, I failed.

"The office is near the airport and I have a place on the corner of Cortland and Twenty-eighth," he says, taking a hearty bite of what looks to be a club sandwich. My stomach starts rumbling on cue. "There's a few more in there." He gestures at the bag and I dive in.

We eat in companionable silence for a bit, when Grant says something unintelligible in his sleep, and promptly resumes snoring.

"He been here the whole time?" Jake wants to know.

"He wasn't feeling well. He's been asleep almost since they wheeled mom into the OR. He's dead to the world."

The words have barely left my mouth when the door opens, and a doctor I'd seen briefly earlier today walks in wearing surgical scrubs. Grant shoots up in his seat, disoriented, and rubbing the sleep from his eyes.

"Ms. Perkins? Is this all family?" he asks, and I quickly nod. Grant is as good as, and Jake's the one who quietly talked to her to keep her calm while we waited for the ambulance, and the one who held me as I fell apart after. He's already seen the worst of us. "Very well," he responds to my acknowledgment. "The surgery itself went well. We were able to stabilize the neck of the femur, where the fracture was located." He takes a breath and I brace myself, because it's already clear from his demeanor that not everything went smoothly. "Your mother didn't respond well to the anesthesia," he continues, "something that is always a risk in elderly patients. Especially those who already have some medical issues. We had to restart her heart twice in the OR, successfully, and she's been taken to recovery. You'll be able to see her in a little bit, but only for a few minutes. Given the problems she had during surgery, we need to monitor her closely. It's too soon to know what, if any, long-term effects she will have, but I think it's safe to say if you have already looked at possible placements in nursing homes, you may want to narrow it down. If not, you'll want to start looking in short order. Even just the recovery from the hip surgery will require at least a few months of rehabilitative care in a full-care facility."

My head is spinning, trying to process the information without letting panic set in. I can feel Jake's warm hand wrapped around my ankles, but I can't concentrate on anything.

Mom almost died. *Twice.*

Even as I try to come up with questions to ask, the two things that keep flashing in my mind are the facts I almost lost her, and the modest balance line on my bank account statement.

"Will someone let us know when Rosie can see her mom?" Grant asks on my behalf, and I manage to shoot him a little smile.

"A nurse will come get you and we will make sure you're kept up-to-date at all times."

"Thank you," I manage, as he nods and leaves the room, letting the door fall shut behind him.

The nurse finally comes to get me forty minutes later.

I just sent Grant home, he still wasn't feeling the greatest and wanted a shower and his bed. Jake, on the other hand, was unmovable. He insisted on sticking around, no matter what I said.

Hillary popped in to check, on the first break she had since we got here this morning. Apparently things still haven't let up in the ER, and she'll likely be busy for another few hours before she can hand off to the next shift. She promised to check in with me first thing in the morning; after I assured her I'll be all right by myself tonight.

I've also just hung up with the hotel's night manager, to update him on my mother's condition. I mention needing to take some personal time, something Grant strongly suggested and Jake agreed with, to make sure my mother is looked after. He didn't give me too much trouble, said I wouldn't be docked for time missed so far, but since I have no vacation time saved up, it would have to be unpaid leave.

I'd figured that already, but there's little I can do about it. It is what it is. Technically, today and tomorrow are my weekend, but come Wednesday, I'm officially without income.

I don't get much of a chance to fret about it, because just then the nurse pokes her head in and introduces herself as Kim.

"I'll wait here," Jake rumbles when I get up to follow her. Almost instinctively, I open my mouth to tell him there's no need, but just as quickly shut it. I don't know what to expect when I see Mom, and I don't really want to come back to an empty room.

The nurse leads the way down the hall, where she stops in front of a double door that reads Intensive Care Unit, and turns to me.

"Just so you know, your mother woke up briefly earlier but was quite confused and combative when we attempted to do some cognitive tests on her. We had to sedate her so she wouldn't hurt herself, and moved her here to the ICU for now. She will be sleeping and is hooked up on monitors. I want you to be prepared," Kim adds in a sympathetic voice that almost has me in tears, but I steel myself and follow her inside.

"You can hold her hand and talk to her, she may be able to hear you, even if she doesn't respond," she says, pointing at the stool beside the hospital bed that holds my mother.

It's amazing how small she looks; lying there hooked up to IVs and attached to wires. Her hair, which had just been done a few days ago, stood out from her head in clumps, making her face look even more gaunt. She looks like she's aged twenty years in one day.

Tears burn in my eyes as I dig through my purse, looking for the hair pick I usually carry on me.

"Gave me quite a scare there, Mom," I mumble, as I gently work the tangles from her hair. "If you'd have waited for me to come home, I would've gone with you to feed the ducks. I know you love that pond. It's such a pretty spot, like a little oasis in the dry land around us." I prattle on, spouting mostly nonsense. Anything to keep me from focusing on the beeping of the machines she's hooked up to. "That's looking better already," I tell her, running my hand over her soft, rather sparse hair, now spread on her thin pillow like a halo. "You always did have pretty hair."

Not long after, Kim pokes her head around the curtain.

"Looks good," she says, smiling at me.

I know it's time to go and kiss the top of Mom's

hand, noticing how papery thin her skin has become. How fragile she is.

They say roles reverse. That those who raised us, looked after us growing up, become the ones who need to be nurtured in the end. I don't know that my mother could ever have been considered nurturing, that would've been more my father, but there is no doubt I feel fiercely protective of her.

Jake is standing by the window, talking on his phone, when I come in.

"Gotta go." With his eyes on me, he hangs up the phone, just in time to open his arms for me to walk into, planting my face in his chest.

"Ah, Rosie," he rumbles, cupping the back of my head in his big palm.

CHAPTER 10

JAKE

"*I* PUT A few towels by the sink for you."

Rosie throws me a little smile and disappears into my bathroom, pulling the door shut behind her. Other than Dimas, I've never had anyone in my house before.

It had been surprisingly easy to get her to come with me. She looked worn, emotionally drained, and plain exhausted when she walked into the waiting room, and it took me all of one second to see she'd had enough. All I did was mention my house was close, and that after a shower and a little rest I'd have her right back at the hospital, for her to concede. We stopped by the nurses' station to tell them we were leaving and made sure they also had my name and phone number, just in case.

She let me guide her to my vehicle, not even mentioning her piece of shit I left parked at the hotel this morning when I grabbed my truck, and stared blindly out the window for the five minutes it took me to drive home.

Thankfully, my fridge holds half a carton of eggs that still fall within the best-before date, and I keep some bread in the freezer. It's been a while since I've been home, let alone grocery shopping. I'm also not a great cook, by any stretch of the imagination, but I can do the scrambled eggs and toast she seems to like. The woman currently naked in my shower— something I'm trying not to linger on—needs to get some food in her before she collapses. I think she took two bites from the sandwich I brought her and that was a few hours ago.

I'm about to go check on her, when twenty minutes later I hear the shower finally turn off. It takes her another ten minutes to come walking into the kitchen. She's changed out of the work clothes she'd still been wearing, into the clothes Hillary packed for her. Some stretchy pair of pants and a large T-shirt with a scoop neck, which seems to keep sliding off her shoulder. Not sure if it's supposed to or not, but it makes for an enticing picture.

"Have a seat." I point to the stools tucked underneath the kitchen island.

My kitchen isn't huge—it's just a small, two-bedroom, adobe bungalow—and when I'm here, I either eat at the island or on the couch in front of the TV. I never bothered to invest in a dining room table, since I don't really spend much time here anyway. In fact, I don't have much furniture at all, other than a couch, coffee table and TV, and a bed and dresser in the master. The other bedroom holds only my treadmill and weight bench. It takes the crew of two, who come here once a month, maybe an hour to clean the place.

"Want some eggs and toast?" I ask, already popping the bread down in the toaster, without waiting for an answer. I take out the pan of scrambled eggs I kept warm in the oven.

"Sure." It's the first word I've heard her say since she saw her mother. A small blush makes the freckles stand out on her pale cheeks, when she catches me watching her braid her wet hair. "If I don't, it turns into a Brillo pad," she explains. I doubt that gorgeous red hair of hers could look anything but lush, but I keep it to myself and just smile.

"I'm out of jam," I mention as the toast pops up. "But I have some butter." Not sure why I said that, I've never bought a jar of jam in my fucking life. I don't even like the stuff, it's too sweet, but I find myself wishing I could offer her some.

"Butter's fine."

She ends up eating only some of the eggs and half a piece of toast, but it's something.

I install her in front of the TV on the couch, since she says she's too restless to sleep. I busy myself washing the few dishes we dirtied, and doing some work on my laptop sitting at the counter. I don't know how long it's been but I find myself yawning constantly, and when I look over at the couch, Rosie is curled up on her side, fast asleep. At some point she must have loosened the braids in her hair, because most of her face is covered with the curls.

It's getting dark outside, and a quick glance at my computer screen shows it's almost nine. I'm willing to bet she hasn't slept much in the past few days, and frankly, I haven't either. Resolutely I close my computer, turn off the TV, and carefully scoop Rosie in my arms, carrying her to the bedroom. She is dead to the world and doesn't even flinch when I lay her down, covering her with only a sheet. I'd love nothing better than to crawl in bed with her, but I'm not so sure that's a good idea. I leave the room, pull the door almost shut behind me, and hit the bathroom for a quick shower.

It's tempting—standing under the hot stream and thinking of Rosie, naked in my shower a short while ago—to slide a fist over my hard cock and jerk off. Something about that seems wrong though. Doesn't matter that the woman, at the top of my current spank bank list, is currently sleeping on the other side of a very thin wall—I can't bring myself to rub one out.

Fucking hell.

Still tired, but now painfully frustrated as well, I step out of the shower and quickly dab myself dry. I slip into the bedroom, dig a pair of boxers from my drawer, and bend over to put them on, dropping the towel from around my hips. I thought she was sleeping, but the sharp intake of breath from the bed behind me tells a different story.

"You're awake." I point out the obvious as I

quickly tug my underwear over my ass. Not that I have an issue being naked, but she may.

"Erm…yes." Her voice is thick and drowsy with sleep. Sexy as hell.

"Go back to sleep," I urge her softly, as I head for the door.

"Where are you going?"

Something in the tone of her voice has me stop in my tracks and turn around. She looks like a fucking wet dream; her long shiny hair draped all over my pillow, one of her legs slightly cocked at the knee and falling open, and her eyes sparkling under heavy eyelids.

"The couch," I answer after clearing my throat. "I'll crash on the couch." I'm not sure why I'm repeating myself; I guess I need the extra push. I still stand unmoving with the door in my hand, but my eyes feasting on her, when she pushes up on an elbow.

"You don't have to go."

In two steps, I'm by the bed, any and all resolve easily forgotten as I slide in beside her. She easily molds herself against my side, her arm anchored around my stomach and her head tucked under my chin. Working hard to ignore certain insistent parts of my anatomy, I tilt my head down, press a kiss in her hair, and wrap her tightly in my arms.

I can't remember anything else until the faint sound of a phone ringing wakes me around seven in the morning. Grudgingly, I untangle myself from Rosie, who wrapped herself around me like an octopus and seems oblivious to the ringing. By the time I get to the living room, the sound has stopped, but starts up again as I locate my phone, which I left sitting in the charger on the kitchen counter. I snatch it up and answer.

"Mr. Hutchinson?" The voice on the other side is tentative, and I don't blame them; I may have grunted when I answered. I clear my throat and try again.

"This is he."

"Ah…this is Bergland, Grand Junction PD? I'm sorry I missed your calls yesterday, but I was out most of the day. I'm used to dealing with Ms. Graves, it took me a minute to figure out you were calling from PASS."

"That's right," I confirm curtly, not hiding the fact I'm not thrilled with a call at barely seven in the morning. Clearly Officer Bergland likes to have the upper hand. Trying to keep my voice down, I explain the film crew will be shooting in McInnis over the next few weeks, and we were merely notifying as a courtesy.

"That might be a problem," he says. "We've just received a report from the lab on some forensic evidence that was found at the scene. Some new questions have come up that suggest we may need to have a closer look at a few of your people."

"If there's anything I can help you with, I'm sure I can relay any questions you have to the appropriate people. Unless you prefer to wait until they return? That should be in a week or two."

"I'll need a list of all vehicles associated with the production," he presses on. "Your security fleet, trailers, support vehicles, limos, and any personal vehicles belonging to staff. Make, model, color, and year."

"I'll do my best to get that to you as fast as possible." I don't make any promises as to how fast, because given this bit of information; I have some clean up to do in a goddamn hurry.

"I'm afraid you'll have to do better than that." He sounds less than impressed, but I don't give a fuck. I understand it's important to stay on the good side of the local cops, especially now, but diplomacy has never been my strong suit.

"And I'm telling you that's the best you're gonna get."

I end the call and toss my phone on the counter. I'm in need of some very strong fucking coffee.

"Is that the hospital?"

I turn around at the sound of her raspy voice. Her eyes are worried as she comes shuffling into the kitchen, her hair in wild tangles around her pale face.

"No, honey." The endearment almost slips unnoticed from my lips. "It was work. Sorry if it woke you."

Still half asleep, and likely without much conscious thought, she once again walks right up to me, pressing her face in my chest, and slipping her arms around my waist. The anger I had buzzing under my skin disappears at her touch.

Pulling her close is fast becoming a habit.

ROSIE

He smells good. Like man and soap.

Feels good too. Warm, a little fuzzy, and solid, but not uncomfortably ripped. I mean uncomfortable in the sense I'd be uncomfortable if he were too perfect. Although, as I was able to ascertain last night, despite the minimal light, his ass is a picture of perfection.

I'm not sure why it is I throw myself at him all the time. Men like him used to intimidate me. They still do. Yet despite the fact Jake is sometime bristly and mostly confusing—not to mention self-admittedly deceitful—I find safety and comfort in his arms. Like when Dad was alive.

Oh crap! Don't tell me I have unresolved daddy issues? Clearly I haven't been hugged enough since he passed away, and Mom was never one for physical demonstrations. *Mom!* I can't believe I almost forgot.

"You didn't hear anything?" I ask, pushing out of his embrace abruptly to look for my purse.

"On the couch," he says dryly, easily reading the random twists of my mind. "Want some coffee?"

It isn't until I fish my phone from my purse, dial the hospital, and wait to be connected to the ICU desk, that I take a second to appreciate a scantily clad Jake putzing around his kitchen. Wearing only boxers. Sure, I just had my face planted between his pecs and my hands on his strong back, but still groggy, I never quite got a decent visual.

"Ms. Perkins, are you there?" The disembodied voice is almost yelling to get my attention.

"Gosh, yes. I'm so sorry; I'm still half asleep. How is my mother?" I ramble, lying through my teeth. Something that apparently doesn't go unnoticed, since half-naked Jake catches me ogling him, and smirks. I quickly swing around and focus my eyes out the window.

"Stable. She made it through the night without issues. This morning we're slowly letting her wake up for some tests the doctor would like to run."

"Will I be able to see her?"

"After the noon hour is best. We may have a better idea of what we're dealing with by then."

I thank her, hang up, and shoot off a quick message to Grant, who may still be asleep, to see how he's feeling today. I'm just reading his response—**_Stopped puking blood, that's good, right?_**—when Jake walks up and hands me a mug.

"Just cream?" he asks, and I just nod. I'll drink coffee any damn way he thinks I take it, as long as he serves it to me wearing next to nothing. Or nothing—whatever works.

"They're doing tests on Mom this morning and Grant's puking blood." One of Jake's eyebrows lifts up when that random message comes flying from my mouth. To illustrate, I flip around my phone and show him Grant's message. "I should probably call him."

"You do that," Jake suggests, "and I'll get some

clothes on."

"Okay."

I wait for him to turn and walk away so I can admire his rear assets in daylight, but he stays standing there, looking down on me.

"Morning, Rosie," he rumbles in a low voice as he tags me with a hand on my neck and pulls me close.

"Morning…" I manage whispering, but already his mouth is on mine in a gentle, deliciously lazy kiss with soft lips and subtle heat. "…Jake," I finish when he finally breaks away, and I watch, a dopey smile on my face, as he turns and walks out of the room.

By the time he's dressed and back, I have assured myself Grant is still alive and going in to see a doctor today. I am on my second cup of coffee, and I have French toast cooking on the stove. The man has oatmeal and powdered coffee creamer in his cupboard, three eggs and half a jar of mustard in his fridge, and three and a half loaves of bread and what looks to be half a cow in his freezer. French toast was the only legit option.

"I was going to take you for breakfast," he says as he walks into the kitchen. "But this works for me too."

"Where is my car?" I ask, as I slide a few pieces on a plate and set it in front of him.

"Left it in the parking lot at the hotel," he says, half a piece of toast already in his mouth.

"I'll need it, if you could drop me off there after? I should probably use this morning to go home to grab

Mom's insurance stuff and start looking for a care facility for her."

Not a task I'm particularly looking forward to, mainly because I'm also planning to have a long good look at our finances. Once I've paid the deductible on Mom's insurance, I know there will be just crumbs left in that account. I also have to prepare for the worst-case scenario, should she not make it. I remember from when my father died, they had a special insurance policy that covers expenses should one of them pass away. I just don't know whether that would still be sufficient today, twenty-some years later. Now I feel a bit stupid that I've never really checked that policy before, I kind of assumed it would cover any needs when the time came. Well, that time could be here, I'm already on very thin financial ice, and the last thing I need is to be unprepared for an expense that is sure to come up. If not now, then at some point in the not so distant future.

All in all, I have a fun morning ahead of me, but it's better than twiddling my thumbs in a hospital waiting room.

"I can do that," Jake responds. "I've got some stuff to take care of downtown anyway."

"You need some new wheels. *That,* is a crap car."

I turn on Jake, who is leaning out of the window of his fancy truck, eyeing my PT. Sure, it's a piece of shit, but it's *my* piece of shit. I'm the only one who gets to make fun of it.

"I also need a vacation in Maui, a new Eileen Fisher wardrobe, the legs of a five foot ten woman, and an ungodly amount of liposuction, but that's also not going to happen, because I have a mother I need to find a decent home for."

With a closing huff to my mini rant, I focus on unlocking my car with the key, since the remote locks for some reason aren't working.

"Who is Eileen Fisher?"

I turn an angry glare on him as I finally wrestle open my obstinate car door.

"Really? That's what you got out of that?" Shaking my head, I slip behind the wheel, but just before I slam the door shut, I make the mistake of glancing over and spot the half grin on his face.

Rude.

CHAPTER 11

I'M STILL SMILING when I pull up to the run-down looking building housing Brick's Rod Body Shop.

The quiet, hardworking Rosie may have caught my attention, but this feisty and passionate version I'm getting to know, is holding it.

Brick—his real name is Ernest Paver—is a friend of the Mazur brothers. A massive man almost as wide as he is tall, with a loud booming laugh, and a ready smile, but don't let that fool you. Underneath that jovial exterior, he is definitely someone to reckon with, both in terms of his high quality work and his questionable associations.

It's one of the reasons Yanis likes him looking after our fleet; Brick has no issues straddling or even overstepping the law. A man like Brick lives by his own sense of justice, and being part of the local chapter of an influential MC in town, he's a man you want on your side.

"Someone got laid," he booms from the open bay,

where he's working on what looks like a 1969 GTO in rough condition.

"Not that lucky," I return, grinning as I walk up to him, adding as an afterthought, "yet. I'm working on it." Brick seems to find this hilarious.

"Losing your touch?"

"Don't think I ever had one," I admit, slapping my hand in the shovel-sized one he's holding out.

"Good-looking fellah like yourself?"

"Jesus, Brick—don't be saying shit like that holding my hand." I pull out of his hold as he cracks up again.

"What can I do you for?" he asks, finally turning serious. "You here for that Lexus?"

"How'd you guess?"

"Cop by the name of Bergland called a few days ago, looking for any cars with damage to the front end dropped here in the past week or so." Brick shrugs his massive shoulders. "Course I explained to him I build hot rods—specialty cars—I don't waste my time on run-of-the-mill body work."

That's the beauty of having someone like Brick on the payroll. He's able to sneak in all kinds of aftermarket upgrades on our cars, which are not always legal. On the flip side, we provide him with a regular paycheck for easy, but steady maintenance work, so he can work the rest of the time on his designs.

"Appreciate it."

"Don't mention it. You want that ride to disappear? Body work is done, I have it in the back under a tarp waitin' for ya, but you may not want it back."

"Thought about that," I admit. "But I think it might create problems down the road." Truth is, there are too many people who might have seen Steele with his sporty ride and having it suddenly disappear might raise more questions. I don't need to share all this with Brick. I'm sure he can guess. "I'm thinking a paint job," I say instead. "Something close in color but not the same. Something close enough, it would be hard to see from a distance."

"Shouldn't be a problem. When do you need it by?"

"Two weeks enough time?"

"Doable," he answers, clapping me on the shoulder. "Give you a call?"

"Please. And thanks." I shake his hand and start walking toward my truck when he calls after me.

"Hey, handsome! Lose the scowl, you may get lucky!"

"Kiss my ass!" I yell over my shoulder, making him laugh harder.

"Don't you wish!"

After a quick stop to check in with the two guards we left at the warehouse, I'm ready to head up to the office, but give Rosie a quick call first.

"Where are you?" I ask when she answers the phone.

"At home. Pulling my hair out."

"What do you need me to do?" The urge to jump in and fix whatever shit she's dealing with is strong, but I doubt it'll be welcome.

"Nothing," she quickly responds, confirming my thoughts. "Just stuff I've got to sort out myself."

"You sure? I'm about to head to the office, but I can easily swing by."

"I'm good. I'm heading to the hospital shortly anyway."

"Okay. Stay in touch."

It's quiet on the other side and I'm starting to wonder if she's hung up on me.

"I'm setting up appointments to see a few homes later this afternoon, so I'll be out and about," she finally says. I'm not quite sure, but it feels like she's trying to shut me down. I wonder what happened between this morning and now, but I can venture a guess.

"That's fine," I casually respond, not about to be sidelined. "Just call when you're done."

Another pause, and then, "I'll probably just come back here after and do some more work."

Most definitely cutting me out.

A few days ago, maybe even as recently as yesterday, I might've let her, but after waking up with her body tangled with mine, and her scent imprinted on me…I don't think so.

"Sounds good. Talk later." Fully intending to make that sooner than later when I show up at her place with takeout tonight.

"Yeah, later," she replies, ending the call, but I don't miss the slightly wistful tone to her voice.

⌒

Plans change.

"I was just about to call you," Radar says when I walk in the office. "Got a call from DDI. They need a security detail for a few of their engineers heading to Bolivia."

DDI is one of our regulars, an engineering company that specializes in mining. With projects all over the world, their engineers sometimes work in less than friendly environments, necessitating security. That's where we come in.

"Didn't they finish that project last year? Or is this a different one?" I ask, dropping down on a seat across from him.

"Same one. One of the shafts collapsed early this morning. Twelve miners buried. The locals are pissed and the handful of police has better things to do than crowd control. It's not gonna be pretty."

"Jesus, what a clusterfuck. We've got just about all our guys tied up in McInnis," I complain.

"Already talked to Yanis." Radar tosses a pad with scribbled notes across the desk to me. "He says to take the two guys we have downtown. You'll need the muscle. I've already put a call in to the temp agency to get a couple of bodies to cover the warehouse."

He points at the notes I'm reading. "Those are your travel details, and any pertinent names and numbers you might need."

Last thing I want now is to head to fucking Bolivia to babysit a couple of suits and protect them from a volatile mob. Doesn't sound like it'll be a quick trip either. "Do we have a timeline?"

"In and out, from what I understand. Two, three days tops."

Luckily, I always carry a bag with extra clothes and toothbrush in the back of the truck. I grab what I need from the office, and toss it in the back as well.

I don't feel good about leaving Rosie, but I don't really have a choice. I briefly contemplate calling her back, but then have a better idea.

"Can you get me a number for Grant Peabody?" I ask Radar, who takes all of two seconds to produce it for me.

"Grant. It's Jake," I start when he answers. "I need a favor."

"Anything for you, sugar," he purrs, which I try to ignore.

"It's about Rosie."

"Spoilsport," he pouts audibly.

"Something came up and I'm going to be out of town for a few days. Could you check up on her?"

"Was in the plans already, my man," he says, changing his tone. "But pleased to know you're not just looking to use her up and toss her like yesterday's garbage, like that other guy did. No worries, I've got our Rosie covered."

An interesting bit of insight about her I'm filing away for when I get back and have time to explore. Right now I have a plane to catch.

ROSIE

It's overwhelming.

Having everything laid out in front of me on the kitchen table, it is almost paralyzing how dire our situation is. Not exactly news to me, but finding the old funeral policy in Mom's name totals a mere $1,500.00 is enough for me to want to throw in the towel. Not that it's even an option, because the situation is what it is and needs to be dealt with.

How ironic not only Mom's care while alive, but also Mom's care should she die are equally unaffordable.

There's really only one solution I can see; sell the trailer. Mom's house. The place she and Dad lived, the house I was born and raised in, the house she insisted on keeping since she wanted to stay close to Dad after he died.

It would kill her.

Just then Jake calls and it is too much. When he wants to know what he can do for me, I find myself tempted to ask him to take over. To just step in and make the difficult decisions I don't want to make. But I don't. Of course I don't. This is not something you hand over to someone else, especially someone you barely know.

I'm alone—no family left, other than an estranged uncle on my father's side who lives somewhere in Alaska, who I've never met—I'm facing this alone. Jake has offered up as savior a few times already in the disaster that is my life, and I don't even know if that is the root of my draw to him. But it also makes me vulnerable to him, and that is something I cannot go through again. Especially not now, another blow like that would end me. He makes me hope, and hope is a dangerously soft spot when you need a spine of steel.

Jake is a temptation I can do without.

"Yeah, later," I say when he finally gives up on me, and I quickly hang up, dropping my head on my arms.

I allow myself two minutes of mourning for what might have been, before I resolutely wipe my tears and get back to solving my problems. Not letting myself think about it too much, I look up the number of a well-known real estate agent, Caroline Bullock, and call her to set up an appointment.

"How is she doing?"

I made a beeline for the nurses' station when I saw Kim's familiar face. She smiles up at me from the computer screen.

"Hi, Ms. Perkins…"

"Rosie, please."

"Of course…Rosie. Well, we managed to get a few tests done, but it was taxing on your mother, so we ended up giving her something to help her sleep."

"Do we know anything more?" I want to know.

"The doctor will be able to tell you, he asked to be notified when you arrive. I'll give him a call now."

"Can I see her?"

"Of course, go right ahead, she's in the same place. The doctor will come and find you."

"Thanks," I mumble, already on my way down the hall to the ICU.

Mom looks comfortable, still hooked up, but her face is nice and relaxed and her color is a lot better than it was last night. I pull the stool up beside her bed, take her hand in mine, and rest my cheek on the mattress beside her. I try to clear my head and just breathe, focusing on my mother's scent. Talcum powder. For as long as I can remember, that is the smell I've always associated with her. From my very first memories of her.

"Ms. Perkins?"

I startle awake, shooting up straight on the stool, and frantically wiping at the drool on the corner of my mouth.

"Sorry," I mutter. "I must've dozed off."

"Understandable." The older man in the crisp white coat is not the same doctor who performed surgery on her. He must've spotted my confusion because he holds his hand out in greeting. "I'm sorry, we haven't met. I'm Dr. Kleber, I'm the neurologist looking after your mother. If you wouldn't mind following me?"

I nod and follow the man down the hall and into a small office where he shows me a chair.

"I try to be careful what to discuss in front of patients, even when we think they can't hear us."

"Of course," I agree, and listen as he goes on to explain his preliminary findings from this morning's testing.

"Your mother had to be resuscitated twice while on the operating table. Surgery in elderly patients, especially those who already have health issues, holds risks. I'm afraid as a result of those complications; your mother has sustained some brain damage. Her speech is affected; she appears to have trouble forming words. It's difficult at this point to assess what other centers in the brain have been damaged— only time will tell." He leans forward and kindly pats my knee. "I don't want to subject your mother to any further prodding or probing at this point, Ms. Perkins. By shift change this afternoon, if her vitals have remained stable, we will move her to a semi-private room. We'll keep her there for at least a few days to monitor her surgical recovery, and after that she will need to be moved to a nursing care facility. If you need any help, I can—"

"No need," I quickly interject, jumping up from my seat. "I'm working on finding her a spot."

"Very well then," he says, standing up as well. "If

you have any questions, don't hesitate to get one of the nurses to get in touch with me."

I leave his office, and instead of going back to sit beside my sleeping mother, I walk straight out the door. I need to stay busy on this or the weight of it will bring me to my knees.

Once in the car, I dial Hillary. I haven't seen her since yesterday morning, but she's been in touch a few times since.

"What are you doing tonight?" I ask her when she answers.

"Nothing important, why? What do you need?"

"I need help cleaning up and cleaning out the trailer."

It's quiet on the other side of the line for a moment before she speaks.

"So it's like that?"

"It's like that," I confirm, hanging up the phone. I don't need to go into details, Hillary knows the deal; she's practically lived with us for almost eight months.

On the way home, I stop at the grocery store and pick up a frozen lasagna, some salad in a bag, ice cream, and I splurge on a six-pack of beer, trying not to think of the pitiful condition my bank account is in. If I'm going to be packing up a lifetime of memories, I deserve beer and ice cream.

"Where do you want this?" Hillary asks, holding up one of the knicknacks Mom has cluttering up her room. It's disheartening to see how much junk has been packed into this double-wide over the span of a lifetime. And how little time there is to sort through it all.

Even with possible coverage or temporary coverage for a nursing home for Mom, the reality is care will have to be paid out of pocket first, so speed is of the essence in selling the house.

"Toss it in a storage box. I don't know where Mom is going to end up, so I don't know what she's allowed to have in her room. I can't focus on those things right now, so unless something is clearly garbage, just box it up, mark up the boxes so I can find it easily. When sometime down the road, things have settled a bit, I can go through all of it and take my time."

"Fair enough. Do you have a place in mind you want to store all this?"

"That's on the list of things to do for tomorrow," I confess. "There are a couple of places I've looked at, but they're all so damn expensive."

"What about you?" she asks carefully. "You're welcome to my couch any time."

"Thanks." I smile, trying to keep my chin from wobbling. "I may have to take you up on that, at some point. I've been so focused on getting Mom's stuff in order, I haven't really put that much thought into it."

Before she has a chance to say anything else, and break my fragile hold on my sanity, I turn and go back to my own room, where I've been radically purging. I'm tying up the third industrial-sized garbage bag I've hauled out of there, when a knock sounds at the door and my heart skips a beat.

All afternoon I've ignored the niggles of doubt and pangs of self-recrimination, but all that effort is gone with one knock on my door. I swing around and jerk it open, only to be met with Grant's big smile as he pushes his way inside with two large pizza boxes in his hand. I rest my forehead against the door, slowly letting it fall shut.

"Who were you expecting?" Grant asks from the kitchen, where he's already pulling down plates and finding napkins.

"No one." I plaster a smile on my face and join him at the counter.

"Liar," he growls, leaning down with his nose almost touching mine. "And just so you know, he called me this afternoon on his way to the airport. He's out of town for some kind of assignment." Suddenly straightening up, he opens the fridge and pulls out the beers I was saving for dinner. "Ah, you got booze! It *has* to be serious then." He easily pops off the top and takes a deep swig. "Yeah, your man is off doing his GI Joe thing. I've gotta tell you, girl, that man is so scrumptious, I'd drop pretty Olaf like a hot potato if there was any chance I could have your dude swing my way. Hm…hm…mmm."

"He's not mine," I protest, to which Grant lifts one gracefully plucked eyebrow high.

"Really? Cause that's not the vibe I'm getting."

"Pizza? Damn I'm so hungry," Hillary exclaims as she walk into the kitchen and dives right into one of the boxes. "Ahhh…meat lover's! Do you have any beer?"

"Kitchen full of meat lovers, honey," Grant teases with a wink at me, before he turns back to the fridge and pulls out two more beers, handing one to Hillary and one to me.

I try glaring at him, but he just shrugs his shoulders and opens the second pizza box.

I give up.

Sipping on my beer and nibbling on a slice of pie, I sit back quietly, as those two chatter on about their dating lives. Both pretty active, at least in comparison to mine. Apparently Hillary's Dr. McSteamy has lost his shine quickly, canceling their dinner and a movie date this past weekend because of work. Except his idea of work was getting hammered with his buddies at Fever, a strip club at the edge of town, and getting into a brawl, as she found out yesterday from an EMT friend who was called to the scene for cuts and bruises.

Grant seems to be faring just a little better with Olaf, but he's in McInnis with the film crew for a few weeks.

"So why not take a few days, grab a tent and a sleeping bag, and head into the park for a couple of nights? It'll be romantic," Hillary suggests and I can barely stifle a snicker. Grant in a tent—I would give good money to see that.

"Sweetheart," he starts in complete diva mode, waving his hand up and down the front of his body. "See this six foot six frame of carefully honed muscle, coated in a rich coat of cocoa, polished and waxed to a perfect shine? This here body will not stuff itself in any sleeping bag, it does not fit in any tent, it is not intended for rough terrain, and it does not find the idea of peeing in a bush at all romantic." He takes a deep drink of his beer, slams his empty bottle on the counter, and belches loudly, only adding to our hilarity, before he finishes. "This is a body designed for feather beds and the soft slide of twelve hundred thread-count, Egyptian cotton sheets. I'll sleep in the wild when I'm dead."

"I stand corrected," Hillary hiccups, wiping tears from her eyes. "No offense."

"S'all good, girl." Grant claps her on the shoulder. "None taken."

I'm still chuckling when I collect the bottles; Grant in full diva mode is a sight to behold. I start washing the few dishes and clearing things away, and don't notice both sets of eyes following me around. Not until Grant plucks the dishrag from my hand, tosses it in the sink, and hugs me hard against his chest. It's then I feel the wetness on my face.

"Let it all out, Rosebud," his deep baritone vibrates in his chess. "Give it all to Grant."

My tears of laughter at some point had turned into just tears. A carefully controlled physical expression of emotion, inadvertently triggered by something as innocent as laughing.

"My life really sucks," I mumble in his shirt.

"Sure seems that way," Hillary says, putting a comforting hand on my back.

My life may suck right now, I may be homeless soon, and I've blown off the first decent man who's looked at me in decades, but I'm not alone. Not with friends like these.

CHAPTER 12

MANY HANDS MAKE light work.

I remember Dad saying that, but I've never really felt its full meaning until these last few days.

"Last box," Grant says, jumping down from the back of the U-Haul truck we rented to move my stuff to his garage.

Yeah, that had been his idea, when I had my post-pizza, post-beer, and post-laughing fit meltdown and literally spilled my guts all over my kitchen floor. With astonishing ease, both my friends relieved me of some of the massive weight resting on my shoulders.

Hillary offered to use her connections to help find a suitable spot for Mom, and even is quite knowledgeable about what to expect in terms of insurance coverage. She's already narrowed it down to two homes and is working to get Mom to the top of the list.

Grant alleviated any concern around temporary storage and a place for me to stay. Both his garage and the small studio above it are empty. He lives close to downtown, actually just four or five blocks up from the hotel, on Chipata Avenue. It's actually the house he grew up in, an older bungalow sitting on a large treed lot. He inherited it after his parents died. He'd been living in the small apartment over the detached garage at the time, which has sat empty since.

"I really appreciate you taking a day off to help me do this," I tell him, handing him a bottle of cold water when he steps back outside. It's a hot Friday in late summer and probably not a good day for this kind of physical exertion, but as Grant pointed out earlier when I mentioned it, it's gonna have to get done.

It does. I met with the realtor on Wednesday and she seems to think we can get a quick sale if we stage the trailer with minimal furniture to play up the space, maybe give it a lick of paint. I have that planned for tomorrow and Sunday, but first I needed the place as empty as possible. Much less time wasted moving shit from one end to another while trying to paint around it that way.

Grant's offer of his garage was a godsend. The cheapest storage space I could find would still run me almost a hundred bucks a month for the size I'd need, and that would be pushing it. The garage on Chipata Avenue is twice the size and wouldn't cost me any extra. I balked when he refused to consider any compensation, but we ended up compromising. Once Mom's house is sold and she is settled in a home, and I have a good handle on what needs to go out every month, we'll sit down and hammer out a rental amount that suits us both. The only reason I agreed—other than I can't afford any other solution—is I'm not going to be in anyone's way. The place has a stairway to the apartment on the other side of garage from the house, offering some privacy for both of us.

The plan is for me to move in after I'm done painting the trailer.

"I had some leave days saved up. I rarely have a chance to use those and end up loosing them at the end of the year," he says after taking a drink of the cool water. "Anything else you want brought over here now? Otherwise, I suggest we bring this truck back so you only get charged half instead of a full day."

"I think we're good. My bed comes apart pretty easily and should fit in the back of my PT, and any furniture I want to keep is already here. The only thing, other than my bed, left at the house is either going with Mom to whatever home she ends up in, or to the dump. Besides," I point out to him, "if worse comes to worst, I can always rent a truck for a couple of hours again, but I don't think I'll need to."

Sweaty, dusty, and tired, I hop in my car, take one more pleased look at my new home, and follow the truck back to U-Haul.

"Morning, Rosie."

I turn to find Les Shipman, Mom's neighbor, waving from his driveway. I've just come back from the hardware store down the road and am unloading paint supplies.

"Morning, Les," I return, watching him approach. "I was going to come by to thank you again for helping me find Mom earlier this week and to give you an update."

"Of course," he answers, pushing his glasses back up his nose as he smiles sweetly. "You know we've always tried to keep an eye on Connie, ever since your dad passed away."

"I know, and I so appreciate that."

"How is she doing?"

"I'm afraid she won't be coming back home, Les. The broken hip alone would have been enough, but the surgery set her back some too, so we're moving her into a full-care facility."

"We figured," he says, putting a hand on my arm. "Dora sent me out to check with you on that." I look over his shoulder and see his wife in the window, waving. I smile and lift my hand before turning my attention back to Les. "She's wanted me to put a bug in your ear ever since she saw you moving boxes and furniture out. She was worried you may have already sold the place and yelled at me last night, but I guess you wouldn't be painting if that were the case, right?"

"Right?" I echo, a little confused. "Actually, I am afraid I am selling. I have no choice, unfortunately. I am just getting it ready so it can be listed by the agent next week."

"Before you do that, I think maybe we should have a talk before you do anything else."

As it turns out, the Shipmans have been looking at something a little larger than their own trailer to fit the growing number of grandkids they boast. Preferably a bungalow, something without stairs, because of Dora's arthritis, but with a nice big kitchen and living space so they can have the family over all at once. They haven't had much luck so far; mostly because they don't really want to leave the neighborhood they've lived in most their lives.

"If we could combine your lot and ours, we could build a house right here and still have a nice yard left over for the grandkids to play," Dora informs me over the cup of coffee the Shipmans lured me in for.

"You'd tear down the trailers?" I blurt out.

"Well, actually," Les interjects. "That's the beauty of it, we wouldn't have to. We have a friend who is a contractor and works with Habitat For Humanity. He buys old trailers and moves them to his yard where he fixes them up. Habitat For Humanity then places them on one of their project properties, and uses them for affordable housing."

I smile, because this is a much better plan than destroying the house I grew up in. The idea it would provide another family, a struggling family, with a roof over their heads, hits just the right spot with me. Having just received kindness myself, it feels good I get to pay it forward somehow.

"I like that."

Les quickly points out they're prepared to pay fair market price on Mom's place, and if they used the same realtor, we could split the cost of her fee. Clearly my neighbors have thought this through thoroughly, and I have no problem giving Caroline a quick call to get her take on this deal.

By five o'clock on Saturday afternoon Les, Dora, Caroline, and I are sitting at the small table in our kitchen, and I use my power of attorney to sign my name to the Shipmans' offer. Les runs out to their house to grab a bottle of Prosecco, they were saving for a special occasion, to celebrate.

My head is still spinning when I hit the pillow, and only partially from the sparkling wine. Sometimes life feels like a boulder rolling down a mountain, slow at first, but picking up speed on the way. Right now I feel my life has hit warp speed and a crash is imminent.

The next morning it hits. I'm standing in the kitchen, waiting for my Keurig to brew me a cup of coffee, and suddenly I need to get out. Away from this place that holds so many memories, some good, but those are mostly buried under the years and years of unpleasant ones.

I yank the plug on the Keurig, stuff it in the box that is waiting for the final bits and pieces from the kitchen, and empty my travel mug in the sink. I'll pick up some coffee on the way. First I need to pack up my car.

My dismantled bed is already in the back of my PT, only the mattress, which I slept on last night, is yet to be fitted in. I quickly grab the last of my toiletries, and stuff those along with the sheets and my remaining clothes in the big duffel bag I have ready. I haul it outside and manage to cram it in the passenger seat, along with the box from the kitchen.

The mattress luckily is just a double, but still a bit of a challenge. With the help of a long packing strap and the Kelim rug I had under my bed, I manage to get the mattress outside. Driven by frustrated tears and a building urgency to get away, I finally am able to close the gate on my PT. Without even looking back, I jump behind the wheel, start the car, and peel out of the driveway.

JAKE

"Can I get you something to drink?"

I just got on DDI's corporate jet and am leaning back to let the cold air from the little vent hit my face. I lift my head to look at the flight attendant leaning over my chair.

"Water is fine, thank you. With ice if you have it. Lots of ice."

July in Bolivia is not my idea of a fucking good time.

Hot, humid, and hostile.

The good news is; the twelve miners stuck in the collapsed shaft were rescued late last night. The bad news is; the local mining company, that originally hired DDI on the construction of the mine, is now firing up local authorities to charge them with willful negligence. It only made the situation more tense than it already was, and it fast became clear, it was better we leave the country in a hurry.

I'm hot, I haven't slept in days because the situation was so volatile, and I'm beyond ready to get out of this shithole. Next time they can take someone else. I've been in enough hot, humid, and hostile places to last me a fucking lifetime. Enough.

Once we take off, I tilt my seat back, close my eyes, and sleep most of the flight back to Colorado.

I didn't allow myself to think much about Rosie, and I purposely didn't call. It would've been a distraction I just couldn't afford on this particular assignment, but while the plane is still taxiing down the runway back in Grand Junction, my mind is on her. I hated having to leave right when shit was hitting her on all sides, and I certainly didn't mean to be gone for almost a week. She'd been pretty clear on our last phone call that she wanted some space. I never intended to give it to her, but I inadvertently did anyway.

Now that I've had a few hours of sleep, my first stop is the office. It's nice and early, just coming up on six. I want to write up my report, and get it finalized so I can forget about it. I'm almost done when Radar walks in with a coffee in each hand. It's almost eight thirty.

He sets one coffee down in front of me and takes the seat across from me.

"Thanks," I mumble, taking a sip of the perfect brew. "How'd you know I was here?" I indicate the coffee.

"Every time someone disables the alarm, I get a notification on my phone. I was standing in line at the coffee shop when I got yours," he explains, smugly sipping his cup.

"And you knew it was me, because?"

"I checked the air traffic control log this morning."

"You mean you hacked into it," I accuse him with a grin.

"Potato, potahto…" He shrugs. "Besides, I was waiting on your ass to get home because I found something I'm thinking you're gonna want to see."

He gets up and moves to his desk; a large conference table with one side shoved against the wall. There are at least five or six computers set up on the large table, and the rest of the surface is littered with paper and empty cups. On the wall, one large screen is mounted, to which he is directing my attention. On it appears a still-frame of an empty hallway in the hotel.

"What are we looking at?"

"Security tapes. I was bored this week and decided to go over some of the surveillance tapes again. It got interesting when I got to the ones from the night that chick got jumped in the pool."

"Rosie," I correct him. "Her name is Rosie." Ignoring the wide grin on his face, I point at the screen. "Run it, let's see it."

At first the hallway is quiet, the only visible movement is the odd dust particle floating in front of the camera. Then, on the bottom right corner a hand appears, holding a can, and a jet of black paint obscures the image. Next clip is from the gym, showing the same basic thing: the hand, the can, and then black. Ditto for the pool area. I don't see anything identifying on the hand, and whoever it is knows exactly where the cameras are and how to stay out of range.

"Run it again."

Again I watch, this time I try to focus on what I can see behind the hand that appears, but again, I see very little.

"Okay, I give," I concede, throwing my hands up. "What am I looking at?"

"You've been looking at Steele for this, right?" Radar turns in his chair, tapping a pencil to his chin. "That somehow he was trying to silence Rosie?"

"Maybe," I admit. "And don't forget she'd shut him down the night before, right there by the pool, when he was coming on to her. And I'm not so sure he'd have taken no for an answer had I not been there to shut that shit down."

"Fair enough. Now with all you know about Steele, every little habit, every innocuous detail— watch the clip again and see what seems off about it."

He runs the clip again, and I watch it, making note of the type of nozzle on the can, the fact he's spraying from left to right for me, so right to left from his perspective. I note how he moves his hand in the direction of his fingers, not his thumb. And then I see it.

"Fucking hell," I whisper, watching the same movement on each of the three cameras he disables.

"Right?" Radar grins, swinging around in his chair. "So simple and yet we missed it."

"Left-handed. How did we miss that?" It was more of a rhetorical question, but Radar answers anyway.

"Because we are looking at it in mirror image. I'm usually good at details like that, but I missed it too, for the longest time," he admits.

"You know what that means?"

"Sure do," he says with a grin.

"Rosie…" I shove my chair back, and Radar looks at me oddly before realization washes over his face. "I've gotta check on Rosie."

The moment my ass hits the seat of my truck; I dial her number. It rings twice and then goes straight to voicemail. I'm already driving when I dial Grant's number. Again, relegated to voicemail. Where the fuck is everyone?

From the office to Rosie's place would normally take ten, fifteen minutes, but during morning rush, it's taking entirely too long.

When I finally pull into Rosie's driveway, I see her neighbor coming out her front door and walking straight up to my truck, a worried look on his face. I met the man briefly when we were looking for Mrs.

Perkins. A night that already seems so long ago.

"She's gone," he says, a confused look on his face. "I just dropped the wife off at an appointment and came back home to find her front door wide-open, but she's gone."

"Wait here," I tell the clearly distraught man and walk into the trailer. It's fucking empty, or close thereto. From what I recall, there was at least twice as much furniture in here and every available surface was littered with knickknacks. There's nothing, just an old couch, the kitchen table, and an empty travel mug in the sink. Nothing left in Rosie's bedroom but the old little side table.

"What's going on? Why is the trailer almost empty?" I ask the older man, who is still wringing his hands by my truck.

"The wife and I bought the place off Rosie. Last night. We were in her kitchen signing papers. She mentioned she was going to get the rest of the stuff out of there today. Said she had a place to stay."

Sounds like she's been busy while I was gone, and I'm surprised how disgruntled I feel at being so uninvolved.

I need to find her, and not just because it looks like she's moving on, but also because I thought she was safe while Steele was away filming in the mountains.

She may not be safe after all, because whoever attacked her is a lefty.

And Kyle Steele is right-handed.

CHAPTER 13

ROSIE

I'M NOT SURE how I managed to get to Grant's place in one piece.

All I can remember is this loud rushing in my ears, like something was closing in on me fast. I drove right by the coffee shop I'd planned to stop at and somehow was able to navigate my way here without any rational awareness.

Grant's car is in the driveway, but he's left room on the far side for my old shitbox to fit. I don't even bother grabbing anything but my keys and rush up the stairs to my new sanctuary. It's a small open space, with a couch, coffee table, and single chair by a wall-mounted Ikea table that flips up in the small kitchenette. A single door opens a passage to the bedroom and separate bathroom beyond. The best part of the apartment is the small balcony off the bedroom, which overlooks the lush garden in the back. Enough to fit one chair and a small side table. Ideal for morning coffee.

But right now all I see is the couch, where I curl up in a ball, my eyes closed tight.

JAKE

I tried calling the hotel, without any luck. Grant had worked his shift but already went home, and no one had seen Rosie. I called the hospital as well, but according to them, Ms. Perkins had not been in today yet.

"Radar, do we have a landline for Grant Peabody?"

"Just a sec." I hear the sharp click of fingers on the keyboard in the background. "Here it is." He starts rattling off a number that I struggle to remember.

"Send me his address by text too," I tell him before I hang up and dial the number I remember.

Apparently I got it right, because after only four rings, the familiar, but sleepy, voice of Grant rumbles in greeting.

"Who the hell is this?" Is the friendly greeting I receive, but I don't give a rat's ass.

"Jake. Where's Rosie?" I barge right in, wasting no time explaining.

"Rosie? She's at home. Not supposed to be here 'til tonight. Why? What's going on?"

"That's what I'd like to know. I get back this morning, head over to see her, and the front door is wide-open, the place is all but empty, and her fucking car isn't in the driveway. What the fuck have I missed and where the fuck is Rosie?" I realize I'm yelling, when the driver of the car stopped beside me at the light, glances over suspiciously.

"Hang on. Let me see if she's here." I listen to what I assume is the rustle of bedcovers.

Here is Chipata Avenue just west of Third Street, as I can tell from the text I just got from Radar. I was already heading in that general direction. I'm only about five minutes out.

"Her car's in the driveway, she must be here. I'll get some clothes on and head right over."

"Head over where?"

"Apartment over my garage. She needed a place, I had it empty."

"On my way," is all I say before hanging up.

I pull up in front of his small bungalow, a few minutes later, just in time to see Grant step out of a side door and cross the driveway. I catch up to him right as he starts up a set of stairs on the side of the garage.

"I'm not so sure she'll want to see you," Grant says, blocking me as I try to pass him.

He may be massive, but there's no way he's gonna stop me from making sure for my fucking self Rosie is okay. Without any compunction, I draw my gun and shove it in his gut.

"Move, Peabody. Now!"

Far from intimidated, the man raises a manicured eyebrow and steps aside, gesturing up the stairs with dramatic flair.

"Didn't know you felt that strongly," he mutters

as I rush by, tucking the gun—safety still on—back in its holster.

Yeah, he's not impressed at all. Grant, for all his stereotypical effeminate posturing, is more man than many I've encountered.

I barge through the door at the top of the stairs and am halted in my tracks when I see Rosie, unharmed from what I can tell, curled up in a ball on the ratty couch. Apparently fast asleep. Or at least she was, because she's pushing herself in a sitting position, rapidly blinking her eyes now. Grant shoves me from behind so I almost stumble into the room, and now it's his turn to rush ahead of me, sitting down on the couch beside a very rough looking Rosie.

"What happened?" I ask, sitting down on the coffee table, facing her. "What's wrong?"

"Best answer him, Rosebud," Grant mumbles, putting his arm around her. "He pulled a gun on me just so he could get to you. The man is *se-ri-ous*."

"You pulled a gun on him?" she asks me incredulously. "On Grant?"

"It worked. He got out of my way." I shrug before I explain. "You left your front door open at home. I thought something happened to you."

"I was in a hurry," she justifies guiltily. "I must've forgotten."

"It's okay, sugar," Grant interrupts, tugging her close. "You've got a lot on your mind."

"Do you mind giving us a minute?" I direct at him, meeting his eyes and holding them. An entire sharing of the minds takes place with that look alone, and by the time he leans over to kiss her on the head before getting up to leave—we've come to an understanding—without ever exchanging a single word.

"I'll be cooking breakfast. Come find me when you're ready," he says from the doorway, more to Rosie than to me, but I'm the one who says, "Thanks." Rosie still seems a little shell-shocked.

Relieved she seems unharmed, at least physically, and glad not to have her kick me out right away, I take the spot Grant just vacated on the couch. Much like he did, I wrap my arm around her shoulders and tuck her against me, feeling relieved when she seems to settle in my hold, with her cheek resting on my shoulder and my chin touching the top of her head.

We sit like that for a while. Her scent, the feel of her body, and the steady puff of her breath against my neck go a long way to settling my heart rate back to an acceptable level.

"Want to fill me in?" I try gently, but the sharp shake of her head is instantaneous. Clearly not ready to share. She is curious, though.

"Where were you?" she asks without moving, but still I can feel a little tension creeping in her body. "Grant mentioned you were out of town. I'm surprised you're here at all."

"I was in Bolivia," I tell her honestly. DDI's involvement in that mine disaster is already public information, so there's no reason for me to hold that back. I give her a brief synopsis of the week.

"That's horrible," she says, shocked.

"It could've been much worse," I quickly point out, before I move to the next point I want to make. "PASS is spread pretty thin with the production back at McInnis. It pulls almost all available bodies away from Grand Junction and limits options when an emergency like this one comes in." I cup her jaw with a hand and tilt her face so I can look her in the eye. "When I told you I'd talk to you later, I planned to show up at your place that night with dinner. I know you were trying to blow me off, and I wasn't gonna let you." She lowers her eyes, trying to avoid the scrutiny in mine. I patiently wait until she lifts them again. "When this job came in, I called Grant right away to make sure he'd keep an eye on you while I was gone. So you shouldn't be surprised I'm here."

I know I should probably tell her about Steele. However, that's not as important at this moment as finding out why she was rolled up in a protective ball when we walked in, and still looks like she's about to come apart at the seams now.

"Your turn," I tell her softly, holding her eyes with mine. "What all happened in your life?" A hard snort escapes her and immediately her eyes brim with tears. I catch her chin with my thumb and gently shake her. "Take a deep breath, concentrate on facts, and tell me from the start."

She does. She clearly steels herself, audibly breathes in through her nose, and proceeds to tell me;

a little shaky at first, but by the time she gets to her visit to the paint store, her voice is steady. I'm pretty stunned at the massive amount of change that has taken place in what felt like a long fucking time for me, but was—in fact—not quite a week.

"It still doesn't explain why I find you here in a fetal position on the couch," I push, and am rewarded with a flash of anger darkening those bright green eyes. She tries to shove me away, unsuccessfully.

"I was tired."

"Perhaps, but you were rolled up tighter than a coiled wire." She gives me another shove and this time I let her go. Luckily she doesn't go far, just curls up, pulling her knees up to her chest, on the other side of the couch. Needing that distance again.

"I had to get out of there. I suddenly just couldn't wait another moment. The memories, the silence, it overwhelmed me, sent me into a panic, so I took off."

"And left the door open, scaring the crap out of me," I tease, reaching out and tugging on her long hair, trying for some levity, but she's not biting. Her serious eyes are fixed on me as she keeps her distance.

"Why?" she suddenly asks. "At the very least I should find you questionable, for protecting someone who killed another human being. Something for which he can surely be considered morally reprehensible. Instead you make me feel safe. I had convinced myself I didn't have time in my life to be sidetracked by fantasies, and yet here you are." I reach out to her, but her hand comes up defensively as she curls up tighter, her arms wrapping around her knees in a purely protective pose. What concerns me most is the fact there are no tears, just a tight, white face, and eyes that seem to sink deeper while I watch. "I'm not even sure who I am anymore," she continues, her voice monotone, "since my own moral compass has been unbalanced for many years now, and if I don't know who I am, how could I possibly know who you are? I'm scared, because I should be worried about that poor innocent man, who may have family somewhere waiting for him, but instead I'm sad about leaving a house that hasn't felt like a home since my dad died. My head is so full of thoughts, I don't know what to do to shut them up, and I don't know why you're here." She leans forward a little, studying me intently. "Why are you here, Jake?"

I'm not sure I followed half of her ramble, but it's clear Rosie is standing on a slippery slope. I'm well aware how I answer can either give her purchase, or give her a final shove.

"Because I'm drawn. Because you were first on my mind when I got off the plane. Because I've always been okay with a quick fuck, but it's not all I want from you." I pause when I see her flinch, and reach for her hand. I'm surprised she lets me, although she keeps to her corner of the couch. "I don't know what that means, honey. I have zero experience, so I can't tell you, but I know I'm here because I want to be. Simple as that." I meet her eyes, and instead of the storm of confusion that was visible there earlier,

I now see a hint of curiosity. I decide to share one more thing. "As for morals; I have them. The life I've led—the work I've done—may have blurred the edges some, but they're there. Could be I didn't have much reason to look for them before, but I do now."

This time when I give a light tug on her hand, she lets me pull her closer.

ROSIE

There is something whispering at me that, once again, I'm letting myself be seduced by pretty words and faint hopes, but that voice sounds a lot like my mother's, so I ignore it.

Jake's arms come around me protectively, and for a little while I let myself lean. The steady thud of his heartbeat under my ear, and his firm hold, anchor me. I let myself be in the moment, just enjoying the feel and touch of a man's body. It feels natural to tilt my head back, slide a hand to the back of his neck, and pull his head down so I can steal a kiss.

The instant my lips touch his, I feel the band of his arm tighten around me as his mouth opens hungrily over mine.

"Rosie…" The deep rumble of his warning voice only serves to spur me on, and without losing his lips, I twist in his hold and turn so I can slip a leg over his lap and straddle him.

A hand slides into my hair and tugs my head back, as he runs his open mouth along my jaw and down the column of my neck, making me shiver. Pressing his tongue in the hollow between my collarbones, he tastes me.

Without a coherent thought in my head, I'm letting myself drown in sensation, curling my fingers in the short hairs of his neck, as I grind my hips down on the hard ridge in his jeans.

"Please," I mumble, not quite sure myself what it is I'm asking for. He makes the world disappear and it feels so good, I don't want him to stop.

"What do you need, honey?" he asks, and goosebumps break out all over my body when he slips a hand down the back of my yoga pants, curling his fingers into the soft, naked flesh of my ass.

"I thought I'd start bringing some stuff in, while my frittata is cooking," Grant says from the doorway, barging in with the duffel bag and box from my front seat. "Oopsies," he adds, when he notices our position on the couch.

I try to scramble off Jake's lap, but all he does is slip his hands out of my pants and from my hair, only to grab my hips and hold me in place.

"Give us a minute?" Jake asks pointedly, as he glares at Grant, who looks right back at him, but with a huge grin on his face. He's not moving, though. "Grant?" Jake prods and that seems to do the trick.

"Right, I'm uh…just gonna grab the rest." With a dramatic wink at me, his big bulk disappears out the door.

Jake releases his hold on me and I climb off his

lap, unable to miss the bulge in his pants. He catches me looking and smirks.

"Yeah," he says dryly. "Didn't want to give the man a complex." I roll my eyes, unable to contain a chuckle, as I get up and straighten my clothes. I try not to watch as Jake does the same, adjusting himself in the process as he heads to the door. "I'll go give him a hand."

Forty-five minutes later, I pop the last piece of toast in my mouth and look surprised at my empty plate. Last thing on my mind had been eating, but between the easy banter the guys developed while assembling my bed for me, and the delicious smells from the oven when Grant finally coaxes us into his kitchen, I was ravenous. That little gropefest on the couch may have played a part as well. The result is a tentative feeling of well-being, despite this morning's meltdown.

"Whelp…" Grant draws our attention with that dramatic intro. "I should be hopping in the shower, because I have a long standing appointment with Trent, the esthetician who does a fabulous job keeping me appropriately groomed…" I hear Jake groaning beside me and I bite down a snicker. "…and flush with naughty fantasies that last me until my next appointment. But since the man will be nose to tip, waxing my fun stick and love spuds, and he's not a fan of jungle crotch, I need to scrub my junk."

"Grant!" I exclaim, slapping my hands over my ears. "TMI, please!"

"*Jesus*," Jake grumbles beside me.

With his fingertips pressed to his lips and his eyelash extensions fluttering, Grant disappears down the hall.

"Let's get out of here." Jake snags my hand and drags me to the door.

I stop him at the bottom of the stairs to my apartment.

"What exactly are we doing?" I ask, not even trying to hide my suspicion.

"I would've known the answer to that ten fucking minutes ago, but now I just want to get out of here and bleach that visual from my brain," he groans, pinching the bridge of his nose with a pained look on his face. It's all I can do not to giggle. "Why don't you grab your purse and things you might need from upstairs? We'll swing by the hospital and play the rest by ear."

I melt a little. It's sweet he offers to take me to the hospital, but I'm not quite sure…

"Okay, let me get my purse, but…what things?"

He hooks an arm around the small of my back and pulls me flush against him, bending his head so his lips almost touch mine. "Stuff for tomorrow morning. We're staying at my place tonight."

"Hold on a minute," I stop him, pushing him back with a hand in his chest. "You're leaping light-years ahead here. I don't think I've even started processing the fact you showed up. Besides," I say quickly when I see he's getting ready to interrupt. "This was going to be the first night in my apartment." I admit I stick my bottom lip out a bit, something that instantly catches Jake's eye.

"New plan," he says, his eyes never leaving my mouth. "Hospital, then we go grocery shopping—we both need some—we drop mine off at my place, *I'll* grab a few things, and then we head back here and cook dinner."

I look at him sternly, but when his eyebrows slowly rise in a plea, I give in to the chuckle bubbling up.

"So you're still on the fast train, but you're conceding on the location?" I tease.

"And that's a big deal," he says solemnly before adding, "since your bed is tiny."

CHAPTER 14

JAKE

ROSIE'S MOTHER CAN'T verbalize her feelings, but the fury in her eyes speaks loud and clear.

"Hillary helped me find you a great place, Mom. Your room will have a view of the beautiful garden. They even have a pond with ducks, and a small bench where you can sit and feed them, when you get better."

Rosie seems oblivious to her mother's anger as she goes on to describe the nursing home she's apparently decided on. Mrs. Perkins is mildly sedated, but clearly not to the point where she doesn't feel any emotions at all.

"We'll bring a few of your things there, so when you move in, you'll feel right at home." She gets up and grabs her purse, bending down to kiss her mother's cheek, but she twists her head away and looks pointedly out the window. Rosie straightens and with a sad smile steps back from the bed. "Hillary said she'd come by and see you tonight when she's done her shift, and I'll be back tomorrow."

"Tough visit," I mumble as we walk out of the hospital. Rosie shrugs her shoulders

"I guess," she says as she gets in my truck. "Before this happened, she was pleasant and mostly couldn't remember who I was, she only got angry or agitated with me when she did remember. Now she doesn't seem to remember anything, but is constantly agitated. I'm not sure which is worse, although I guess it doesn't really matter; watching your parents decline really hammers home your own mortality."

I have nothing to say to that, I've been face-to-face with the reality of my limited time here many times before, but I don't tell her that, I just reach out and squeeze her hand.

"What about you?" she asks, turning to face me as I pull out into the street. "Are your parents still alive?"

The question surprises me, but I guess this is all part of starting something. Building a relationship. I'm not used to sharing, but I understand the need for it.

"They're dead. I barely remember them." I realize my response has come across as a little curt, when I sense Rosie stiffen in the seat beside me.

"I'm sorry," she whispers, and I turn to look at her, but she keeps her eyes firmly on the road ahead.

"Why are you sorry?"

She flicks a sideways glance at me before focusing forward, lightly shaking her head. "It's just one of those things, you know? For the last twenty years, since my father died, I've all but forgotten I had loving parents for the first twenty. A bit shameful when you're reminded there are people like you who never even had that."

"But when you grow up without them, you also don't know what you're missing," I counter, sliding my hand between her clenched ones in her lap, twining my fingers with hers. "It wasn't as bad as you may think. At sixteen I ended up with the Mazurs. They gave me a taste of family life and left me with two brothers."

"Dimas?"

"And Yanis," I add. "Dimas and I are the same age, we shared a room and became friends almost immediately. Yanis is a few years older and has always been protective. They both are."

The rest of the drive is silent, but when I pull the truck into a parking spot in front of City Market, Rosie leans over the center console and presses a kiss to my cheek. She smiles, stroking her hand along my jaw, where I trap it with mine.

"They're your family, and you're just as protective as they are," she whispers.

I turn my head and kiss her palm.

"Come on," I prompt. "The sooner we get these groceries done and back to your place, the sooner we can test that ridiculously tiny bed of yours."

As a distraction that works well, Rosie blushes bright and almost launches herself out of the cab of the truck. One of the things I find irresistible about her is the way not only her freckles, but also the slightest of blushes, stand out against her pale skin. Chuckling, I follow her into the grocery store.

Does anything ever work out as planned?

It takes less than five minutes to throw a few groceries in my fridge and grab a quick bag for tomorrow, another fifteen or so to get back downtown to Rosie's apartment. I rush her through storing away groceries, and just when she slams shut the fridge and I stalk toward her, with only one thing on my mind, the door flies open and Grant barges in.

Fuck! Forgot to throw the deadbolt on the door. Rookie mistake.

"So how do I look?" Completely ignoring me, he moves in front of Rosie and lifts his shirt. "Feel it," he urges her, grabbing her hand and slapping it on his chest. "Smooth as a baby's butt. Not a freakin' hair left on my body. I kid you not. That boy knows what he's doing, I tell you. Gets into all the crevices too. Here, check this out." He starts undoing the buttons on his fly in front of a now snickering Rosie.

"All right, that's enough," I bark, putting an end to this…whatever it is. "Keep your damn pants on."

"Ease up, G-man. Just introducing the lady to the multitude of talents my boy, Trent, boasts. In fact," he says, turning back to Rosie. "I should make you an appointment. He can make you smooth all over…"

He drags those last words out for emphasis, throwing a sideways look in my direction.

"Over my dead body," I snap.

"Not inconceivable," he retorts, and I almost chuckle.

"Bite me, Cupcake."

"Didn't we have this conversation before?" he taunts, his hands on his hips. "I thought I made it clear; I like my men less…hetero. In fact, maybe you should get in with Trent too. He might give you a twofer. Get you groomed up a bit."

I have no idea what a *twofer* is, but if it involves the illustrious Trent, I'm pretty sure I wouldn't like it. Rosie, who's been giggling during most of our banter, suddenly comes to my defense.

"No way," she aims at Grant. "I like the fuzz on him. It's manly."

I grin at her while Grant rolls his eyes.

"Like I said, too hetero," he explains. "With that scruff, he's like catnip for soccer moms."

"Are you calling me a soccer mom?" she protests.

"No. I'm calling him catnip."

"I need a drink," I announce, chuckling as I dive into her fridge, where I just shoved a couple of six packs.

Another thing I discovered about Rosie, she's a beer lover.

I can live with that.

ROSIE

"Hey, Grant?" I call down the stairs after him. "Can you let them know I'll be back for my shift starting Thursday?"

"Sure thing, Rosebud," he yells back.

Grant stayed for a quick dinner, easy spaghetti and meatballs, even though Jake seemed less than pleased when I invited him. I know he had different plans, but I've been out of the game for so long, I was nervous. With the tension building high all afternoon, I welcomed the temporary distraction. And to be honest, those two are hilarious together.

I close the door and turn to where Jake is cleaning the last of the pans in the sink, his eyes on me.

"Back on Thursday?" he repeats.

"Mom is scheduled to be transferred on Wednesday, after I move some of her stuff to her new room on Tuesday," I explain, sitting down on the couch where I can watch him. "Thursday I'll try to sleep during the day so I can get back into my nighttime routine."

"Why not try and get a day shift?" he asks as he walks over to the door, and throws the deadbolt before turning to me. "You don't *have* to work nightshift anymore."

He's right, I don't—and it's not like I haven't thought about that, because I have—but with my entire life in flux, it's nice to have one thing remain predictable. At least for now.

"Eventually," I tell him, shifting a little restlessly in my seat as I watch him stalk toward me. "But for now I welcome the familiar routine."

"Fair enough," he mumbles, bending forward and bracing himself with his hands on the couch on either side of me. "Now where were we, before your buddy busted down the door?" He rubs his nose along mine, and I feel his breath against my skin.

"I believe it was the kitchen," I whisper, but that quickly turns into a squeal when he playfully pinches my side, before pulling me up off the couch.

"Right, but we were on our way to the bedroom." He walks backward, pulling me along with him.

"We were?" I echo, not quite knowing where to look or how to act. I'm nervous.

"Absolutely," he says, opening the bedroom door behind his back and leading me inside, where he folds me in his arms. "Relax," he mumbles, his face in my hair as his hands start kneading my back and shoulders. "Stop thinking."

Easier said than done. I try, I really do, but when I feel his tongue on my neck and the vibration of his groan, I freak.

"We don't really know that much about each other. I mean, I don't even know your favorite food, or where you were born. I don't know where you went to school, or even how old you are." While I ramble, Jake lifts his head, eyeing me with a bemused look on his face.

"Pizza, Salt Lake City, I went to lots of schools but graduated Central High, right here in Grand Junction, never went to college but headed straight into the army, and I'm thirty-eight years old. Now where were we…"

"Thirty-eight?" I mutter, planting my hands flat on his chest when he leans in.

"Last I checked."

"I'm forty-two," I share slightly nauseated, waiting for shock to register on Jake's face, but all I see is measured patience.

"I'm aware," he announces. "Not sure what your point is."

That shuts me up. I'm not really sure what my point is either. Especially not when Jake returns his focus, and his mouth, to the sensitive skin of my neck. So I'm a couple of years…fine, I'm four years older. Big deal.

"When's your birthday?" I ask, and this time his irritation is obvious as he lifts his head once again.

"October."

Awesome. His is before mine in February, so technically only three-and-a-half. I can live with that.

"Stop talking," I tell him, wrapping my arms around his neck and lifting my mouth to his. I barely notice the roll of his eyes, but I can feel the vibration of his groan when I slide my tongue between his lips.

Our mouths and hands explore both over and under layers of clothing. Touching and testing. Jake's skin is soft over the firm muscle underneath and I want to taste. Shoving up his shirt, I expose the short, course hair on his chest, narrowing to a strip running down his belly. I bend forward, touching my tongue to his skin; tentative at first, but bolder when I hear the hiss of his breath. I sense more than see him take the shirt off the rest of the way before his hands tangle in my hair.

I'm not quite sure what possesses me, but my hands are already working the button on his jeans when I sink down on my knees in front of him.

"Fucking hell."

Jake's muttered curse sounds more like a plea than a protest, and I'm happy to comply.

His cock is hot and hard when my hand closes around him, while the other is shoving his pants down to his knees. Commando. I always thought it was a myth—I guess not.

The head dark red, almost purple, the veins bulging along the thick shaft. I feel bold and empowered when he twitches in my hand, and I softly kiss the tip before pressing the flat of my tongue to the base of his shaft, dragging it slowly from balls to crown.

"Rosie...*Jesus.*" His voice sounds pained as I slide him into my mouth. His hands on either side of my head, he firmly pulls me back, dislodging himself from my mouth with an audible pop. "Baby," he coos when my eyes lift to find his, heavy-lidded and dark, burning with heat. "My turn."

I'm not very worldly, sexually speaking, and to say I'm not used to being on the receiving end would be putting it mildly. Giving is easy, but having the focus turn on me is a different ball game.

I let Jake pull me to my feet and take the opportunity to admire his strong body. I haven't seen many men naked, but I can safely say—in most cases—they look better with clothes on. Not so Jake.

I'm so distracted by his body, running my fingertips over his skin in discovery; I barely notice I'm being divested of my own clothes. Not until he backs me up to my bed, and pushes me to lie down on the mattress. Now I feel exposed, with him standing there, looking down on me. I can feel his eyes and touch taking in every inch of my pale, freckled skin. I'm not a small woman; I'm short, but not small. The swell of my belly and thighs are always a cause for insecurity, but the way Jake trails his fingers from the tips of my breasts to my stomach, testing the softness, feels more like worship than criticism.

He remains standing when he opens my legs, draping off the edge of the bed, and trails his fingers through the newly trimmed patch of red curls at their apex, slipping one finger inside my tight channel. My mouth falls open at the intrusion, as his eyes close and his head tilts back.

"So wet," he whispers. "So hot and wet, I could come just from feeling your hold on my finger."

My heart pounds in my chest and I hear the blood rush in my ears. My skin is charged, hungry for the rasp of his touch.

He slips in a second finger, and my hips come off the mattress as my eyes roll back, and I give myself over to sensation.

Suddenly his hand is gone, and when my eyes snap open, I see him reach down for his jeans. Seconds later, he steps back between my legs, a condom rolled neatly down his thick shaft, as he slips his hands under my knees and slides me to the edge of the mattress, lifting my legs wide. He leans in and kisses my lips sweetly, before straightening up. Just by flexing his hips, he rubs the head of his cock along my slit before sliding inside. Just the head, but already I feel full. Jake stops right there.

"I'll go easy," he says, his eyes betraying a barely contained restraint as he looks down to focus on our connection. By small increments, he feeds his cock inside me, stretching me to facilitate him with a slight, satisfying burn. He rocks his hips deeper and deeper, until finally he's fully seated in the cradle of my hips and stills. The effort to hold back has sweat running down his body, as his eyes come up to meet mine. "About to lose it here, baby. Won't be able to hold back, you feel too good. Need you to put a hand to that pretty little clit. That's it," he says, encouraging me when I slide my fingers over the slick little button.

He strokes me twice, deep and slow, before losing all control, and his hips piston, slapping skin against skin as I work my clit furiously to keep up. The groans, whimpers, and grunts intensify, as we both seem to barrel toward climax. I feel his body jerk inside me as he yells his release, while I teeter on the edge for an endless moment, before bursting apart on a scream.

Without a word, but with infinite gentleness, he cleans me up after, lies down and tucks me close, his nose buried in my hair, before drifting off almost instantly.

I lie awake for hours after, reliving every second, afraid if I fall asleep I might lose this feeling of peace and utter contentment.

JAKE

I wake up with the sun, only disoriented for a second when I open my eyes to an unfamiliar bedroom. The woman wrapped around my back, like she never wants to let go, is very familiar, though. Even more so since last night. Probably why I can't remember the bedroom, my eyes were glued to her.

Still stuck between time zones, I lean over to check my phone I put on the nightstand last night. Five o'clock: too early to go to work and too late to go back to sleep. Normally, I love to go for a run at this time of morning, but I didn't bring any gear.

Rosie huffs out a sleepy complaint when I roll to my back, quickly reattaching her luscious body to me, pulling her knee up over my legs. I feel the heat coming from her core against my hip, a heat I've touched and been inside, but have yet to taste.

With my face clenched between her thighs, my tongue buried deep in her pussy, and her taste bursting in my mouth as she climaxes awake, I discover I have a new favorite pastime to indulge in at the crack of dawn.

It's not until much later, when I walk into the PASS office and see Radar sitting at his desk, I realize I never told Rosie about the security tapes. Perhaps it's best. The film crew won't be back until next weekend, and with Rosie back at work on Thursday night, which means I only have a few more days to give her my undivided attention. What good would it do to spoil that now?

CHAPTER 15

ROSIE

I DON'T KNOW if I'm ready for work today.

It's been another very busy week, but this one is much easier to handle than last week. Probably because this week I'm being kept well-stocked with oxytocin and endorphins, thanks to a dark, brooding, and supremely talented, personal security guard. Seriously, I think I've come more these past couple of days than I have my entire sexually active life. Not that it's saying much, but still.

I've been on cloud nine, making it so much more tolerable to deal with the legalities of a quick sale of the house and the logistics of moving Mom and her things to the nursing home. When every aggravating day ends in bed with a man whose solitary focus is pleasure, his and yours, any frustrations or hurts are quickly forgotten.

I've never had that: someone who is there at the end of the day. Not ever. It was promised to me before, along with the sun and the moon—by the man

I allowed to lead me along for way too many years—but all Chad Pendergast gave me in the end was a black hole. Empty promises of a married man, who wanted his cake and to eat it too.

And I was the naïve girl who kept swallowing it down.

Jesus, I'm morbid today. It may have been the afternoon spent in the nursing home. Nothing like a quick trip down memory lane to squelch any positive sparks. A subtle feeling of panic nags just below the surface. What if I'm falling in the same trap again and am making too much of whatever is happening with Jake? I don't even know if what we have is sustainable, once life settles back down in a normal routine. I don't know if he even wants that.

We haven't really talked much.

We haven't even gone on a real date. We've barely surfaced from either my bedroom or his. And even though it's not the once-a-week-and-only-at-my-condo I was limited to with Chad, the singular focus on sex feels familiar and has me a little concerned.

Don't get me wrong, I love the sex—I'm all for the sex, in particular with Jake—but don't I want there to be more?

Frustrated, mostly with myself, I turn into the hotel parking lot. I find a lucky spot, not too far from the back door, but before I can even get out of the car, my door is pulled open and I'm hauled out by my arm.

"I missed you," Jake growls, immobilizing me in

the tight band of his arms. I barely have a chance to react before his mouth is on mine, kissing me like I'm his last breath, before he leans back, his eyes closed.

I haven't seen him since early this morning, when I cracked one eyelid as he left to drive up to McInnis. Some company lawyer was flying in from LAX, on the red-eye, who was needed on location. Jake mentioned he had no idea what that was about and didn't care, but he looks pulled through the wringer now.

"Missed you too," I echo, feeling a hint of relief to my earlier concerns. "I didn't expect you back until tomorrow."

He was supposed to drive back with the rest of the team, at the end of their last shooting day.

"I know," he mumbles, pressing a kiss to my forehead before dipping his chin to look into my eyes. "But I needed a chance to talk to you before then."

"About what?" There is something in his look that makes me uneasy, so my voice has an edge to it.

"Blackmail."

JAKE

It's been a long fucking day and promises to get even longer.

The only instructions I received last night were to pick up one Simon Berry, legal counsel for the rich and famous, from the airport at five forty this morning, and to drive him straight up to McInnis Canyon.

First of all, the guy was cranky as shit at that

hour of the morning, without much sleep, and even crankier when he found out there'd be no stopping for a couple of hours of sleep in a comfy hotel bed. My instructions had been clear: no delays.

After an hour of complaining, the guy finally fell asleep in the passenger seat and snored the entire way there.

Yanis, Dimi, Drexler, and an unusually subdued Steele are waiting in Drexler's trailer. I thought I was just required to drop Berry off, but when I try to back out of the door, Yanis calls me back.

"Best sit down and listen in," he orders, giving me a glare I can't quite place.

I slip into the seat beside Dimas and throw him a questioning look, to which he shrugs apologetically. Now I'm really confused.

But not for long.

"We all know that our fucking golden boy here," Phil Drexler starts, jabbing a thumb in Steele's direction, "made an ass of himself in a titty-bar, drove drunk, then hit and killed a bum in an alley. We also know that while he's been pouting in his scotch, fucking any two-legged creature he could lure into his suite, the rest of us have been trying to clean up his goddamn mess." With every word, Drexler's face turns a deeper red, while Kyle shrinks farther and farther into his seat. "To top it all off, it turns out Mr. Steele was trying to pay off someone claiming to have damaging information, and he never bothered to *tell anyone until fucking yesterday!*"

I'm genuinely concerned with Drexler's well-being as he falls back in his chair, pulls a wad of tissues from his pocket, and starts mopping the spittle from his mouth. The table is quiet for a moment, more to give Berry and myself a chance to process this information, than anything else. It appears this is not news to the others.

"Kyle was contacted the Friday, after the incident in the alley, with a note that was slipped under his door. In the note was a newspaper clipping of the police scene in the alley, the name *Fever*, and a phone number," Yanis continues, taking over. "He tried the number, but there was no answer. Next thing a text popped up from that same number, with instructions to set up a cash drop. Instead of notifying us, he had his agent fly out with fifty grand in a messenger bag. Saturday morning, he paid a barista from the coffee shop in the lobby five hundred dollars to drop the bag at the bottom of a food bank bin inside the Safeway on Horizon Drive."

There is so much fucked up with this scenario, the damage already done hurts my head.

Apparently, another text came in yesterday morning, from the same number, that time asking for two hundred thousand. That's when Kyle panicked and confessed to Drexler. He thought he'd be able to handle things on his own and nothing would have to get back to Guild Film Productions. Clearly that didn't work.

"We're behind the eight ball on this one, folks."

Yanis continues. "We're going to have to do damage control, and at the same time, get on top of this before it blows up in all our faces."

"Exactly," Drexler agrees, his color having returned to a much healthier shade. "And we'll wrap up shooting today and pack up tomorrow morning, but first we have to do some contingency planning for the future of this production." He turns to Simon Berry, who's been listening quietly, and nods his head in response.

"You don't need us for that." Yanis stands, motioning both Dimi and me out, following right behind us. "Hold up," he calls when I head in the direction of the catering tent. I haven't had anything more than a breakfast sandwich at the drive-through on the way to the airport this morning—I'm starving.

"Just grabbing a bite," I call back.

"Need to talk to you, Jake. Command center in five."

With that, he turns on his heel and marches off to the big truck we use as our headquarters when we're on the road. It's a compressed and completely self-contained version of our offices, with monitors, computers, a small armory, and the latest communications hardware; all operational and ready to go no matter what remote outpost we end up in.

I continue on my quest for food, and Dimas falls into step beside me.

"Brace yourself," he mumbles from the corner of his mouth.

"For?"

"Spanish Inquisition. Yanis doesn't want to do it in front of Drexler, but he's going to want to know what the chances are our little Ms. Rosie has anything to do…umph." Dimi looks up from the dirt where I just dumped his ass. All it takes is one well-aimed kick at the healthy knee of a one-legged man.

"Don't even finish that goddamn thought. She has nothing to do with this for fuck's sake."

"Fuck you, asshole," he grunts, grabbing his knee. "You know we've gotta check everything. And cheap move."

"Quit your whining," I bite off, reaching out a hand to pull him up, even as I chew him out. "You invented the cheap moves and you know it. If the roles were reversed, you would've fucking aimed for my balls."

"I thought you were hungry?" Dimi hobbles to keep up with me, as I do a one-eighty and head straight for the PASS truck.

"I just lost my appetite."

I find Yanis alone in the truck; Bree is nowhere to be seen.

"It's not her," I barge right in. Yanis throws a pissed look over my shoulder, presumably at his brother. "She's got nothing to do with it."

"At the very least we'll have to question her, Jake. I get you're invested in the woman," he starts—only adding fuel to my fire.

"You don't get anything," I spit back. "She's had

other fucking things on her mind with her mother in the hospital."

"I realize that," Yanis says in a soothing tone that works like nails on chalkboard. "Which is exactly why we have to look at the possibility. Hospitals and nursing homes cost money, which Ms. Perkins doesn't have a whole lot of."

I surge forward, ready to plant my fist in his face, but I'm grabbed around the waist and lifted off my feet. Fucking Dimas abusing the four or so inches he has on me.

"Gotta think, Jake. She's the one person who can tie him to the hit-and-run," he mumbles behind my back. "And she's gotta be scrambling to find funds to pay for…ah fuck!"

This time I do what he would've done, aim for the balls as I sharply pull up a heel. The result is immediate release, as Dimi needs his hands to cradle his tenderized package.

Without saying another word, I shove him aside and march out the open trailer door, almost bumping into Phil Drexler coming up the two steps. Ignoring him too, I head straight for my truck. Fuck them, I need to give her a heads-up before they can blindside her with accusations. She's barely hanging on as it is.

After the first hour on the road, I start calming down a bit and decide to answer my phone, which has been ringing off and on since I left the set.

"Yes," I bark.

"Where are you?" my boss wants to know in a

clipped voice.

"About thirty minutes out of Grand Junction."

"Goddammit, Jake. Why'd you have to pick fucking now to grow a heart? Your timing sucks." He sighs deeply when I don't say anything. "For whatever it's worth, I don't like your Ms. Perkins for this."

"She sold the house."

"I know," he answers much friendlier. "Radar told me. We still need to talk to her, though. It's possible she mentioned something to somebody else."

"She didn't."

"You don't know that for sure."

"Highly unlikely."

"Have to ask, though. We have a responsibility to our employer," Yanis persists. "We can't afford to miss anything."

"I've gotta go." I hang up before he has a chance to say anything else. I got the message already.

I've been waiting in the alley beside the hotel's back door for Rosie to get here.

When I arrived in town earlier, I went straight to her apartment but her car was not there. Grant saw me parked at the end of the driveway and came outside.

"She's at the nursing home. She had meetings with Connie's doctor, the social worker, and a physical therapist, to discuss a plan for her mom's care."

"She still planning to work tonight?"

"Said she'd be heading straight there after."

So I've been hanging around the hotel, grabbing a quick bite to eat, and warning hotel security we'll be invading their space again as of tomorrow, generally killing time.

The moment I see her car pull into the parking lot, I move, catching her off-guard, as much with my presence as I do with my words. Fuck, I surprise myself. I'm not sure I ever told anyone I missed them—I can't be sure I've ever actually felt that before.

She's visibly confused when I explain why I'm already back and doesn't protest when I pull her to where my truck is parked, helping her inside.

"I'm gonna be late."

"I just need a few minutes," I assure her.

"Can't we do this inside?"

Rather than explain the *why*, I decide to tackle the *what*.

"Steele is being blackmailed. He's already paid once, a relatively small amount, but this week he was contacted again, this time for substantially more." If I weren't already sure she had nothing to do with the extortion, the expression on her face would have made it crystal clear.

"You're shitting me..." she whispers, shocked.

"I shit you not."

"But..." I see the wheels start turning as her eyebrows pull into a frown and her eyes drift off into the distance. "Who else would know?" She's barely finished the thought and her gaze snaps back, eyes slitted. "You think it's me." It's more a statement than a question, and she shifts her body instantly, pressing her back against the door.

"Not even for a second," I tell her with conviction, reaching over to grab her hand.

"Does your boss?"

"He doesn't think it's you, necessarily, but he still wants to talk to you, just to clear a few things up."

"Oh my God—do they think because I haven't been at work…?"

"Yanis and Dimi both know what happened to your mother, so no, they don't think anything of the sort. But they have a client—with over sixty mil riding on this—who needs to be satisfied on that front too. Hence making sure they can eliminate you from suspicion, right off the bat."

I pull her on my lap the moment I see her lip tremble.

"This has been a really fucking shitty day," she mumbles, her face pressed into my neck. "Nothing like I'd planned for. I haven't even started my shift and already I'm exhausted."

"Do you have to go in?"

"I already told them I'd be there."

"Call in sick," I push.

"I could lose my job," she counters, but I can hear capitulation in her voice.

"Would that be so bad?" I suggest carefully. "I realize this job may give you a sense of stability, when your world's been spinning on its axis, but isn't this also an opportunity to find something you really want to do? For you?"

She lifts her head and looks me in the eye, a smile playing on her lips.

"You just want to get me home and back in bed."

"That too," I admit, grinning. "That too."

In the end she goes inside to talk to her manager, while I wait not so patiently in my truck. I hop out when she comes back out fifteen minutes later, with her shoulders a little straighter, and walks straight toward me.

"Well, he wasn't too happy with the short notice," she says, slipping her arms around my waist. "But he said they'd manage. One of the girls on days apparently has been wanting to go on nights. He says if I want, we can do a straight switch, but he'd prefer I take a few days to consider and make sure. Says to let him know by Monday."

She lifts her much more relaxed, smiling face up at me, and I cover her smile with my mouth.

"My place or yours?" I ask when I finally come up for air.

"Yours," she answers with a grin. "We both fit in your kitchen at the same time and your bed's bigger."

CHAPTER 16

ROSIE

"I HAVE TO get to going." Jake sits on the edge of the bed and brushes the hair from my face. I quickly wipe the back of my hand over my mouth in case of stray drool. "With the entire film crew invading the hotel again, I need to make sure security is in place."

"Okay," I mumble, still tired. Almost ten hours of sleep hasn't made much of a dent in the fatigue that feels like it's settled bone-deep.

Jake had thrown together a taco salad when we got to his place, while I talked to Grant, who was already blowing up my phone to find out where I was. By the time I ended the call, Jake was walking in from the kitchen, carrying two metal mixing bowls and handing me one. I teased him about the interesting presentation of his culinary creation, to which he pointed out he was just being practical.

I fell asleep halfway through an episode of *Person Of Interest* he put on, and somehow dreamt that Jim Caviezel carried me to bed.

"Honey," Jake's voice drags me back from the edge of sleep. "You're welcome to stay in bed all day, in fact, I'd fucking love knowing you were waiting here for me, but you don't have wheels here in case of an emergency."

I groan, but still shove the covers off and swing my legs over the side. Somehow I ended up wearing one of Jake's shirts. His doing, I'm sure, since I can't remember much beyond falling asleep to Jim Caviezel's sexy rasp.

"I'm wearing this home," I tell him, tugging on the hem of his shirt, which nicely covers my butt.

"Fine by me." He grins while I put my uniform pants back on.

I'll have a shower when I get to the apartment. With a bit of luck, I'll catch Grant making breakfast before he crashes for the day.

"I need to brush my teeth," I announce, running my tongue along my fuzzy teeth. God, I hope he didn't get a whiff of that. My mouth tastes like old taco salad. Not appealing at all.

"Check the third drawer by the sink. I usually throw the crap they give me at the dentist in there. Should be a spare toothbrush somewhere. I'll pour a coffee to go for us."

"The dentist?" I question. For some reason it strikes me as so ordinary, when nothing about this man really is. He turns around at the door.

"Twice a year for cleaning."

"Sorry," I mumble at his hint of sarcasm. "I just

couldn't imagine your badass self in a dentist chair, that's all."

"I got one set of teeth, I'd prefer to keep them as long as possible. Now—third drawer," he orders, pointing to the bathroom. "I'll get the coffee."

It's almost nine by the time I pull my PT in the driveway next to Grant's car.

I expect him to be asleep already, but when I peek in the kitchen window on the side of the house, I'm surprised to find him still awake and behind the stove. His head shoots up when I knock on the window, and he motions me to come inside.

"I didn't expect you back this early."

"Jake had stuff to do at the hotel and my car was still there," I explain, stealing a few pieces of the apple Grant is meticulously slicing wafer thin. "What are you all doing? I half-expected you to be in bed already?"

"I felt the need to cook," he says, blinking his eyes innocently. It takes me a moment, but then I clue in when one side of his mouth tilts up in a suggestive grin.

"Ah, you heard," I conclude with a grin of my own.

"I heard, although not from the man himself. He's been pretty quiet these past few weeks, busy from what I understand, but in his last message he said he'd been dreaming of my apple tarts."

"And so you're making apple tarts." I look around the kitchen where it's obvious he's been busy already. "To go with the quiches and the…what are those?" I poke my finger at the mounds on a baking tray that appear to be rising under a towel.

"Don't poke them!" He slaps at my hands. "Those are *Bapao*, they're rising."

"But what are they?"

"It's a stuffed bun. I put some of my Cajun pulled chicken in there, but from what I gather, you can fill it with just about anything. They're supposed to be steamed."

"Your first time making them?" He looks a bit sheepish at my question.

"Got the recipe off a Dutch cooking website, and don't look at me like that." He points a finger in my face when I grin.

"How am I looking at you?" I tease. "Like I just deducted, quite smartly I might add, that your boyfriend is not as we assumed Scandinavian, but Dutch? And that you are aiming to impress with your culinary skills?"

"Whatever," he grumbles, turning back to his apples. "I discovered they're originally Indonesian anyway."

"What is?"

"The freaking buns!"

Grant is testy, and other than the fact he hasn't slept yet, I'm guessing he's testy because he didn't hear from the man himself that he'd be coming back to town today. I'm thinking I might be pissy too.

"Here, move over," I tell him, grabbing one of his man-sized aprons off the hook and putting it on; mostly to protect Jake's shirt, which I'm really starting to love. Grant gives me a look, top to bottom, before stepping aside and grabbing another paring knife from the block.

"You peel, I slice," he grumbles. "And for God's sake, don't cut your finger off. I don't want blood all over my kitchen and have to throw all this food out."

"So noted." I nod affirmatively, biting on my lip not to grin.

"Nice shirt, by the way." He bumps my hip with his, without taking his eyes of his hands.

"Right?" I grin wide. "It's Jake's."

"Nice. Would look better on him, though."

"Grant?"

"Hmmm…"

"Bite me."

"Wrong flavor, Rosebud."

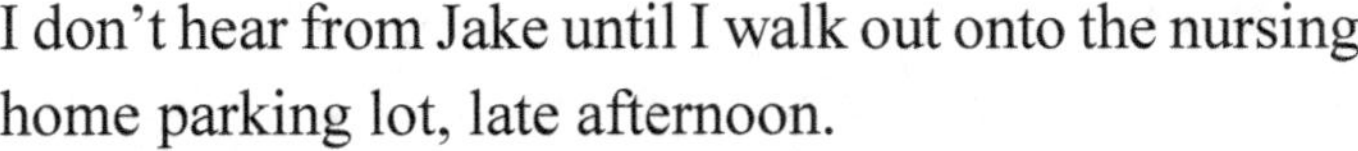

I don't hear from Jake until I walk out onto the nursing home parking lot, late afternoon.

"Hey you," I answer, a smile already on my face.

I'd finally convinced Grant to at least take a nap, since he'd have to work again that night, and headed up to my apartment to have a shower and finally change. I left Jake's shirt folded and tucked under my pillow. I'd be sleeping in that baby tonight.

Visiting with Mom had been rather one-sided since she was sleeping a lot. The nurse told me it could be a result of her medication, and they would have the doctor take a look in the morning.

My plan was to maybe splurge on a couple of steaks, grab some baking potatoes and sour cream, and use Grant's grill and backyard for a nice meal. I have the fixings for a salad in my fridge.

"I was just thinking of picking up some food and cook for you. I assume you like steak? I think Grant may have inspired me, I found him cooking up a storm this morning. He heard Olaf was coming back today. Is everyone back at the hotel yet?"

I realize I'm rambling and he hasn't said a peep yet.

"Jake?"

JAKE

The only saving grace today was finding out that this coming week will be the final week of shooting.

There is something about the air of entitlement these movie people collectively carry, that just rubs me the wrong way. Shortly upon arriving to the hotel, Steele caused a ruckus when he insisted on settling in the bar, presumably to catch up on any drinking he may have missed out on the past couple of weeks. All it took was one groupie to spot him, snap a picture, and plaster it all over social media, and within ten minutes the bar was overrun with a mob of fans. We finally had to extract him and he had the fucking balls to get upset. The day went downhill from there.

It's only been two weeks that the cast and crew were on location, but apparently it was enough for everyone to forget security protocols. It wasn't only Steele who went looking for some diversion, after spending two weeks in a trailer down a canyon. I spent the day tracking down and collecting more folks, who were eager to break free for a couple of hours. One of the other actors got into an altercation in a restaurant and ended up needing a ride to the emergency room to get stitches.

I just dropped him back at the hotel when I find Yanis waiting for me in the lobby.

"A word?"

He tilts his head in the direction of the coffee shop, and I follow behind, ordering a plain coffee when we get to the counter.

"That was the one and only time you get a pass for taking off like that," Yanis says, in a deceptively calm voice, when we take a seat at a corner table. "I can't have my people running off in the middle of an assignment because of a temper tantrum." I have to bite my tongue not to jump in and defend myself, but the truth is; he's right. So I suck it up and let him get on with ripping me a new one. "I have to be able to trust every member of my team implicitly, or things go to shit. I can't have one of you go off on a tangent and leave the rest of the team hanging. If you have an issue with an assignment, with me, or anybody else, you fucking talk it out, you don't bail."

Being accused of bailing on my team hits a nerve with me. If the three tours in the Middle East taught me anything, it's you're only as strong as your weakest team member. I bet Yanis knows it would hit home, but that doesn't make it any less true.

"Agreed."

He looks at me to make sure I'm not just blowing smoke before he prompts, "So fucking talk to me."

"It's wrong," I start after a pregnant pause. "We protect Steele's guilty ass at all cost, and yet don't think twice about throwing accusations at an innocent, hard-working woman who devotes her time taking care of her ailing mother. That's fucking wrong." I expect him to jump on that, but all he does is nod. "I'm having a hard time justifying that in my head— and not just because I happen to be involved with this particular woman."

"Involved?" Yanis bounces back with a grin. "Anyway," he continues, his expression turning serious. "I hear you. The sooner we can wrap up this assignment, the better. One more week of feeding inflated egos, and making sure we fulfill our contract, then our responsibilities end. But for now we've gotta please the customer, even if it's not always pleasant… which brings me back to Ms. Perkins."

"I'm guessing you want to talk to her?"

"Look," he says, leaning over the table so he

can keep his voice down. "Drexler and his sidekick, that Berry guy, are impatient to shut this blackmail issue down. I've not mentioned Rosie, but Drexler is no fool; he will eventually wonder about her if he hasn't already. I'd rather be ahead of the game, before he decides to take matters into his own hands. Sixty plus million dollars is a heck of an incentive to play hardball and not care about who gets bowled over in the process. I don't want your girl to be at the receiving end of that, so give me a chance to clear her name off the list of suspects."

I walk outside for some privacy when I call Rosie, who answers instantly. Her upbeat chatter puts a smile on my face, and I hate having to bring down her good mood.

"Jake?" I hear her ask.

"Still here. Steak sounds great, Rosie, but how about we do that tomorrow, unless you don't mind an extra mouth to feed?"

"Extra mouth?"

"Yanis wants to clear things up with you, as soon as possible, and I thought maybe we could grab a bite somewhere? Neutral ground? Unless I bring him over…whatever works better for you."

"Oh." The single syllable, and the silence that follows, hold many messages. I don't prompt her but quietly wait her out. "I guess maybe going somewhere public might be best then?"

"Want me to come by and pick you up? You think of someplace you want to go, and I'll let Yanis know."

"We could do Mexican at that place down Main Street? I'm actually just getting in my car, I'm up at St. Mary's, I'll just drive myself there."

I'd rather pick her up, but I'm not going to argue about that now. "I know the place. Fifteen, twenty minutes?" I suggest instead.

"Sure."

Yanis is where I left him, sitting at the table in the coffee shop, except Drexler is standing next to him. The two seem to be in a rather heated discussion when I walk up and fall silent the moment they spot me.

"I have a conference call in a few minutes," Drexler announces. "We'll get back to this later." The last is directed at my boss, whose face is blank, but I can tell from the scathing glare he throws at the man, he's not a happy camper.

"What was that all about?" I ask Yanis when Drexler walks away.

"What you'd expect, the man wants answers I don't have. Not yet." He watches as Drexler gets on the elevator before turning to me, switching topics. "And? Is this a good time?"

"She'll meet us at that Mexican place down the road in fifteen. It's not even a ten minute walk from here."

"Then let's walk. I could use some fresh air."

We've been sitting in a small booth in the back of the

restaurant for fifteen minutes, talking shop, when the waitress stops at our table again.

"I'll just leave these here," she says, dropping menus on the table. "In case your guest doesn't show up."

Getting worried, I pull out my phone to check on Rosie when I spot her walking in the front door. She finds us easily and shoots me a repentant smile as she approaches.

"Sorry," she apologizes, right off the bat. "I couldn't find a spot and ended up parking the car at the hotel. I just walked over."

Yanis jumps up and offers his hand in introduction. "Not a problem. Parking around Main Street is a nightmare in the summer," he says, clearly trying to ease the tension coming off her. Still, Rosie smiles nervously as she slips into the booth beside me. I wink and give her knee a little squeeze under the table in support. "Your mom doing all right?" he asks, as he takes his seat across from us.

"She seems to like her new digs."

"Ah, I see your guest has arrived." The waitress, who's been hovering around our table interrupts, and turns to Rosie. "Can I get you a drink while you look at your menus?"

"Sure. I'll have an iced tea."

"Sweetened or unsweetened?"

"Half and half, please." Rosie smiles and opens her menu, pretending to be focused on the options, but I can see the slight shaking of her hands. Yanis notices too, and gives her a moment to get settled as he grabs a menu himself.

"I trust Jake explained why I wanted to meet with you?" Yanis waits until the waitress shows with Rosie's drink, and our orders are placed.

"You think I have resorted to blackmail," Rosie responds with surprising calm, but clearly on the offensive. I can't blame her.

"I'm not gonna lie," Yanis admits. "My initial thought was exactly that, but both Jake and my brother convinced me otherwise. I'm not going to apologize for doing my job. As the one ultimately responsible for my client's security, I can't overlook any possibility, even if you don't exactly strike me as the type."

"Okay. So then why am I here?" she challenges.

"Simple, I trust Jake and Dimas with my life, but my client may have other ideas. He's put his trust in me, so in good faith, I owe it to him to follow due process." Rosie nods her understanding.

His questioning of her over dinner is casual, asking mostly things I already went over with her. She confirms what she told me—she didn't see anyone else in the alley—she didn't tell anyone about what she witnessed, and she absolutely has nothing to do with any blackmail plot. She even offers Yanis insight on her bank account and access to her apartment, which he somewhat sheepishly declines.

"I don't think that's necessary, but I appreciate the offer." He drops his napkin on his empty plate and gets up. "I should probably head back, I still have to find whoever is behind this. You two take your time finishing your meals." He leaves with a nod for me and a smile for Rosie.

"You okay?" I turn to face her, reaching out to tuck a strand of hair behind her ear.

"I am. I'm actually quite relieved. Are you going back to work?"

"For an hour, two tops. I have a few things to finish up. Are you going to be home?"

"That's the plan. I'm wiped."

"Too wiped for company?" I probe, and smile when I see the twinkle in her eyes when she turns to me.

"Don't know," she teases. "But I won't stop you from finding out for yourself."

After we finish our dinner, we discover that Yanis already paid for our meals on his way out. I tuck Rosie under my arm as we make our way back to the hotel, where her car sits in the parking lot. I open the door for her and wait until she's seated behind the wheel, before I lean in and kiss those lips that have been tempting me all night. Like every time I kiss Rosie, I have a hard time pulling myself away.

"We'll pick up on that later," I mumble against her lips as she groans sweetly.

I wait until I see her taillights disappear around the corner before heading inside.

CHAPTER 17

ROSIE

IT'S ALREADY GETTING dark by the time I leave the hotel parking lot. I stop at the light to cross Grand Avenue, still dazed from the brain-numbing assault of Jake's kiss, when the sharp sound of a horn behind me startles me. A glance at the light shows green and I quickly pull into the intersection, peeking in my rearview mirror to check out the impatient driver behind me. All I can make out is a figure behind the wheel of the big, dark SUV behind me. Turning left on Ouray, I notice the vehicle turns behind me and sticks with me as I take a right on North Second Street.

I'm not overly concerned, but I have to admit I feel a touch relieved when I see the SUV's left turn signal in my rearview mirror. You hear about these road rage incidents where irate drivers follow you around for the singular purpose of giving you a piece of their mind…or their fists. Apparently this guy is heading for the RiteAid parking lot and I easily dismiss him.

I start making the turn onto my street, when my

engine starts sputtering, and I barely manage to pull off to the side where it dies. The fuel gauge still shows half a tank, so that can't be it. Just what I need, more expenses to a car that's long past its expiration date. It never fucking stops. I can manage without when it comes to work, but if I want to visit my mom, I'll need wheels.

Frustrated, I pop the hood and get out of the car. Not like I know what the fuck to do with whatever is underneath, but I can try to shake and rattle a few things. It works for my toaster. I lift the hood and use the flashlight on my iPhone to have a look. Just as I lean in and reach in to jiggle a hose, I hear the rev of an engine and the crash of impact.

I'm thrown to the sidewalk as the front of my car is hit from the side, the impact shoving the front wheel onto the curb. I yelp as I land hard on my side, but manage to look over my shoulder to see the dark SUV take off down the road.

"Are you all right?"

An older man comes rushing down the sidewalk toward me.

"I'm not sure," I confess, trying to get up.

"Don't move," he says, putting a hand on my shoulder. "You're bleeding, I'm calling an ambulance." He indicates my arm. I look down to see the sleeve of my shirt is torn. My skin is a bloody mess underneath, but nothing looks or feels broken, just the painful sting of road rash.

"Don't," I plead, holding up my hand to stop him.

"It's just a scrape."

"Are you sure? I still think you should—"

"I'm positive," I cut him off. "I'll call a friend, if you can help me find my phone; it must've flown from my hand. He can contact the police."

When he hands me my phone, which ended up behind me on the sidewalk, I notice the screen is cracked, but the phone still works. I quickly dial Jake's number.

"Impatient," he answers my call with a smile in his voice.

"I need your help."

Immediately serious, he snaps, "What happened?"

"I had a bit of an accident; my car broke down on the corner of North Second and Chipeta, and a car just hit me."

"Stay put, I'll be there two minutes."

"Jake? Maybe call the police? I think it was intentional."

There's dead silence on the other side of the line.

"Jake?" I prompt.

"Two minutes," he bites off. I hear some shuffling and then Dimi's voice is on the line.

"Hey, sweetheart, Jake will be there in a flash, are you all right? Is anyone with you?"

"One of my neighbors heard the crash and came to help."

"Are you hurt?"

"Just knocked around a bit, scraped up a little."

"Good, that's good, honey. The car that hit you, is

it still there?"

"No. It sped off."

"Can you tell me what happened?"

I recount everything, starting with the honks and ending with the taillights of the same dark SUV speeding off down the street.

"You sure it was the same car?"

"Not positive, it's dark out, but pretty sure. I think it's a Ford? I remember seeing the emblem on the grill in the rearview mirror. Either black or navy blue; it was hard to tell."

"New model Ford Expedition, and I noticed part of the license plate, but I couldn't get it all," my Good Samaritan interjects.

"Did you hear that?" I ask Dimi, who asks to speak to my neighbor. Just as I hand over the phone, Jake's familiar truck comes to a screeching halt behind my car. His face is grim and his eyes are focused as his long strides eat up the distance between us.

"Shit," he hisses as he crouches down beside me and examines my arm. "You call an ambulance?" he barks at my poor neighbor, who is still on the phone with Dimi.

"I'm fine," I assure Jake, putting a soothing hand on his arm. "I asked him not to. Please, no more hospital." For a moment, it seems like he's going to force the issue, as he glares at me with clenching jaw.

Next thing I know, I'm scooped up in his arms and carefully placed in the passenger seat of his truck.

"Took a few years off my life," he growls, before

pressing a hard kiss to my lips.

"Sorry," I mumble, as he backs out of the vehicle.

"Stay," he orders with a warning finger in my face. "Don't move a muscle."

JAKE

"Ouch!"

Rosie flinches as I try to remove some persistent debris from the wound on her left arm with sterilized tweezers. I give her a stern look when she tries to pull away, and I may have grunted in frustration. They would've had the appropriate tools to do this at the hospital, but she was adamant about not going. Stubborn woman. It had been twenty minutes before the cops showed, after I got to the scene, and needless to say, I was less than pleased. When I noticed they weren't taking this as seriously as the situation warranted, my blood started boiling. With Rosie safely tucked away in my truck, I made sure to let my feelings be known. It took a phone call to Yanis, and the resulting pull of some impressive GJPD strings, to get the officers to ditch the flippant attitude and do their fucking jobs.

It was another twenty minutes to take her statement, during which time a flatbed truck arrived, but by then I'd had enough. I told one of the officers if he needed to talk to Rosie, he could call my cell.

"Where are we going?" she wanted to know when I drove right by her apartment.

"My place, where I have a proper first aid kit and a real bed."

I ignored her protests all the way home. There's no way in hell I was going to let her out of my sight anymore. It seems every time I do, something happens.

"All done," I announce, taping down the end of the gauze wrapping on her arm. "Now let's see the rest of you." Rosie insisted on walking from the truck into my house under her own wind, but I noticed she was limping quite distinctly. "Drop those pants." I shoot her a cheeky grin, trying to make light of the situation.

I know what happened from her neighbor, and from the account Rosie gave the police, but we have yet to discuss the implications. Someone has it out for Rosie, and I think the connection is pretty obvious.

A sharp hiss escapes me when I see the marks on her left leg and hip. There are no tears in her jeans, but a scrape underneath the denim is oozing and the skin is already starting to discolor on her hip.

"Shirt off too," I instruct, and she strips it off without objection. Aside from some small scuffs along her ribs, her shoulder looks like it got a direct hit from the concrete as well. A deep blue hue is forming around the joint, and I'm pretty sure that will be black by tomorrow. Black and blue, not to mention stiff and sore.

"Shit," she whispers, catching a glimpse of herself in the mirror. "If I didn't have bad luck, I'd have no luck at all."

"Bad luck has nothing to do with this. Bad karma does, and the son of a bitch responsible for this has a serious dose coming."

A bit more cleaning and few sterile pads later, I help Rosie into my bed. I'm about to lock the house down for the night, when I hear a knock at the door. A glimpse through the window shows Dimi and Yanis both standing on my step.

"Little late for house calls?"

Dimi grins unapologetically as he pushes past me into the house. Reluctantly, I step aside and invite Yanis in.

"This'll be quick," Yanis says, by way of excuse, as he settles down on the couch. I take my recliner across from him. "The partial plate and make of the vehicle don't match. Someone has done a switch. Grand Junction PD is keeping their eyes open for a new model Ford Expedition, with damage to the front passenger side, but you and I both know that car is probably already at a junkyard being stripped. Radar is calling around, but given the time of night, he's not having much luck so far."

"Fuck." Frustrated, I shove my hand in my hair. "What about witness description of the driver?"

"There isn't much; the guy was putting out the garbage when he heard the crash. He just got a quick glimpse of the suspect as the vehicle was speeding by and passed under a streetlight. He's pretty sure it was a white guy, wearing a light-colored ball cap, and no facial hair. The one odd thing he noticed was the driver was wearing sunglasses, despite the almost dark. All in all, not a hell of a lot to go by."

"Beer?" Dimi comes walking in with three bottles from my fridge, handing one to each Yanis and me. "How's she doing?"

"*She* is doing fine."

We all turn to see Rosie standing in the door, wearing a tee and sweats from my dresser. The grin that starts forming on my face vanishes instantly when I see the edge of the bandages on her arm peeking out.

"Hey, Gorgeous." My eyes snap to Dimi, who is doing his best to blind Rosie with his smile, and I can't hold in the warning growl. Fucking guy flirts with anything in a skirt.

"Rosie," Yanis greets her. "Glad to see you moving about."

"Thanks," she mumbles, a bit more subdued now all the attention is on her, shooting a pleading look in my direction. I reach out my hand, trying not to look smug when she moves toward me, right by Dimas without looking, and lets me pull her down. Ignoring the guys' soft chuckles, I carefully settle her on my lap. They can think what they want; I don't give a rat's ass.

"Can I get you something? I'm afraid Jake doesn't stock wine." Clearly Dimi can't quite leave trying to one-up me alone.

"Good thing he stocks my favorite beer then," Rosie fires back, her eyes sparkling.

I don't bother trying to hide the satisfied grin this

time, especially when Yanis bursts out laughing.

"Looks like she's got your number, little brother," he pokes at Dimi, who has trouble keeping a straight face himself.

With her own beer in hand, the atmosphere turns serious again when Rosie asks, "Other than keeping an eye out, what are the cops doing?"

"Canvassing neighborhood houses, checking if anyone saw anything," Yanis answers her. "Someone in my office is keeping tabs on their investigation, so as soon as they know something, we'll know it too."

"I don't get why someone would want to hurt me. I haven't done or said a thing to anyone. Why would anyone come after me?"

I'm about to open my mouth to break the heavy silence that follows her question, when loud knocking sounds on the front door.

"Expecting someone?" Dimi asks and I shake my head no. He stalks to the door and checks the peephole before turning around to us with a big grin on his face. "Looks like this just became a party."

ROSIE

"Get out of my way, goddammit, I know my girl is in here. What the eff, Rosebud!"

Dimi barely has a chance to open the door, and Grant pushes his way inside, his eyes tracking and locking on me.

"How did you get here?" I want to know, confused.

"Well, let's see," Grant taps his index finger to the dimple in his chin and rolls his eyes dramatically to the ceiling. "By the grace of God, I managed to change my shift in favor of a hot date, when I ended up home, twiddling my thumbs, after my Dutch boy called to say he wouldn't be able to make it. I was waiting for my girl to get there so she could help me drown my sorrows. A cop shows up to the door—great teeth, shoulders for miles, and an ass they should sell tickets to see—asking if I happened to see the accident. 'What accident?' I asked, batting my eyelashes; because you never let an opportunity to flirt go past. 'A woman in an old PT Cruiser was run off the road,' he tells me. I about grab the poor boy by the collar and get all up in his face, demanding more information." Grant pauses to snatch Dimi's bottle he left on the table, and takes a deep swig. "Thanks, darlin'," he coos at Dimi, who looks shell-shocked, as he gets a half empty bottle of beer pressed into his hand. "Anyhoo…I run outside, and lo and behold, your poor, decrepit, little dinky toy is crumpled up against the sidewalk halfway down the block, but there's no sign of you. Cover model cop has no idea what happened to you, and I trot off down the sidewalk. Rupert from across the road stops me and tells me he saw you getting hit and you were bleeding. *Bleeding.*"

"Honey, I'm sorry, I…" I try to get up off Jake's lap, but he holds me tight. Grant shakes his hand in my face to cut me off, while pressing the other to the middle of his massive chest.

"Imagine the hurt when I find out my best friend, my roomie, my Rosebud, doesn't call me to the rescue—just steps away down the street—and injured and bleeding, sets off into the night with dark, broody GI Joe instead. I tried calling: no answer. I left a message: nothing. Finally I called your office—" He points a scathing look at Jake. "And threatened whoever was unfortunate enough to answer the phone, that I would sit on them, hold them down, and roll rubber bands through their chest hair until they're as smooth as a baby's butt—to get this damn address." Out of breath, Grant plucks the bottle from Dimi's hand, and tosses the remainder back, wiping his mouth with the back of his hand. "Here I am, hot and sweaty as a whore in church. I could use another drink, got anymore of these?" He waves the bottle at Jake, who points in the direction of the kitchen. "But first I'd like to know; what the fuck, Rosebud?"

"I'd just left Jake at the hotel and he was the first person who popped in my head, sorry…" I wince as I make my excuses. "I'm sorry I didn't answer your calls, but I think the neighbor may still have my phone."

"Actually," Jake interrupts. "I have your phone, but I left it in the car."

"Oh, well, anyway I'm especially sorry I didn't think to call you immediately. I thought you were going to be busy with Olaf and since I just have some cuts and scrapes, nothing major, I figured it could wait until morning."

Jake takes over and explains what happened, which gives me a chance to detangle myself from him and hobble to the kitchen to get us more beers. With his second beer in hand, and more or less over his snit, Grant settles in beside Yanis on the couch, who looks a little pale around the nose, especially when Grant repeatedly puts his big paw on the guy's knee.

Back on Jake's lap, I finish my own drink and snuggle in with my head on his shoulder. I follow along with the general conversation, ranging anywhere from the underbelly of the movie industry, to the merits of microbreweries, to the poor performance of the Colorado Rockies so far this season. Just listening to the heavy drone of the men's voices makes me sleepy. Within minutes, my eyelids flutter and I doze off.

The next thing I know, I'm being tucked into bed by Jake—who presses a kiss to my hair—before I let my eyes drift closed again. The bedroom door closes and I hear Jake in the hallway, talking to someone.

"Trust me, I'm not letting her out of my sight. She'll be staying with me."

I should probably protest the fact decisions are being made about me, without my input, but I'm too damn tired to open my mouth. Instead I let myself slide into a deep sleep.

CHAPTER 18

JAKE

"NEXT TIME YOU'RE arm wrestled into giving up my address, you wanna give me a heads-up?"

Radar smiles a toothy grin when I walk into the office.

"And what would be the fun in that? The guy was in a state, and I would've given good money to witness him giving the three of you some of what he handed out to me." He ducks when I try to give him a slap upside the head, and adds, "Just so you know, I did offer to call you to check, but he wouldn't hear of it, he insisted he see Rosie for himself. How is she, by the way?"

"Other than she's pissed as all hell right now, she's fine," I confess with a grin, as I gather up some files and slide them in a messenger bag with the laptop.

***

It started first thing this morning when I woke up in a cold bed. Sounds from the kitchen alerted me to the fact Rosie hadn't skipped out at some point. I wouldn't have put it past her. Not after the weekend we'd had.

She wasn't at all happy I had Grant pack up and bring over her clothes and toiletries on Friday night. So Saturday morning did not start swimmingly when she found out, but her snit didn't last long. Then Grant knocked on my door again that night, after dinner. Seeing him triggered her anger, and she gave him hell for colluding with me to keep her *prisoner*; her words, not mine.

Sunday things seemed more relaxed; we stayed in watching movies and eating junk food. The only time she was upset was when she slid her hand down my boxers after we'd gone to bed, and I stopped her. Trust me, I would've liked nothing better than to take her up on her invitation, but with her body still black and blue, I didn't want to chance hurting her. I wasn't too sure if I'd be able to restrain myself.

In the end she huffed a little, turned her back to me, and finally fell asleep shortly after I wrapped my arm around her, tucking her into my body. The whole night was some kind of torture with her soft ass pressed into my painful erection. Sleep didn't come until the faint light of morning started filtering in through my blinds.

I tagged a pair of jeans and followed the smell of coffee into my kitchen, where I found Rosie fully dressed in her uniform.

"Where do you think you're going?"

She turned to me with one eyebrow pulled high.

"Work," she stated, daring me to respond.

"You're off until we find who is responsible for your injuries."

Clearly that did not make her happy. Thus followed a discussion where I had to explain her boss was made aware of the attack on her, and—after Yanis reminded him of the kind of business PASS provided the hotel by housing all their clients there—the man very graciously agreed to let Rosie take a week.

It's true what they say about the temper of redheads. As shy and easygoing as Rosie appears initially, once the gloves come off; she is fierce. A little scary even. But what is scarier is even the woman's anger seems to be a turn-on for me. The more I see of the real Rosie, the deeper I fall.

By the time Grant called to see if she wanted to go with him to see Connie, she had calmed down a little. When he swung by to pick her up, I mentioned running into the office to grab some work for the week, which earned me a particularly dirty look and a tightly closed mouth when I tried to kiss her goodbye. The fact I could barely contain my amusement at that only fueled the flame. Grant just chuckled as he tucked her into his car.

"Already, huh?" Radar points out. "Didn't take you long to alienate your woman. At this rate you'll break my record."

I don't react to his calling Rosie my woman. I reckon it's pretty accurate, there is no one else who would fit that bill.

"By the way," Radar continues. "The Ford was reported by a security guard at Colorado Mesa University, yesterday morning. He noted it had been left parked without a tag in a lot by the Welcome Center, sometime early Saturday morning, and had remained unclaimed for twenty-four hours by the time it was called in. The Ford was towed off by GJPD for processing."

"Any news from there?"

"Matter-of-fact, there is." He turns to his screen and opens a link on his desktop. "The VIN number on the car was traced back to a lawyer in Glenwood Springs. He reported the car stolen Friday morning at the local golf course. The license plates were traced to a guy who is apparently on vacation with the family in Mexico and left his car in the long-term parking lot at the airport, here in Grand Junction."

"Let me guess," I offer, "his car was sporting the Ford's plates?"

"Bingo. I pulled up the DMV record for Peter Lavoie, the owner of the Ford, and judging by his picture, I can safely confirm he was not behind the wheel."

I take a look at the image on the screen of a black man in his fifties. "Looks that way. So where do we go from here? Whoever stole the Ford had to have had some way to get to the golf course, and some way to get off university grounds after he abandoned the Ford there."

"Bree managed to find out the GJPD checked with their Glenwood counterparts for any reports of an unclaimed vehicle at or around the golf course. Of course, someone may well have dropped him off and picked him up again."

"Could be, which would also raise the possibility the driver could be working for someone else."

"Exactly, but that might make him much harder to trace. For now, I'm going to assume he was on his own and had to find his own way around. Either he was well-prepared and had a second vehicle waiting nearby, but if we're lucky he grabbed a taxi. I'll get started on the cab companies to see if anyone has a record of a pickup at the university early Saturday morning."

"Thanks, appreciate it. Could you shoot everything you find to me in an email? I'll be working from home." Carrying the messenger bag, I head for the door, but stop just short. "By the way; since I'm trying to keep Rosie safe at my place, you may want to hold off on giving out my address to random people for a bit."

Radar turns his infectious grin on me, but when he sees the dead serious expression on my face, sobers right up.

"So noted."

"Can I help you?"

The woman behind the counter smiles when I walk into the store.

"I'm just looking around."

"Let me know if you need any help." I nod at her and walk over to the cooler alongside the back wall, housing a wide range of options.

Jesus, I had no idea there'd be this many choices. It's not like I have much experience buying this stuff. My eye catches on something red, white, and blue. Patriotic—every warm-blooded American likes those colors. Pleased with myself, I grab it out of the cooler—the thing is as heavy as a goddam paver— and walk over to the counter.

"Is it for a special occasion?" The woman throws a concerned look at the replica of the American flag in my hands.

"Not really, just something for someone special," I explain, puzzled when her face drops even further.

"I'm so, so sorry for your loss," she mumbles.

Wait. What?

"Loss? I'm afraid I don't understand."

"It's a beautiful choice. If you'd like we can have the flowers sent straight to the funeral home." She turns soulful eyes on me.

Confused, I examine the piece in my hands, only now noticing a ribbon with the words Rest In Peace, fluttering at the bottom.

Minutes later I walk out, the admonishing glare of the florist burning a hole in my back, clutching a bouquet of white and yellow flowers she ended up picking in my hand.

Apparently funeral flowers are not the way to go when you're trying to make nice with a woman.

How the fuck was I supposed to know?

ROSIE

I shake off Grant's hand when he tries to help me out of his car. "I'm not an invalid."

"You move like one," he fires back, before adding with a smirk. "You wouldn't have lasted an hour at work."

That earns him a dirty look, but I'm determined not to engage. Grant likes to push my buttons, but I've done my fill of arguing this weekend. The truth is—although I'd rather swallow my tongue than admit it—I'm glad for the time off. My hip is killing me, and the bruising and swelling of my shoulder makes using the arm on that side virtually impossible. It would've taken me forever to get my work done, if I could've managed at all.

But I'm not going to let Grant in on that. The men in my life—I'm still getting used to the fact there is more than one—already think they know everything best. Drives me nuts, even if sometimes they're right.

"Have you heard from Olaf?"

"I don't know, Rosie. That man is fine as fine can be when he's around—attentive, funny, and shit; he scorches my damn sheets—but it's like he forgets

I exist when I'm out of sight. I finally got hold of him last night. Says he had to fly out to LA on Friday unexpectedly; something about meetings for a next project, won't be back until Wednesday for the last days of shooting. He forgot his charger and his phone ran out of juice, but I'm calling bullshit. Boy sees me as a temporary diversion, and you *know* I'm worth more than that."

"Damn right you are," I commiserate, patting his knee soothingly. "He doesn't know the pure diamond he holds in his hand."

"Right?" he agrees with flair. "He gets one more chance, but that's it. He better bring his A game."

"Isn't this the last week of shooting, though?"

"For the cast, yes, but the camera crew will stay behind until Wednesday next week to shoot scenery around McInnis and downtown Grand Junction. Of course I work, but I switched a few shifts so I actually have Saturday and Sunday off to spend with him."

"Wow," I smile at him. "For once a proper weekend with everyone else."

"Let's hope it's a good one."

He returns my smile but when he turns his attention back on traffic, it disappears into a straight line. I feel bad for him; Grand Junction isn't exactly a hotbed of the gay community. Especially for a black man built like a tank. He would've been better off in San Francisco or even Phoenix. Despite appearing out of place, his family roots in this town are deep, and I can't see him trying to build up a life elsewhere.

It's just slim pickings here.

"He doesn't appreciate you the way you deserve, you give me a call; I'll give that boy a come-to-Jesus he won't ever forget."

Grant snorts beside me. "Rosebud, you're five nothing and weigh maybe a buck fifty—wet. Have you seen Olaf?"

"One seventy-five, and I'm five-two. He may be bigger, but he hurts you, you can bet your patootie I'll have that Dutch boy singing soprano in the damn church choir."

We walk into the nursing home, my best friend still chuckling beside me. I'm glad I was able to make him laugh.

Mom is dozing in her bed, with one eye half-open when I come in the door. The moment Grant walks in behind me, both eyes pop open and a bright smile appears on her face.

"Hey, Beautiful," Grant coos, as he pushes past me and takes a seat next to her bed.

She barely gives me a second glance as he easily draws her into conversation, trying to pull me in as well, but Mom doesn't bite. I should probably be used to it by now, but it still stings.

My whole life, I've been made to feel inadequate and her dementia has not changed a thing. Sometimes I'll just sit there and tell her about my day, while she either glares at me or avoids looking at me altogether, until I finally give up. Most days she barely acknowledges my presence, and I spend those visits as I do today, sitting quietly in a chair beside her bed.

There isn't much I can do for her anymore—everything I did before has been taken over by the staff here—but I can at least come and visit. I have to admit it's more for myself than her. At some point in this process, I've gone from merely a disappointment to an actual enemy for Mom, and I doubt she'd miss me if I didn't show, but *I* need to know I'm doing all I can. For me.

There are times when I feel utterly alone.

"Ready to go?" Grant's voice startles me out of my daze, and I glance over at the bed, where Mom has fallen asleep. With a kind expression on his face, he pulls me out of the chair and hooks my hand in the crook of his arm. "I'm taking you for lunch."

"I should probably call Jake. Knowing that man, he'll have a posse out looking for me before we get our food."

"Already messaged him."

I look sideways at Grant's profile. "You like him," I conclude.

"He's good for you."

"He's bossy."

"Like I said; he's good for you," he repeats, throwing me a glance from the corner of his eyes.

"You're bossy too."

This time a wide grin appears on his face. "That's why I like him."

"Chad was bossy," I point out as we get to the car, and Grant opens the door for me.

"Chad was a self-centered, controlling, lying piece of shit," he fires back before adding, "Buckle up."

"Yes, Dad," I mumble, as he shuts my door and stalks around to the driver's side, and suddenly I'm hit with a wave of sadness. I miss him almost as much now as I did when he'd just passed. He was always my safe, soft place to fall. Part of me wonders if unconsciously I look for him in the men I let into my life. Chad, who fell miserably short, and now Grant, even Jake. They all—well, at least Grant and Jake— seem to be able to make me feel safe, and cared for. Each coming at it from a different perspective.

I guess bossy is not so bad when it comes from the right place. All the things that irritated me these past few days—things I felt as belittling—suddenly feel comforting when I look at them under a different light. With that realization, I suddenly feel petty and ungrateful.

"Instead of eating out, can we perhaps pick something up for all three of us and eat it at Jake's? He's probably home by now."

Grant's large hand reaches over and pats my knee. "Sure thing, Rosebud. Let's make sure that boy of yours keeps up his strength. God knows he needs it with you around." I choose to ignore the barb, determined not to let anything touch my charitable mood.

Thirty minutes later, we pull up to Jake's bungalow with two bags of Chinese takeout from Bamboo City.

"Honey, we're home!" Grant calls out, as he marches in the door first. I follow behind a bit slower, but halt in my tracks when I see the sunny bouquet of flowers in a plastic juice pitcher on the kitchen counter.

"Couldn't find a vase," Jake says from behind the stove where he is stirring a pot.

"Doubt you have a vase," Grant answers, plunking the bags of food beside the flowers.

"True enough." Jake's eyes never leave mine.

Ignoring Grant, I make my way over to Jake and slip my arms around his waist, tilting my head back to look at him. "Those for me?"

He rolls his eyes but when they come back to mine, they're sparkling with humor. "Sure as fuck am not gonna buy that tree-sized fruitcake any flowers."

"Hey! I resemble that remark," Grant reacts, as he shamelessly opens every kitchen cupboard until he finds plates.

"Thank you," I whisper for Jake's ears only. He wraps an arm around me, and gives my shoulders a squeeze, before dropping a hard kiss on my lips.

"Are we eating or what?"

We both turn to Grant, who has spread the boxes of takeout on the counter and is loading his plate.

"I didn't know you'd be cooking," I tell Jake, indicating the pot on the stove. "We brought lunch."

"Just chili, which will be better tonight anyway."

"Am I invited?"

"Nope," Jake informs Grant firmly. "After lunch

I'm kicking you out. Rosie and I have plans."

"We do?"

He tilts his head down, looking me straight in the eyes. "Damn right we do."

The gruff sound of his voice, and the promise of his words, head straight down my body, making my spine tingle and my knees weak.

"Easy, boy," Grant protests, his mouth full of chow mein. "You're ruining my appetite."

As it turns out, those plans get delayed, when right after Grant leaves; Jake gets a work call. He spends the next half hour, while I'm cleaning up the kitchen, sitting in front of his laptop with the phone to his ear.

I just catch snippets of the conversation, but it's clear they're talking about the SUV that tried to run me down. Something about the cops coming up empty on a search of the vehicle. I assume that means they found it and am itching to hear. I make myself some tea, grab my Kindle, and curl up on the couch, trying to concentrate on my book while Jake works.

"You keep falling asleep on my couch, I've gotta be doing something wrong."

I blink my eyes open to find Jake on his knees beside me, on the floor. "Nothing wrong with you on your knees." Still sleepy, I accidentally voice my thought out loud, and immediately realize my mistake. I scramble upright in my seat. Jake's expression holds the middle between shock and amusement. Embarrassed, I start rambling, "I didn't mean to imply…I mean…that came out wrong. I wouldn't presume…I didn't even think of it…well, clearly I did think of it, but more in a way of observation, rather than wish. That's not to say I wouldn't want that, but not now. This…" I start waving my hand between us, "whatever this is *here*, it may or may not end up *there*. But not now…or maybe ever. So forget I said anything. Please…"

To my abject horror, amusement wins and Jake busts out laughing; his head thrown back and the strong column of his throat exposed. He looks beautiful like this, and I feel even more like a superior idiot.

"Rosie," he starts hiccuping, and I wait for the next words to come but instead he dissolves into laughter again.

Irritated—with myself and with him—I launch myself off the couch, mumbling under my breath, "Fuck this, I need to pee."

CHAPTER 19

I ADMIT, SHE scared the snot out of me when she made that reference to me going on my knees for her, and laughter felt like my only option. But damn…she makes me feel like a dirtbag when she beelines it out of here.

The moment the bathroom door slams shut; I get up and follow behind. I wait outside until I hear the toilet flush and try the door. It's locked, so I knock softly.

"Rosie, let me in?"

"I'm peeing." Her voice is muffled by the closed door.

"You just flushed," I point out, grinning.

"I have to go again."

The door would be easy to open with the end of a paperclip, but instead I back off and give her the space she clearly wants. I head to the kitchen to check on my chili, and start pulling out ingredients for my jalapeno cheese cornbread. By the time I hear the click of the bathroom lock, I have my oven hot and my batter ready to go in the loaf pan. I'm tempted to turn around when I hear her walk into the kitchen, but decide against it. I sense her moving closer to peek at what I'm up to. Sliding the cornbread in the oven, I set the timer for thirty-five minutes.

"Did they find the car?"

I turn to the sound of her voice. "Parked on university grounds," I explain. "Radar just called to say the cops weren't able to secure any evidence in the car to help find out who was behind the wheel, but they did find damage to its front end and the flecks of paint left behind appear to match your PT."

"What about the license plate?"

"Nothing quite that easy, I'm afraid; the car was stolen in Glenwood and the plates at the Grand Junction airport, off a car left in long-term parking."

"So how do you find him now?"

"Radar just looped me into a tape from a university security camera, showing the vehicle pull in to the parking lot, just after midnight, early Saturday morning. Then, just ten minutes later, you see a guy in a light ball cap walking out to the street. From the angle of the camera, you can only see the bottom half of his face, but we've got a good look at his clothes and can put together a better physical description now."

I grab two beers from the fridge and hand one to Rosie, who takes a deep tug, doing her best to avoid my eyes. I'll give her that play, but as soon as dinner is over, I plan to haul her into the bedroom and set her clear on what happened earlier.

While we wait for the cornbread to bake, she asks me questions about growing up without my parents and my service years. The first is easy enough; I've long since come to terms with the rough period I had in my teen years, before the Mazurs took me in. Whatever Mami and Tata Mazur didn't knock out of me, the military did.

Talking about my tours in the Middle East is more challenging. Guilt still taints those experiences. Plus, some things I've done and seen, I'd rather not remember, let alone share with Rosie. Still, I share as much as I'm comfortable with, and she listens attentively, asking pointed, and at times, uncomfortably intuitive questions.

The simple, "Thank you for your service," she expresses at the end, feels like a soothing balm. Almost like an absolution, for lack of a better term. It has impact, coming from someone who holds more pieces of me than even Dimas does.

The chili isn't too spicy, but I make up for it with the cornbread, which holds enough kick to have Rosie dive into the fridge for another beer.

"Yikes, the bread is good, but it's got a bite," she admits after downing her drink. "I'm tasting something different in the chili, but I can't quite place it. What is that? Almost a hint of sweetness."

"Two tablespoons of pure cocoa powder."

Her eyes grow big. "You put chocolate in your

chili? I love chocolate, but I never would've thought to put it in chili."

"The Mexicans put chocolate in their mole sauce, so why not their chili? Gives it a nice rich flavor."

"I'll have to remember that," she says, shoving another spoonful in her mouth.

It pleases me she likes it. I've never given two shits about what I throw together, but I find I like cooking for her. Something very satisfying about feeding someone. I finally get why Mami was never happier than when she had her 'boys' around the dinner table.

Feeding someone is the most basic form of caring for that person, and there is no denying I care about Rosie. More than I planned for. More than I ever thought possible, in fact, although I'm not quite sure what to do with that. Yet.

Once our dishes are washed and the leftover dinner is stored in the fridge, Rosie heads for the couch. I manage to catch her by the hand, just before she sits down, and tug her behind me to the bedroom.

"Jake, what's gotten into you?"

Silently I lead her toward the bed, pushing her gently so she falls backward onto the mattress, and I lower myself on top, pinning her down.

"We had plans, remember? But first we've got something to clear up." The instant I mention that, Rosie shifts her eyes to the side, avoiding mine. "You overthink things," I start, and I immediately have her eyes back, but they are sparking with defiance.

"Hear me out. When a situation or a person makes you uncomfortable or unsure—like this afternoon—you don't let it play out. You draw a conclusion based on your own assumptions and run with it, most of the time in the wrong direction. In this case, quite literally, straight to the bathroom." She squirms underneath me, but I'm not about to let go of her, instead, I press a hard kiss to her lips. "You're still working up things in that head of yours, thinking you know where this is going, but you don't." A dirty look is thrown at me. "Here's the truth of what's playing out inside me; you are a surprise, a very pleasant one I might add. One I wasn't looking for, or ever expected, but here you are, and I don't want to let go of you."

"Oh. But I thought…"

"Sweet Rosie, get out of your head. If you're not clear on what I'm thinking, ask and I promise I'll tell you the truth. So far the truth is, you're opening my mind to a whole lot of possibilities I would never have considered otherwise. Including, but not limited to, going down on a knee." She blushes at that and I rub my nose along hers before continuing, "And for the record; you rambling is funny and cute."

"Whatever. I babbled like a dweeb."

"A very funny, cute dweeb. Now, what about those plans we had?"

"*We* had?" she throws back at me. "From what I recall, you're the man with the plan."

"Fuckin' A I am." I grin and run my hand slowly down her body as I lower my head.

"For the record," she echoes my earlier words, stopping my kiss with her index finger against my lips. "I wasn't looking for you either, but I'm starting to think I'm pretty lucky I found you anyway."

ROSIE

His eyes go from light gray to dark in an instant.

Before I can take a breath, his mouth slants over mine and takes away any opportunity. His kiss is hungry, and the hand he skims over my body restless, imprinting himself on my skin everywhere. In seconds, I'm floating on sensation: touch, taste, and lightheaded from lack of oxygen. When he finally breaks the seal, I draw in a lungful of air as he rests his forehead on mine.

"What you do to me," he mutters, his breath ghosting over my face, and his hands tugging on my clothes. Seconds later, I'm divested of my shirt and bra, when he sits up, his knees on either side of me, looking down. "Are you still sore?" he asks, his eyes scanning my left arm and shoulder.

"I can't feel anything but you."

"Good."

He leans over and presses his face between my breasts, inhaling deeply before drawing first one nipple between his lips, softly stroking it with his tongue, and then the other. "Beautiful." He straightens up and leaves his hand high on my chest, his fingertips dipping in the hollow at the base of my throat, where my pulse drums rapidly against his touch. Torturously gentle, he drags his hand down the center of my body, and I squirm when he finally reaches the waistband of my pants. Suddenly he grabs either side of my hips and flips me onto my stomach, tugging down both my pants and underwear at once. "Lush." I hear him whisper, as he runs both hands up the back of my legs to the globes of my behind, which he gently squeezes.

"Jake," I beg in anticipation.

The sharp sting of a bite on my ass cheek has me hiss in response, and he follows with the same treatment for the other.

"Yesss…"

"On your knees," he orders, as he gets off the bed.

I hear the rustle of his clothes and quickly comply, spreading my knees wide on the edge of the mattress, primed and uninhibited.

"*Christ*, Rosie…" His voice is quickly muffled as he presses his face between my legs from behind.

The first stroke of his warm, wet tongue from front to back sends a violent shiver through my body.

Decadent, dirty, and delicious—so very, very delicious.

By the time I feel the blunt head of his erection prod the slickness at my core, he has me whimpering for mercy. Intent on torturing me, he fills me ever so slowly, driving me insane with need. Rooted deep, Jake bends his body over mine and I feel his lips brush the center of my back. "My sweet, sweet Rosie."

All of a sudden his soft touch and languid pace

is gone. He firmly holds onto my hips and with a powerful rhythmic surge, drives first to my, and then his own release.

⌣‾‾‾‾‾‾

After being off work and inside Jake's house for days, I'm bored senseless. The week is slipping by and I haven't done a single worthwhile thing.

Don't get me wrong; I love his place, the quiet, the views, and yes, the company. Just this morning I woke up to being hauled out of bed and into the shower, where he showed me once again how much he appreciates my not so perfect body. But the rest of the day, he works, while I twiddle my thumbs.

I tried reading, which really isn't that relaxing when you're in the same room with someone who is working on his laptop or talking shop on the phone. I tried my hand at baking bread to keep myself busy, but I can tell you baking bread is not fun when you suck at it. Three days, three loaves, and all of them solid enough to pave the driveway with.

I honestly thought it would be exciting to learn about his job, but it turns out a lot of it is endless chewing over details, looking at plans, and waiting. The only interesting bit of news came an hour ago, when Radar called to say he'd finally connected with a cab driver who recalls picking up a ride, fitting the driver's description, on the corner of North Twelfth and Orchard, around the time he was caught on the security tape. Radar is taking a copy of the footage to confirm with the guy. He's supposed to swing by after, to let me have a look at it too. Perhaps I've seen the man around before.

That is the only reason why I'm back in the kitchen now, working on a stack of grilled cheese sandwiches and some soup for lunch.

Like I said; June Cleaver.

"Smells good."

Jake's strong arms slip around my front as he folds himself around my back, his chin on my shoulder. He tries to sneak a sandwich while distracting me with his mouth on my neck, but I catch him.

"They're for later," I admonish him, slapping his hand away.

"I'm hungry now," he growls in my neck, while shoving the thieving hand down the front of my pants.

"*Jake*, he could be here any minute."

"So? Not like he can surprise us, he still has to ring the—"

Just then the doorbell startles me. Jake grudgingly releases me and moves to the front door to let Radar in. I quickly ladle soup into bowls from the cupboard and set them on the counter, before sliding the last sandwich from the pan to the plate.

"What smells good?"

A tall lanky guy with nerdy good looks—longish blond hair and glasses perched on a chiseled face—I assume is Radar, walks into the kitchen, sniffing the air like a dog.

"Rosie, this is Radar," Jake follows behind, introducing us.

Radar walks right up and wraps me in a bear hug. I'm not quite sure how to respond to this, so I awkwardly pat his back.

"Jesus…" I hear Jake mutter as Radar takes a step back, his hands on my shoulders, looking at me with a twinkle in his eyes.

"I just want you to know you're already a legend in the office," he informs me.

"How so?"

"Don't mind him," Jake interjects, swiftly stepping between us.

"Never thought we'd see this man discombobulated," Radar responds, not even a little deterred by Jake's attempt to intervene. "Always steady and even-keeled, nothing fazes him, yet you've rattled him good. It's funny as shit."

"All right, enough with the fancy words and the ribbing," Jake groans, elbowing his teammate in the gut. "Sit your ass down, Rosie made lunch."

"Hungry?" I bite down a smile as I direct Radar to a seat.

"Always." He's already bitten off half a grilled cheese sandwich when he answers.

Lunch is a lively affair. I'm regaled with anecdotes of past cases the two have worked on, and although Radar has the floor most of the time, eventually Jake relaxes and occasionally jumps in with a comment. I almost forget this is not a social visit, when Radar suddenly turns serious—after putting away two bowls of soup and two sandwiches—and goes to grab the briefcase he dropped on the couch when he walked in.

"Have a look at this," he says, pulling out a sheet of paper and placing it in front of me on the table. "Sorry for the poor quality, but do you know this man? Seen him before?"

I study the grainy black and white image of what looks to be a fairly big man, wearing a white or light-colored baseball cap with some kind of logo and dark clothing. I can't really make out any features, other than that he appears to be clean-shaven.

"Can't say I have," I answer honestly, as I peek a little closer and shake my head. "Sorry. All I can tell is that it's a white man, who appears to be quite a Rockies fan."

"What?" Radar turns the picture around and leans forward, looking at it closely before standing back, slapping his hand down. "Son of a bitch, I did not catch that."

"What?" Jake takes his turn scrutinizing the ball cap in the image.

"That's gotta be a fairly new ball cap," I explain. "The Rockies changed their logo recently to simple initials. If I'm not mistaken, that's the C and the R."

"Yup. I see it too," Radar confirms, coming around to my side and placing his laptop on the table. His fingers move over the keyboard in a blur, and then a video pops up on the screen. "Have a look at this and tell me what you see."

Jake moves in behind me and looks over my shoulder.

At first, I only see a street light illuminating part of an empty street and sidewalk, and at the edge of the frame you can just make out the corner of a building. A man walks into the image, moving around the corner, into the light of the street lamp, and toward the camera. It's the same guy from the print, ball cap on his head. Now I know what to look for, it's easier to recognize the Rockies logo.

"Same guy," I point out. "He's wearing glasses; you can see the bottom rim just under the bill of his cap."

"Witness said he saw the drive of the Ford wearing sunglasses," Radar fills me in.

"He's fit," I notice. "Broad shoulders, long legs, walks with a confident stride. He's not looking around like he's worried."

"He's a professional," Jake concludes. "He planned and prepared."

"Prepared for what? To scare me?"

"Not so sure scaring you is all he was after." Radar looks at me with an apologetic smile. "The driver's side of your car is crumpled. Had you been behind the wheel, I doubt you would've walked away. According to the GJPD investigator in charge, your engine was messed with, causing it to break down on your way home. My guess is he hung back until he saw your car stopped, but didn't realize you'd already gotten out."

"He's a professional," Jake repeats, his face

solemn. "He'll be back to try and finish the job."

"Undoubtedly."

Radar looks at me with concern on his face, and a shiver runs down my spine, as if someone stepped over my grave.

"Well, shit," I add, leaning down to take one more, good look at the man on the screen.

CHAPTER 20

JAKE

I LOOK OVER to where Rosie is bent over a pad of paper, writing furiously.

She's been at it since Radar left earlier, and for the past few hours I've let her be, but my curiosity is getting the better of me.

"What are you up to?"

Her head comes up off the paper and she looks almost disoriented.

"Writing down everything I remember. From the moment I heard the crash down the alley. Every tiny detail I can recall."

I note a rushed, almost speedy quality to her words, and her body language screams tension. I move over to stand behind her, put my hands on her shoulders at the base of her neck, and feel the taut muscles under my fingers. Carefully I start applying a little pressure with my thumbs, and at her responding moan, I add a little more. The sounds she makes are more than a little distracting as I try to massage the tension from her neck and shoulders. If she keeps this up, she'll have a whopping tension headache tonight.

"Take a little break," I suggest, but she shakes her head no.

"Can't. I'm tired of doing nothing, being useless. It's not like me to sit around while others fix my problems for me."

"It's only—"

Her hand comes up immediately to cut me off when I try to tell her it's only temporary.

"I know, I know—but you wouldn't be doing nothing if someone had it out for you, right? I don't have the first clue how to go about nabbing this guy. Not sure whether he's the same guy from the pool, why he wants to hurt me, or whether he could also be the one extorting money. What I do know is, with his focus somehow on me, there may well be something I know, have seen, or heard, that may be helpful. So I'm writing everything I can remember down."

"Can I see?"

I let go of her shoulders and take the notepad she hands me and read, leaning my ass against the table. Small tidy handwriting fills three pages; lists with times, dates, and detailed descriptions of events. She even has noted down what she remembers everyone wearing.

"I keep remembering stuff," she mentions. "Like the thing with Kyle Steele." My eyes flick over to her as I lower the notepad.

"What about him?"

"Since that time he was being an ass up by the pool and you intervened, I've only seen him a handful of times, and mostly from a distance, but each time I would catch him looking at me."

"That doesn't surprise me; you're not exactly hard on the eyes. You probably didn't notice him looking before." The snort she emits tells me she might require a bit more convincing on that part.

"Well, this is a tad embarrassing," she mutters, a fiery red blush creeping up her face. "I would've noticed. Grant and I may have shared a little crush on him." She holds up her hand with thumb and index finger almost, but not quite, touching. "We had a running bet who would be the first to get to talk to him, and we were watching. Most definitely he never once noticed me before."

"You had a thing for him?" I tease her, pretending to be disappointed. "Wow, and here I was flying high thinking I rescued you by the pool, when all I did was screw up your fantasy."

"Shut up." Her words are accompanied by a slap to my arm. "Whatever I found appealing about him on the screen, disappeared the moment he opened his mouth in person."

She may not quite believe it, but I think Steele is not used to being turned down by a beautiful woman. Like any spoiled rich boy, he craves what he can't get and the less attainable it becomes, the more he wants it. I don't doubt once he noticed Rosie, had a sample of her fire, he'd want a taste of her too. I'm not sure if he would've respected the cold shoulder she was giving him, but he sure as fuck respected my clear message to leave her alone. At least I assumed he did.

Now I'm not so sure.

"What's this scribble about Peabody and food?"

She takes the pad from my hand and checks her notes. "Oh, I was just writing down anything out of the ordinary. Remember when Grant got sick? He thought it was a flu and went to the doctor, but it turned out to likely be some kind of food poisoning from the takeout we had one night."

"You didn't get sick?" I ask.

"Not really, I didn't really like it. Maybe it was the taste of the elk meat, I don't know. I took a small bite of my burger and ended up giving the rest to Grant." Rosie puts down her pad, gets up from the table, and walks into the kitchen. "The whole thing just seemed strange to me," she continues as she dives into the fridge and comes up with a couple of beers. "Not only do I know Grant to have a steel-lined stomach, with what he shoves in there, but he'd just eaten at that place the week before with his boyfriend."

Just as I'm starting to wonder if perhaps the pool and the crash were not the only times Rosie's life had been threatened, my phone goes off.

"Talk to me."

"Need you at the hotel." Yanis' voice is clipped. "Radar intercepted a message to Steele's phone from the blackmailer. The source is right fucking here at the hotel."

"I'm bringing Rosie with me."

"Fine by me. It gets Drexler off my back, he has a real hard-on for your girl for this, but he won't be able to deny she couldn't have sent this last communication.

"I'll see you in twenty."

Rosie's eyes are big as she waits for me to fill her in.

"The blackmailer was in touch. Sounds like things are shaking loose in the hotel, so Yanis wants us there."

"Us?" she asks nervously, and I take the beer from her hand before hugging her to me.

"Us. Looks like it may have been someone in the hotel, and since you haven't been in the hotel—or out of my sight—for days, he can prove once and for all to Phil Drexler you have nothing to do with this."

"That would be one less thing to worry about," she says as she slips from my grip and heads for the door, grabbing her purse on the way. "Well, let's go."

ROSIE

"What are you doing here?"

I swing around to find Grant behind the front desk, leaning on his elbows with his chin on his fists.

"I should ask you that question? Since when are you working a day shift?" I fire back.

"Hutch! You coming?" Yanis is standing by the elevator, holding the door open.

"Honey, I've got to go, do you mind hanging out

with Peabody for a bit, while I get briefed? Shouldn't be too long."

"Sure—go."

I wave him on his way, but after just two steps he turns on his heels and turns back. Facing Grant, he leans over the desk.

"Don't let her out of your sight, yeah?"

"I'll put a leash on her," Grant quips, drawing protest from me.

"Hey—"

But my words are cut off when Jake tags me behind the neck and yanks me to him. With a warning in his eyes, he slams his mouth on mine, bruising my lips with a hard kiss, effectively silencing me. Right there in the lobby of my place of work. In front of God and everyone, to a loud whooping from Grant.

"Yowza, momma—that was hawt!"

"Hush," I hiss at him, as I watch Jake cross the lobby with long sure strides to where his boss is still waiting, but instead of the impatient glare I was expecting, Yanis has one side of his mouth tilted in an almost smile.

"Girl, just watching that almost had me bust a nut."

"Grant!"

I admonish him, but he just raises his eyebrows, purses his lips, and does this little head wobble, clearly unimpressed. With me, of course—he already made it clear he was very impressed with Jake.

"As I was saying earlier, what's with the day

shift?" I change the subject, in hopes distraction will get his mind off my boyfriend and out of the gutter.

Boyfriend.

Christ, I can't remember the last time I had one of those. I'm not going to pretend that's not what Jake is, he's made that much clear, both in words and in actions. And not just because of that kiss. I was used to Chad, and the odd time we were in public, other than for work, he was adamant about his rule; no public displays of affection whatsoever. He also didn't like the terms 'boyfriend/girlfriend' but preferred lovers. In hindsight that all makes sense, but at the time I remember it made me feel insecure.

Jake just blew through all of that with a very public claim. He wasn't hiding me, or ashamed of me. Instead he marked me in front of everyone, including his own boss. If he'd have peed on me it couldn't have been clearer. Fuck, if that doesn't make me feel good.

"Are you even listening?" Grant snaps his fingers in front of my face to draw my attention. "Fine friend you are. Asks me a question and don't listen to the answer. What cloud are you off on?"

"I'm sorry! You were saying?"

"Nothing as exciting as whatever movie reel was playing in your mind that has you looking blissed out, obviously."

"Please," I prompt him.

"Fine," he concedes. "Remember I mentioned switching out my schedule to clear my weekend?" He waits for my confirming nod before he continues,

"Charlene is picking up my nights today, Friday, Saturday and Sunday, and I'm taking her days, today, tomorrow, Monday and Tuesday. As per Wednesday we're back on regular rotation."

"So you came off your night shift this morning and just kept going without sleep?"

"All in the name of love, baby. All in the name of love."

For the next thirty or so minutes, we catch up between guests at the desk, and the rest of the time I amuse myself with Sudoku on my phone.

Grant is checking in a busload of seniors, who just arrived with a tour that stops here a few times during the summer. A weeklong tour of Colorado parks and conservation areas between Denver and the Utah border. Grand Junction is their mid-tour stop before turning back toward Denver.

For the past five minutes, I've been trying to get his attention, but he has his hands full sorting out the old folks. I need to go to the bathroom and waiting becomes increasingly difficult. With a wince I check the remaining lineup in front of the desk. At this rate, it'll be another half hour at least, before he has them all processed, and I don't have that long before my body takes matters into its own hands.

The restrooms are on the other side, right past the elevators. Grant doesn't even notice when I sneak out from behind the front desk and head across the lobby. Just as I pass by, the elevator doors open, and when I turn my head to look, I see Kyle Steele emerging. His eyes lock on mine and a sneer forms on his face. As I noted on my list this afternoon, he makes me very uncomfortable when he's eyeing me without saying a word, but that is when he smiles. The sneer he sends me now is far more unsettling, and I abruptly swing around to face forward, rushing toward the safe haven of the restroom. Normally, I prefer it when I find a restroom empty, but right now I wouldn't complain if every last woman on that senior tour were hit with incontinence issues.

Pushing open the door, I groan when I find it completely empty. Ten stalls, and every last door is open. Irrational panic overwhelms me when I realize I've just cornered myself into an empty space, and I never bothered telling Grant where I was going. I take a quick peek at the main door, hoping for a lock, but find none. When I get to the first stall, I pull the door shut and am glad when it sticks shut. The third and fourth doors to my right do the same. I manage to get one more to stay shut on the left, and end up getting in the furthest stall on the left, shutting and locking the door behind me. Should he be nuts enough to follow me in here, those closed doors won't stop him, but maybe they'll distract him enough to buy me a bit more time.

I wait for a few seconds to see if I can hear anything, but then I have to hurry to get my pants down before I pee them. The relief is only momentary as I empty my bladder. I barely have a chance to wipe before I clearly hear the sound of the spring above the door. Quickly and as soundlessly as possible, I pull up my pants and climb on top of the toilet seat. I wait with bated breath to hear a stall door open. And then another. And another… Whoever is in here is looking. I count three doors, and the sound of footsteps is coming closer. I'm afraid the loud gallop of my heart is bouncing off the tile walls when the fourth door opens. It's the stall right beside mine and I'm poised to scream.

When loud knocking shakes my door, I let loose with a bloodcurdling shriek.

"Rosie!"

JAKE

"Good to have you back," Dimi smirks, as I walk into the surveillance room behind Yanis. "Doesn't look like you missed us much, though," he says, pointing at the monitor showing the lobby and front desk. "That was quite impressive, wasn't it, Bree?"

"I frankly didn't think he had it in him." I turn around at the sound of her voice to find her grinning ear to ear, on the other side of the room.

"Very funny, you guys. What are we, twelve?"

"Never mind them," Yanis intervenes. "That's jealousy talking."

"You sure you aren't talking about yourself?" Dimi fires back at his brother, who just shrugs.

"Positive. No way I'd ever lose my head like that over a woman."

From the corner of my eye I see Bree startle. I've

always suspected she had more than just a normal passing interest in our boss, but the way her body jerks at Yanis' words, you'd think the impact had been physical.

"You called me here, how about you fill me in?" I quickly change tracks and Bree shoots me a grateful look. "What was the message you intercepted?" I ask Radar, who has been quietly observing the banter, processing and analyzing his impressions, much like one of his beloved computers would. He hands me a sheet with the message printed out. It's pretty generic, with a reminder of the threat, a new demand, and instructions for drop off.

"And you picked up on the signal?"

"Came right back to this hotel. Or rather, the city block it takes up," Radar clarifies. "I can't exactly pinpoint location within the hotel."

"So now what?" This question is meant for Yanis, who is keeping an eye on the lobby monitor where a busload of seniors is just filing in.

"Fucking hell," he swears. "Of all days for that damn tour to show. Radar? What time did that bus get here?"

"Sixteen forty-five."

"The message came in at a few minutes after three," Bree fills in.

"Can you see if the conference room is available?" Yanis asks her, to which he receives a curt nod. "Also, check if Simon Berry has left yet. I'd like to set up a meeting with Drexler, Steele, and Berry at some point in the next hour, provided you can locate them all." Yanis points a finger at me. "You bring Rosie and let's rattle those cages. Come fucking hell or high water, we're going to get to the bottom of this." Bree is already dialing before the boss is done.

"Hutch? Get a load of this."

I look at the monitor over Dimi's shoulder and watch as Rosie sneaks out from behind the front desk and zigzags around bodies, suitcases, and a fair number of walkers, to the other side of the lobby.

"Where the fuck is she going?" I mumble.

"Elevators?"

"Keep an eye on her!" I order as I start moving.

Heading through the door, I bypass the elevators and aim for the stairwell. My footsteps echo off the concrete as I run down, two steps at a time. When I shove open the door on the main level, the small hallway in front of the elevators is empty, but I just catch a glimpse of someone walking away and mixing with the crowd in front of the desk. I follow in that direction, scanning for her without success.

She has to be fucking somewhere.

I backtrack to the elevators when I spot the sign for the ladies' room.

CHAPTER 21

Empty.

I thought for sure she'd be in the bathroom. My gut is churning with worry, but also anger. What the hell was she thinking? When I explicitly told her to stick with Grant. I'll have a bone to pick with him as well.

When I head back into the lobby and check the front desk, there are two people assisting guests, but Grant is not one of them. I walk up and interrupt.

"Do you know where Grant went?" I ask the young woman I've seen around the hotel before.

"He just took a break," she responds, clearly recognizing me. "I would check the coffee shop."

I thank her and am about to move in that direction when I spot Dimi coming toward me. I gesture for him to follow and he falls in step beside me.

"Any luck?"

I'm about to fill him in, when I see Grant sitting at a table in the coffee shop. Alone. By the time I reach him, I swear steam is coming from my ears.

"Where the fuck is she?" It takes everything out of me not to haul him out of his chair by force, but my volume draws enough attention. "Where's Rosie?" Agitated, I shake off Dimi's restraining hand that lands on my shoulder.

"Hutch, chill," he warns in a low voice. "Let the man answer."

Grant pushes himself up to his full size and faces me with a carefully blank face. I have to admit; his dead silence is effectively intimidating as he stares me down.

"What's going on?"

ROSIE

The three of them turn in perfect concert at the sound of my voice.

I stop just a few feet away, a tray with two takeout cups and a couple of muffins I bought for Grant and me in my hand. My eyes dart from one to the other, confused and slightly concerned. I could hear Jake's booming voice all the way over by the small counter on the side, where I was doctoring our coffees.

They look pissed; Grant is glaring at Jake, Jake is glaring at me. Except Dimi, he looks amused, biting his lip trying to hide a grin as he winks at me.

Then I notice the other coffee shop patrons, most of them seniors off the bus, who are gawking at us. Our little standoff may well be the most excitement they've seen in years.

"Sit down," I hiss, setting the tray on the table. Dimi pulls out a chair immediately, but the other two stay standing. "For Christ's sake, sit yourselves down," I repeat impatiently, elbowing Grant in the side, who grudgingly complies. I sit as well, but Jake takes the longest, angry vibes coming off him in waves, before finally he sits as well.

"Isn't this cozy?" Dimi says, when the thick silence at the table becomes ridiculous.

"Shut up," Jake and Grant say in unison, immediately falling silent again, and by now I'm working up a good head of steam on my own. Like I don't have enough going on, without the two most important men in my life at each other's throats. I love them both, but right now I want to stick them behind wallpaper.

"Okay, why don't I start then?" Dimi continues, apparently not bothered by the palpable animosity at the table. "We were watching the monitors upstairs and—"

"You were supposed to stay with Grant and I saw you take off on your own," Jake interrupts, before directing his glare at my friend. "And you were supposed to make sure you didn't lose her from your sight."

"All right. Enough!" My voice is loud enough to draw the attention of not just the guys at my table, but the rest of the place as well. Lowering my volume to a more discreet level, I focus specifically on Jake. "I had to use the bathroom and didn't think it would be an issue, but I bumped into a not so friendly Kyle Steele at the elevators. Grant was just looking around the lobby for me when he happened to see that encounter, so he left his post and followed me straight into the bathroom. And now I'm buying him coffee by way of an apology for scaring him." I lean over and nudge Jake's shoulder with my own. "Seeing as I scared you as well, maybe I should buy you one too?"

He turns to me and bends close. "Scared the piss out of me," he whispers, his voice gruff with residual emotion. Grabbing my hand under the table, he tightly laces his fingers with mine. "Not losing sight of you again." I give his hand a squeeze.

"I should get back upstairs," Dimi says, getting to his feet, immediately followed by Grant, who grabs his cup and muffin.

"Yeah, I should get back to work too."

"Hold up," Jake says, putting a hand on Grant's arm as he starts walking away. "I owe you one."

"Sweetheart," Grant coos, batting his eyelashes, but I can still see the steel in them. "You owe me much more than that, but don't worry; my spectacular black ass will come collecting one of these days, and you're gonna need to bring your A game to satisfy me. Pun intended."

I don't know why I'm nervous as I follow Jake down

the corridor to the small conference room on the other side. If the prospect of sitting in the same room with Steele isn't disturbing enough, I'll also be faced with the producer and his legal counsel. For someone who doesn't particularly enjoy confrontation, this promises to be a very uncomfortable encounter.

Jake assures me I have the entire PASS team to back me up, but I still feel like I'm walking to my execution.

"It'll be fine," he promises again as we stop outside the door of the conference room. Voices can already be heard on the other side.

"Hope so."

Gathering my courage, I let go of his hand and push the door open, leading the way inside.

"What the hell is *she* doing here?" The angry, carefully cultured voice comes from my left, and I turn toward the source. I caught glimpses of Phil Drexler before, so I know what he looks like, but he looks particularly intimidating in business attire, flanked by a clearly angry Kyle Steele, and an equally well-dressed man I don't know.

"You'd do well to hold your horses," Jake warns the man as he steps around and in front of me.

Once again I appear to be stuck between two angry men, and frankly it's becoming tiring.

"Have a seat." Yanis comes to the rescue, pulling out a chair beside him. Grateful, I ignore the three scowling men on the other side of the table and slip into the seat, Jake taking up sentry behind me. "*She,*" he annunciates pointedly, his eyes on Drexler, "is here by my invitation. I believe the only people you haven't met are Bree Graves—" He gestures to an almost nondescript brunette with a solid build, but with a smile that turns her from plain to stunning. I automatically smile back. "And Simon Berry is counsel for Guild Film Productions." I look over at the unfamiliar man at the other end of the table, who simply nods at the introduction, ignoring my tentative smile. Well then. "As you all know, we heard from the blackmailer again, a few hours ago," Yanis continues, taking his seat. "This time we were ready for it, and my team was finally able to trace the phone the message was sent from."

"You could've saved yourself a lot of trouble," Drexler pipes up, clearly irritated. "We all know Ms. Perkins was the only one with knowledge, motive, and opportunity."

My stomach rolls at the pure venom in his tone. I don't have to sit here and take this, but before I can react, Jake's hand comes down heavy on my shoulder.

"Actually," Yanis retorts calmly. "Every single person in this room had knowledge and opportunity. It won't take too much imagination to come up with a motive for most of us. Ironically, only two people in this room can be excluded safely; Jake Hutchinson, and…Rosie Perkins."

"Preposterous! Your man is probably in cahoots with that trailer trash. Clearly your company is biased, you are protecting a criminal!"

Yanis calmly stares down a fuming Drexler, who has jumped to his feet, and I'm surprised the counselor beside him is not voicing his own outrage. Instead, Mr. Berry has slightly turned in his chair and is scrutinizing his client, obviously unhappy.

"I would strongly suggest your counsel cautions you before you deign to open that particular can of worms. May I remind you, covering up a crime is what landed you in hot water in the first place?" Yanis finally says.

"Sit down, Phil," Berry says, pulling on his sleeve. Drexler shakes him off, looks around the table, and finally complies when he realizes there's no support to be found in this room. Not even from a clearly confused Kyle Steele.

"Let's put the cards on the table, shall we?" Yanis suggests. "It started with a hit-and-run that left a very unfortunate homeless man dead. We have a hotel employee who was almost run off her feet just seconds later, by your leading man—" He points to a thoroughly subdued Kyle Steele. "—who had slipped his security detail to visit a titty club and get drunk. On your orders, we try to cover your star's tracks, and keep an eye on Ms. Perkins."

I squirm uncomfortably in my seat as sympathetic eyes land on me. Jake moves his hand from my shoulder to my neck and rubs his thumb along the throbbing vein there.

"And here's where it gets interesting, then Kyle decides to make a hard play, up at the pool area, for the woman who holds the power to damage his career and your production." I look up and notice the surprise on Drexler's face as he turns to the actor, who is staring down at the wringing hands on his lap. "Rosie Perkins turns him down but still he persists, making it necessary for his own protection detail to pull him away. Curiously, just days later, Ms. Perkins is attacked in that same pool, and if not for Hutch, she may not have survived."

The heavy silence that has fallen over the room is broken by the scrape of castor wheels over the laminate. Interesting that Simon Berry, for all intents and purposes Drexler and Steele's lawyer, pointedly moves his seat away from his clients.

"And somewhere in there, Kyle receives his first mysterious blackmail note, shoved under his suite door," Yanis adds. "But only when the second comes in the form of a text, does he finally decide it might be a good idea to sound the alarm. Right off the bat, you accuse Rosie, loudly and insistently, when there isn't a shred of evidence supporting that claim," he directs at Drexler.

I'm definitely warming up to Yanis. His supportive words go a long way to making up for making me feel like a criminal. I'm not sure exactly what he's driving at with this synopsis of events, but I know it's making the men on the other side of the table decidedly uncomfortable.

Kyle glances my way furtively, looking away when I catch his eye. Was he behind the attacks on me? Was Drexler? Hearing Yanis lay everything out; I have to admit, it seems like a pretty strange sequence of events that appears to have the star at the center.

"What is odd, though, is that there was never any follow-up from the blackmailer on that second message. Not until after another mysterious hit-and-run injured Ms. Perkins, and we took her in protective custody for her own safety."

"I have no idea what you're talking about," Drexler finally reacts to Yanis' presentation. "I know nothing about any attack on this woman."

Dimi, who is leaning against the wall beside the door, staying in the background, suddenly moves forward and leans across the table.

"Nice shades," he says, reaching over and fishing a pair of folded sunglasses from Drexler's jacket pocket.

JAKE

"Do you like baseball, Phil?" Dimi asks, as he studies the glasses in his hand.

"Dimas," the boss warns under his breath.

His brother ignores him, perching his hip against the heavy boardroom table as he twirls what look to be expensive designer shades between his fingers. "You know? Baseball? The bats, the balls, the caps? Do you wear a cap? Are you a fan?" He continues to badger Drexler, whose face is turning an unhealthy shade of red.

"What the fuck are you on about?" he finally snaps,

looking around in what appears to be confusion. "Can someone explain what baseball has to do with this?"

"Perhaps you can enlighten us," his counsel finally puts in a word. "Otherwise, I'll have to insist this meeting is over."

"I'd be happy to," I jump in, having remained silent so far, although not without some painful restraint. The brothers are good at this: Yanis lulling people into knowing exactly where he's taking them, and Dimas poking at them from different directions, keeping them off-balance. It wouldn't be the first time they managed to crack a suspect. "There was a witness in this last attack on Rosie. A neighbor watched helplessly as a large SUV steered deliberately into the driver's side door of her car. She had pulled alongside the curb when her car stalled, and as luck would have it, was not in her seat, but about to check under the hood." I pause, and observe the varied body language with interest. Drexler impatiently taps his fingers on the table in front of him; completely disengaged from the scene I've painted them. Steele continues to sneak peeks at Rosie, restlessly shifting in his chair. And Berry shows the only expected response, one of shock and concern as his eyes immediately go to Rosie. "The witness saw the driver," I finally continue, drawing their attention. "But that's not all, we also have some interesting camera footage that confirms his description."

"I still don't see—" Drexler starts, but Yanis cuts him off.

"Isn't it true you've been a Colorado Rockies fan for years? Ever since you were part of a movie production that shot on location at Coors Field? In fact, you own a VIP box, don't you?"

"Technically the company does, but yeah," he responds, bewildered. "I'm not sure what that has to do with anything."

"Rosie's attacker was wearing a white baseball cap with the new Rockies logo," I clarify.

"We're in Colorado," the lawyer points out. "I'm sure at least three-quarters of the state are avid Rockies fans, what are you implying?"

"Your turn. Take it away," Yanis says to Radar, who is grinning like the Cheshire cat.

"Right. So not all ball caps are equal," he explains. "When the Rockies introduced the new logo, they had a limited number of caps printed specifically for their skybox owners. It has the new logo on the front, but the outline of a golden star on the back of the cap." He pulls up two, side-by-side close-ups taken from the video feed, showing the front of the suspect's ball cap, as well as the back. Clearly he did some work to improve the quality because you can clearly identify the Rockies' logo and VIP star. "At about forty boxes, and four caps issued per box, there are only a total of one hundred and sixty of these ball caps worldwide. Even just in Colorado, the odds of randomly bumping into one of these are very slim."

Rosie is quiet all the way to my truck. She barely acknowledges Grant, who is waving at her from behind the front desk. It's not until we pull onto Third Street that I decide to break the silence.

"What's going through your mind?"

"I'm still trying to wrap my head around what just happened," she finally says, followed by a deep sigh.

What just happened was instead of taking what we pulled together to the authorities, who likely would've taken one look at the thin circumstantial evidence and dismissed it as grossly insufficient, we successfully negotiated an agreement. Without anything concrete to pin on one person or another, Yanis had suggested unbalancing both Drexler and Steele with what little we did have—which was mostly conjecture—to such an extent, when we offered them a way out, they would jump at the opportunity. Contingent on that had been Rosie's cooperation.

Per the agreement, Guild Film Productions would wrap tomorrow, and pull up stakes immediately. Drexler, Berry, and Steele would be on a plane back to LA before sunset, and only a handful of people would stay behind to finalize and clean up. They would also compensate Rosie for the loss of her vehicle and one year's salary—that had been Dimi's idea—and in return Rosie promised to retain her silence.

She surprised everyone, including myself, when she proposed to include a separate clause. One that stipulated the old warehouse by the railroad—which had been used as a makeshift studio for the movie—

would be turned into a homeless shelter for the disenfranchised, in and around Grand Junction. The cost of renovations to the building should be paid by Steele, as restitution for the hit-and-run, causing the death of the unidentified man in the alley that night.

"You did good," I tell her, reaching over to take her hand in mine.

"Did I? I keep thinking I'm letting them off the hook. Perhaps it would've been better to let justice take its course."

"Except in this case, there likely wouldn't have been any justice at all. Not for those guys. With the kind of money they have access to, they'd have been able to buy the best representation, and the case probably wouldn't even have made it past the grand jury hearing. In the meantime, the movie would have been doomed, which would have had consequences for everyone."

"I realize that," she mumbles. "Or I wouldn't have signed the papers. I can't help feeling guilty, though."

Guilt is an emotion I understand, since it's plagued me most of my life, as well.

"Perhaps there's something you can do to alleviate that," I propose, an idea forming in my head.

"Oh yeah? Like what?"

"Run the shelter."

"You're nuts! I don't have a degree, I'm not a counselor, I have no experience. I'm simply not qualified."

I patiently listen to her list all the reasons why she

thinks she can't, before I list the reasons why I think she'd be perfect.

"To run a place like that, I don't see why you wouldn't be. You don't have to, you can hire therapists, you don't need a degree, and you have proven you're not afraid to get your hands dirty. You have plenty of experience in hospitality and you have home-turf advantage. You grew up here and have a lot of connections to the community others might not have, not to mention a fair bit of leverage over the moneyman. Plus," I add as an afterthought, "you looked after your mother. You may not be a counselor, but you have the patience of a saint. You might just be perfect."

I glance over to find her looking at me, her eyes wide and face open, and I have to bite down a grin. She looks like a kid on Christmas morning, full of promise and anticipation. That hint of innocence is what drew me to her. The inner light she shines has served to eliminate all the shadows on my soul.

Falling in love with her was inevitable.

CHAPTER 22

ON THE COUNTER is the result of yet another attempt at home-baked bread.

I think I'm starting to get the hang of it, because on this one the crust is beautifully even with a deep golden sheen. It would make a pretty picture—just don't try to pick it up.

Today's sampling could sink a pontoon boat.

I read at the bottom of one of the recipes, if you're not happy with the results, you shouldn't throw the bread away, but instead use it for bread pudding. I tried that with Wednesday's sample. It says to cube the bread—that was hard, I ended up using the meat cleaver from the knife block—and then soak the cubes in milk to soften them.

Well, they soaked. All day yesterday and this morning. I was going to make the bread pudding for breakfast, but Jake had to leave early to make sure the last day on the set went without a hitch. All I remember is the slow lazy kiss he woke me with, just so he could make me promise to stick around for today. I must've fallen right back asleep.

It doesn't matter, it's not like I have a car. That's going to have to be first on my to-do list: finding some new, affordable wheels. The amount Drexler had agreed to pay would be transferred some time next week, so I'll have to dip into the proceeds of the sale of the house for now.

It's funny how the mind works; this past week, being confined to Jake's house, being free to go where I want was all I could think about. Now I have that freedom, I find I don't really want to leave. The small apartment over Grant's garage is cute enough, and I love being that close to my friend, but Jake's place is roomy, has these beautiful views, his bed is super comfy, and well—it has Jake.

We've just known each other for a couple of months, at best, and haven't really had a chance to consider the long-term with everything going on. I don't doubt he cares, but how much of that was for me as a person, or as someone who needed protection. Something that seems to come natural to him. Those lines are suddenly a little blurry.

I poke at the cubes that look no softer than they were before. I bet if I dropped those on Jake's hardwood floor, they'd leave divots. How is it, someone who can put together a decent meal, bake a passable pie—with the help of a frozen crust—and whip up a tasty batch of chocolate chip cookies—thank you, Pillsbury—I cannot produce an edible loaf of bread?

Disgusted, I shove the loaf away from me. A little too far, and before I can get a good grip on the pan, it falls off the counter and lands on the floor with a loud bang.

"Jesus, what was that?" Jake storms in the front door, a large brown paper bag in his arm. "Everything okay?" he asks when he sees my dejected face. "I thought I heard something fall."

"That was my spirit, hitting rock-bottom."

He chuckles, putting the bag down and rounding the counter to wrap his arms around me from behind. "I'm sorry," he mumbles, his face buried in my hair. "But at least it smells good this time."

"Hmmm." I lean back and close my eyes, enjoying the attention he is laving on the soft skin behind my ear, and taking in a deep breath. He's right; it does smell good, like fresh bread, cinnamon… and apples? "Hey, wait a minute." My eyes fly open as I lunge for the bag, pulling out apple turnovers, a bag of fresh croissants, and a beautiful, light and fluffy, Italian loaf. I swing around on a grinning Jake. "How did you know?"

"Well," he says in a conciliatory tone, "it was a pretty safe guess, when I left you up to your elbows in flour this morning, the result would be no different from the other times you tried. Thought we might need some backup, so I stopped at the Homestyle Bakery on my way home."

"I should be insulted," I protest weakly, as I press my face in the hollow of his neck, "but I'm too grateful you brought home goodies."

I feel his muscles tense against me and try to tilt back to look at him, but his large hand cups the back of my head, keeping me in place. "I like that." The sound of his deep voice is gruff, but heavy with emotion.

"What?" He releases his hold on me so I can look up in his face. "You like what?" I whisper, seeing the dark swirl of heat in his eyes.

"Everything about you." One side of his mouth pulls up in a lopsided grin when I pinch his side.

"You were talking about something specific," I challenge.

"You said home. That struck a chord. The only home I have known was with the Mazurs. Even this place," he says, looking around, before his eyes come back to me. "I own it, it's my house, my name is on the deed—but it's only felt like home for the past couple of days with you here."

The warmth of his words seeps into my skin and settles in my bones. Here I had been trying so hard to impress with my culinary skills—and failing miserably. With something as mundane as homemade bread, I'd tried to create some normalcy, some comfort in what—for all intents and purposes—was a forced cohabitation, when all this time simply my being here had apparently been enough. Since my father's death, no one had ever made me feel like I was anything other than falling short. Failing, somehow, at trying to match expectations people around me placed on me.

Forcing myself into a box that didn't fit.

It wasn't an 'I love you,' but it might as well have been.

I take in a deep breath; let it out slowly, and with blurry eyes, the years of feeling inadequate roll off me like the tears from my cheeks. I'm enough just being me.

"Did I say something wrong?" Jake's voice is laced with concern, as he brushes at my tears with his thumbs. I shake my head vehemently and a silly giggle escapes me. "Rosie?"

"I'm fine, Jake" I quickly ease the worry on his face. Poor guy probably thinks I'm one step shy of a breakdown. "More than fine," I add, resting a hand in the middle of his chest where I feel his heart pounding. "You said absolutely everything right."

I open my heart in the smile I give him. No reserves, nothing held back, just pure feeling. He scans my face before settling on my eyes, and I see his gray ones warming as he reads mine.

Quietly, and without losing eye contact, he picks me up and I wrap my legs around him, as he walks me to the bedroom. There he carefully lays me on the bed, undresses us, and covers my body with his larger one. I open my legs so his hips can settle between them, and primed by his words and the rhythmic rub of his erection against my core as he carried me, he easily slides home, deep inside me.

Even as he makes exquisitely slow love to me, we never once look away.

Not even when I harshly cry out my release, and he bucks and shudders through his, do we lose that connection.

That window into each other's soul.

JAKE

For the past twenty minutes, I've watched her sleep.

Her glorious red hair wildly tangled on the pillow, a high flush still on her cheeks, and her lush lips parted and slightly vibrating with every exhale.

She snores.

Not much, just this slight wheeze, with an occasional snort, when she's restless. It's a comforting sound I've become accustomed to in a very short time. A reminder she's here, in my bed, in my home, and safe. A sound I've come to love, like everything else about her. I want her to stay.

It had been on the tip of my tongue to ask her earlier in the kitchen, but I didn't. So far our relationship has been unconventional at best and forged in a seriously fucked-up situation. Divided loyalties, broken trust, and a vast expanse of gray area. A lot has happened in a relatively short time, not the least of which is the discovery I actually have a heart. Who the fuck knew?

Rosie is important to me. Hell, who am I kidding? I love her. But the truth is, we were thrown together by fate, with little choice involved, at least not on her part. I want this to last—I want *us* to last. I need to know when I ask Rosie to live with me, she is free to follow her heart, and not feel pressured by circumstances.

The soft buzz of a message coming in alerts me, and I lean over the side of the bed to snag my jeans to get to my phone.

All parties safely en route.

Well done, team.

Sleep in tomorrow, team debrief at 14:00 @ PASS.

I quickly turn off the sound as thumbs-up are popping up from each team member, and I quickly add mine to the group message. Beside me, Rosie stirs.

"I can't believe I fell asleep," she mumbles, rubbing sleep from her eyes before she aims them at me, a drowsy smile forming on her lips. "Sorry."

"Don't apologize," I return with a grin of my own. "I consider it a compliment to my phenomenal sexual prowess."

"Whatever," she snorts; rolling her eyes but the smile never leaves her face.

"The Hollywood crew is gone." I hold up my phone to show her the message.

"All of them?"

She sits up, and I'm momentarily distracted by the sheets pooling at her waist, leaving her fantastic tits on display. Noticing, she yanks the sheet up to cover them, but just as fast I pull it back down, lean in, and kiss one of the now soft rosy peaks. The instant hardening of her nipple is a testament to her responsiveness to me.

"Mmmmm," I hum, as my cock stirs alive.

"Jake," she prompts me, as she slides out of bed. "So did they? All leave?"

I lie back with my arms folded behind my head, watching her flesh jiggle enticingly as she scoops her clothes off the floor. I realize how much I like them just there. That would be perfect: Rosie in my house, naked all the time.

"*Jake.*"

I grin unapologetically as I swing my legs out of bed and stalk toward her.

"It's the middle of the afternoon, and we haven't even had lunch yet," she tries to deflect, retreating into the bathroom with her hands up.

"We'll eat later."

"Don't you have to be at work or something?" She's backed up against the vanity and has nowhere to go. From the smirk on her face, she doesn't really mind.

"Nope. And since we can sleep in tomorrow, we have all the time in the world."

Her hands land on my chest when I step into her, but rather than push me off, she spreads her fingers, and with her thumbs brushes over my nipples. Guess I'm just as responsive to her, as an electrical charge zaps right down to my package. With my hands on her hips, I swing her around so her lush ass is pressing against my dick.

"Fuck, you're beautiful. Just look at you."

I watch as her eyes slowly lift to find mine in the mirror. She looks like a Rubens painting; lush plump curves, with pale skin, stark against the fiery red of her hair. One rough, tanned hand cupping her breast and the other splayed on her soft belly stand out in contrast. Her yin to my yang. The light to my dark.

"Jake…" she whispers as my lips nuzzle behind her ear, and my hand slips down between her legs.

It's considerably later when we finally get to the bag of goodies I brought back from the bakery. For future reference, eating apple turnovers and croissants in bed, may not be the best idea.

"To answer your question," I mention to Rosie when she walks into the kitchen, wearing some of my old sweats for comfort. "The Hollywood threesome is gone, along with some of the crew. Just a handful are staying behind to finalize some stuff and clean up."

"Was that so hard?" She walks up to me and slips her arms around my waist, tilting her head back to see me.

"Nope, but I had more important things on my mind."

"I noticed." She grins before turning serious. "By the way, do you think instead of sleeping in tomorrow, we could head across the river to the Kia dealership? The prices are reasonable, and some of the cars are cute, and look," she says, pulling from my arms and pointing at a full-page ad on the back of the newspaper on the counter, "they're having a sale."

"You should look for safe and reliable," I point out. "Not cute and cheap. I have a guy who can probably hook you up with a good deal on a decent, previously owned car. Maybe a smaller SUV; a Nissan, or a Ford or something."

I would be happy buy her a safe vehicle, but I get the impression she might not feel that way. But that doesn't mean there aren't ways around it.

"Those tend to be too expensive, even secondhand," she protests as expected.

"Brick is a good guy. He does maintenance on our work fleet. Occasionally, he gets a bead on vehicles coming to auction or company cars coming off lease, and he fixes them as good as new and sells them. We can go see what he has in the yard now, and if there's nothing to your liking, he can keep an eye out. He's trustworthy and he'll get you a good deal."

She narrows her eyes at me, weighing her options and finally nods. "Okay, we'll check him out first, but I really need wheels to get around, otherwise, I have to rent and that's expensive too."

"Want to pick out a movie while I give him a call? I'll throw some popcorn in the microwave when I'm done."

She smiles and lifts up on her toes for a kiss. "Great idea."

I watch her move into the living room and plop

down on the couch, remote in hand. I toss a bag of popcorn in the microwave and slip down the hallway to the bedroom, where I quickly dial Brick.

"I have a 2017 Subaru Forester sitting out back," Brick tells me after I quickly explain what it is I'm looking for. "Came off lease and needed some minor body work, which is done. Thirty-three thousand miles on it, but it's got a long life left."

"What are you hoping to catch on it?"

"Blue book starts at around sixteen grand for this model. Are you downsizing or something?"

"Not for me, it's for a friend."

"Friend?" he chuckles. "You got bit by the bug?"

"Let's just say it's important to me she's safe, in a reliable set of wheels. Important enough to make sure you get fair price, and she can afford it. I'm good for the difference."

"Gotcha."

By the time the microwave pings and Rosie looks over her shoulder, I'm in the kitchen waiting with a bowl.

"What are we watching?"

"There's a rerun of *Postcards From The Edge*, it's a classic with Shirley MacLaine and Meryl Streep."

Not my first choice—not by a long shot—but I'll sit through it for her.

"Perfect," I manage through clenched teeth, as I almost burn my fingers on the damn bag, dumping the popcorn in the bowl. She starts laughing when she catches the grimace on my face.

"Nah. Just yanking your chain. I've got *Dunkirk* lined up; hope you like your history."

For the next couple of hours we watch Allied forces battle for freedom on the beaches of Normandy—at least Rosie does. I miss half the movie; I'm too busy watching the woman snuggled against me.

CHAPTER 23

"*Y*OU'RE GOING SHOPPING without me?"

"Like you could peel yourself away from your Dutch boy," I point out to Grant.

I haven't spoken to him in a few days and wanted to check in while Jake showers. From the way he answered the phone, I could tell he had company.

I forgot he'd made plans with Olaf and am dying to see how things are going, but don't want to put him on the spot, should his lover be around.

"He's still sleeping," Grant replies. "Plumb wore the boy out last night."

"Guess that's good news? I'm glad to hear it."

"Jury's out on that one," he says, a wistful note to his voice. "Don't get me wrong, he's got all the moves, but his mind was definitely not in bed with us last night. It's a little disconcerting when someone has their eyes shut tight the entire time you're doing the horizontal Mambo."

"Yikes." That does not give me good vibes.

Especially knowing the way it feels when Jake can't seem to look away from me as we make love. If he kept his eyes closed the whole time, it would make me wonder what, or maybe who, he was seeing.

"Right? One redeeming factor, he asked about you, which was kinda sweet. Anyway, enough about that. Do you know what kind of car you're looking for? You should go for a sleek little sports car."

We spend the next five minutes arguing about pretty versus practical, until Jake walks in and motions for me to wrap it up.

"Honey, I've got to go," I warn Grant. "Jake's got a meeting this afternoon, and if we want to go car shopping, we've got to get a move on. Best of luck with your little problem."

"What's wrong with Grant?" Jake asks, as he ushers me out the door and to his truck.

"I'm afraid his involvement with Olaf is not destined a long life, and it's not because of Grant; he is head over heels, but I think the object of his affection has one foot out the door."

"Ouch. It sucks for Grant, but I have to tell you, from what I've seen, these Hollywood types are more the love 'em and leave 'em kind."

"It makes me sad. He deserves so much better than that."

Jake responds with a sympathetic grunt as he backs out of his driveway.

The drive is silent, with only the sweet sounds of Fleetwood Mac drifting around the cab of the truck.

Jake pulls up to a business that looks more like a junkyard than a car dealership. Car parts, old tires, and rusty junkers litter the lot, and I turn to him with an eyebrow raised.

"This is the place?" I ask, unnecessarily, since it's obvious from the fact Jake turns off the engine, grabs his phone and wallet from the console, and opens his door, that this is, indeed, *the* place. Yikes.

"This is Brick's," he confirms, grinning when he sees the dubious look I give him.

"Honey, I'm not sure if any of these will be an upgrade for my PT."

"Don't let the front fool you—it's meant to throw thieves and lowlifes off the track—he keeps the nice stuff in the back."

No choice but to trust him, I take his hand and let him lead me into a small office, where a man in a dirty pair of overalls is working on the largest iMac I've ever seen.

"Hey, man," he greets Jake when we walk in. He gets up, moves around the desk, clasping Jake's hand, and slapping his shoulder. "This your friend?" he asks, turning to me.

"Rosie, this is Ernest Paver; Brick to his friends."

"Pleased to meet ya, ma'am," the gruff looking guy says with a salute to his imaginary hat. "Hutch here tells me you're looking for a new ride?"

"New to me, yes, but previously owned is all I can afford." I figure it's best to get that out there right away, before he gets any ideas. "Something not too big, but reliable, that'll last me a few years."

"I may have something. Come with me."

We follow Brick through a back door to a cavernous space. A former warehouse, I'm sure, with one side set up as a workshop, with three bays. Two of them have vehicles up on lifts, with a couple of guys working on them, and the third looks to be a spray booth, with an overhead door.

It's the other side of the warehouse that has my mouth drop open. Clearly this is what the junk outside is supposed to be hiding; an impressive selection of luxury vehicles, maybe ten or twelve in total, in addition to a handful of newer looking cars.

"In addition to fleet maintenance and general repairs, Brick specializes in bodywork on luxury cars," Jake explains.

"This may be a good little car for ya," Brick says, walking ahead to small, canary yellow VW Beetle.

"Fuck no." Jake glares at the grinning Brick. I'm sure he's yanking Jake's chain, and I decide to play along.

"Oh, how sweet! Ever since they came out with the new ones, I've wanted one of these." I wink at Brick. "Does it come with one of those flowers in the dashboard?"

"'Fraid not, no, but I can get my hands on some big fluffy dice to hang off your rearview—"

"All right, enough of that," Jake snaps impatiently, realizing he's being had, and cuts Brick off. "No dice, no flowers, and no yellow cookie tin. Show Rosie a real car, will ya?"

The dark red SUV Brick shows us next is gorgeous, and so far out of my league, it hurts.

"Great vehicle; Subaru Forester, 2017 low miles, good on fuel economy, and one previous owner. It's sturdy, she can take a beating in winter, and these babies last for fucking ever. Pardon my French," he adds as an afterthought.

"You bet, but, erm…Brick? It's gorgeous, but I hate to ask about cost, I'm pretty sure it's way over my budget."

"Well, what's the budget?"

I look longingly at the SUV—no way in hell I can afford something like that. It'll be well over ten grand. I'd hoped to get something under eight, but Dad used to say to never show your bottom line right off the bat. "Between six and seven thousand?"

Brick makes a clicking sound with his tongue, while squeezing one eye shut. The universal 'aw shucks' sign. Dammit, I really love this car.

"Too bad," he says, "it might be a tad steep for your budget."

"Brick…" Jakes gruff voice has a warning tone to it.

"Lowest I can go is eight." Brick shrugs his shoulder apologetically. "Absolute bottom price, it covers cost at auction and bodywork, but it don't leave much for—"

"I'll take it," I blurt out, not quite believing my luck.

"Hold off," Jake jumps in. "Don't you want to check it out first? Test drive it?"

I swing around, walk up to him, and plant my hands on my hips. "It looks like a dream, it's priced like a dream, and compared to my PT, I'm sure it drives like a dream too. Besides," I hiss, "I thought you trusted your friend? Would he dare sell a piece of crap to the girlfriend of a badass like yourself?"

"She makes a good point, Hutch," Brick adds, chuckling.

I can't believe my luck when thirty minutes later; I get behind the wheel of my gorgeous new SUV. A knock on my window shows Jake, a smile on his face. I lower the window.

"How about this; I should get over to the office shortly, but why don't you head over to your place, spend some time with Grant? I'll swing by after the meeting to pick you up, and we'll go out for a nice meal to celebrate?"

"Like a date?"

"Sure is. Safe to say, it's a bit like tying the horse behind the cart, but I'm thinking it's about time. I hear regular dates are what keep loving relationships healthy, best start now."

"I heard that as well, and I'm game." I keep a calm exterior, but inside I'm doing cartwheels.

"Good," he simply confirms, but then leans in to lay a sweet, soul-stirring kiss on me. "Should be there around five, see you then, baby."

"Later, honey."

I start the car and carefully start driving out of the warehouse. In my rearview mirror, I see Jake walk into Brick's office. The men shake hands, and then just before I turn the corner, I see Jake pull something from his wallet and hand it over.

It looks suspiciously like a credit card.

Sonofabitch.

JAKE

"Can't believe you got away with that." Brick eyes me from under his bushy eyebrows and shakes his head. "She looks to me the independent type. Obviously, that girl is much too sweet and trusting for the likes of ya, despite the fiery hair."

"Don't I know it," I agree, taking back my credit card and slipping it into my wallet.

"Hope it don't come back and bite ya in the ass. I know my missus would castrate me on the spot, if she'd catch me in a lie. Did that once back when we were dating, and I swear, she made my life a living hell for months. The woman can smell a lie a mile off, except these days it comes in handy with the kids."

"Not exactly a lie," I defend myself. "I never told her I wouldn't do everything I could to make sure she's got her ass in a decent, reliable vehicle. She knows I'll make sure she's looked after at all times, that includes a safe car."

"Still, wouldn't mind bein' a fly on the wall when she finds out."

"She's not gonna," I end the discussion firmly. "Once again, many thanks for your help, and I'll catch you later."

<hr>

When I turn into the office parking lot, Bree's decked out Jeep Wrangler pulls in behind me. She looks a little rough when she gets out.

"Late night?" I ask, as we fall into step walking toward the door.

"You could say that," she mutters. "Although it wasn't for the fun reasons."

"So no bottomless bottles and endless sex?"

She snorts loudly at that. "Fuck no, that would be bliss. I'd still be carrying the smile, but the likelihood of that happening is nonexistent, especially now."

"Oh?"

"That arrogant asshole is shipping me off to Kenya," she hisses, as we push through the door and walk into the lobby. "Calls me last night to give me a heads-up. I didn't fucking sleep a wink."

Before I have a chance to ask why she's heading to Africa, Yanis opens the door to the conference room and waves us in impatiently. Bree is not happy, and throws the boss a dirty look as she slips past him into the room.

"Glad you could make it." There is a distinct edge to Yanis' voice, although I'm not sure whether that remark is addressed at her, me, or both of us.

"Not a problem." I sit down next to Dimi, who throws me a wink. Radar is on the other side of the table, his trusted laptop already open. As usual, he's deep into what he's doing, barely noticing when we walk in.

"As of today, all our part-timers and short contract folks are on leave," Yanis starts, standing at the head of the table, his fists leaning on the table as he looks at each of us in turn. "This has been our biggest assignment—longest in time and most complicated in scheduling—and the demands on all of us have been tremendous. Especially these past couple of months. The wheels threatened to come off at the end there, but because of the commitment of everyone around this table, we have been able to pull it off." He sits down, running his hand through his hair. "Still…this assignment leaves me conflicted, as I think it does some of you. It's caused some tensions between some of us, which is why I felt it necessary to debrief."

I look over to find Yanis' eyes on me, before he shifts them to Bree, who refuses to look up. The room is uncomfortably silent, and even Radar seems subdued.

"We walk a fine line," he continues. "Our responsibility is to our clients, and although we don't generally participate in anything illegal, the job doesn't always align with the law. But in this case, we stuck our necks out. We challenged our moral compass, at least we did mine, and it really sticks in my craw that a couple of rich, entitled, amoral assholes get to walk away without so much as a wrinkle." Abruptly he stands up, shoving his chair back and moves to the window, staring outside. "An innocent man is dead, and I feel sick to my stomach that the only reason there'll be no justice for him is because he was living on the fringes of society, while the man responsible resides at the top of it. An innocent, hardworking woman was hauled through the mud, targeted and attacked, and she doesn't get justice either. As restitution, she just gets a payoff these guys don't even feel in their wallet, and in return is expected to turn a blind eye." Yanis barks out a derisive laugh. "And we…we walk away with a little bit more of our soul left behind on the job. All for the almighty dollar. *Sonofabitch*, some days I wonder what the fuck we're doing out there."

His words resonate. It's what eats at me too, on some jobs more than others, but I feel that casual erosion of my core values. The slight shifting of boundaries that may seem innocent enough when you look at one case, but when added together make up a total rezoning of what is acceptable. Even if I could argue the death in the alley was accidental, what happened to Rosie was calculated. The fact someone, who tried to kill my girl, is walking around scot-free, gnaws in my gut.

"Perspective," Bree pipes up to my surprise, her voice soft as she gazes over at Yanis, his back to the room and his forehead leaning against the window. Other than a slight shift of his shoulders when she starts speaking, he doesn't move. "There would've been no form of justice that could've brought the dead man in the alley back to life. There would've been no shelter going up, that will mean safety and opportunities for those like him, the marginalized. And I bet if you gave Rosie a choice between erasing these past few months, if it meant she'd have give up Hutch, she would tell you where to get off."

"In a heartbeat," Dimas adds, with a smirk in my direction.

Bree gets up and moves behind Yanis at the window, putting a hand in the middle of his back, in contrast with her earlier anger at him. "We work in the gray zone; that space between light and dark, where only those with a strong moral sense can stay standing. So perhaps, there was no judicial fairness in this case, but it sure reached the best possible outcome under your guidance."

"Bree," he mumbles, turning as he grabs Bree's hand, pressing it against his chest for a moment before dragging his eyes from her upturned face and scanning the room. "All right, enough of this shit. Let's get down to business."

Thank fuck.

The next hour we go over the technical aspects of the assignment; what worked, what didn't, and where to get better. Every PASS job is analyzed, both before and after the work is done, with an eye on improving our performance, both individually and as a team. It allows for effective use of our assets on future gigs.

"There's just one thing that still bugs me," Radar says after Yanis finally proposes to move on to upcoming projects. The rest of us groan; it already feels like we've been beating a dead horse. "The southpaw. I would've sworn whomever was messing with that camera was left-handed. I would've bet my life on it."

We've already gone over this. Both Drexler and Steele are right-handed, but it was argued whoever sprayed the camera up on the second floor, could've used their left hand because they were holding something in the right. It's possible, but clearly Radar can't let it go.

"For the sake of argument, do we know who the confirmed lefties are?" I indulge him.

"None of the main players, but let me find it," he says, shuffling through a notebook beside his laptop until he finds something and taps his finger on the page. "Here you go. Three confirmed lefties, two of the support staff and one on the technical crew."

"Who are they?" Dimi, his interest now piqued too, wants to know.

"Sheila Grimes, one of the caterers, a guy on the road crew by the name of Luc Brassard, and one of the cameramen."

A cold chill crawls up my spine as I listen, almost detached, to the discussion that ensues around the table.

"What's his name?"

My question gets lost in the back-and-forth about

what could motivate any of them, and how unlikely any of those choices would be. So I slam my fist on the table.

"What is his name?" I repeat, looking pointedly at a stunned Radar. "The camera guy—what the fuck is his name?"

Part of me already knows, as I try to sort through the bits of data in my mind, letting them all click into place.

"It's the tall blond guy, Olaf Fens? I think he's Scandinavian."

"Dutch," I correct, shoving my chair back, adding as I walk to the door, "He's got something going on with Grant Peabody. I think Rosie may be in trouble."

Dimi is on my heels as I take the stairs down, two at a time. Without asking, he jumps into the passenger seat of my truck. As I drive off the parking lot, I toss Dimi my phone. "Call her."

Twenty minutes to get from downtown to her apartment feels like a century, and I glance over at Dimi to see if he's had any luck. The slight shake of his head is not encouraging.

"Keep trying."

CHAPTER 24

ROSIE

I KNEW THIS car thing was too good to be true.

Should've known eight thousand dollars for the SUV was way too low. Obviously, Jake concocted some kind of deal with his buddy to manipulate me into buying it.

I get myself worked up to the point I want to turn around, when I catch sight of Grant's house. His car is parked in front of the garage and a second vehicle, one I assume belongs to the flighty Olaf, is parked out front in the street. It's too tempting to slip my new car into the vacant spot left on the driveway, and instead of turning around, I pull in, for once not looking out of place next to Grant's shiny ride. Besides—I tell myself—returning the car wouldn't be fair to Brick. The man is trying to run a business after all. Never mind ending up without wheels again. The Subaru really drives like a dream, and I love sitting up a little higher; for once I can see where I'm going. That doesn't mean I'm going to let Jake pull a fast one on me, he's going to get whatever extra he forked over back. One way or another.

Normally, I walk straight into Grant's kitchen, but not wanting to barge in on whatever the two of them are up to, this time I knock on the side door. I've barely lowered my hand when the door is yanked open and Grant almost bowls me over.

"Let me see!"

I barely have a chance to acknowledge Olaf behind him, and Grant is pulling me along by the hand.

"It looks brand-new," he observes, running his hand along the side as he walks around my car. "Perfect color for you. Red."

Olaf walks up and stops beside me.

"I think so too. Very seductive," he says in his faint accent, throwing me a wink. "Seems appropriate."

I'm not sure what he means by that, but I shrug it off, blaming it on language issues.

"It's not new," I answer Grant, and drop my keys in his open hand. "But it's definitely gently used. It even smells newish." Grant wastes no time getting in behind the wheel, where he examines every nook and cranny.

"Oh look, it's got a moon roof. Sweet!"

Smiling, I admit, my eye caught on that when I first saw it. In my younger years, I'd always wished for some sporty convertible one day, and although the SUV is the more practical choice for someone my age, I like the idea of being able to feel the sun on my head and the wind in my hair. It inspires fantasies of road trips to places I've always wanted to go.

"Come on. Hop in," Grant urges, excitement on his face. "We'll take a little test drive with the roof open."

"You have something in the oven," Olaf reminds him, causing his face to drop.

"Shucks. That's right too—forgot about the baked apples."

"He's been trying to fatten me up," Olaf explains, smiling in Grant's direction as he pats his stomach. "Seducing me with pastries when I try to stay in shape. Good thing I have a strong will, not much can distract me from my goals."

There is something about his words that makes me uneasy. I look up at him to find his eyes on me. His mouth is smiling, but it doesn't reach his eyes; they're hard and cold.

Yikes.

Something is very off in my friend's love life.

"You know—" I turn to Grant, who is getting out of the car. "—maybe sometime this week we can head up to McInnis for a hike? I'll let you drive."

"Let me drive? You know the only way I'll even come with you is if I'm driving. Hiking in McInnis sounds too much like exercise, and as you are well aware, I don't like sweating unless it's for the right reasons."

I snort when Grant coyly bats his eyelashes at Olaf, but when I look in the man's face; it's become a mask of detachment. Definitely something off.

"Anyhoo…" he continues with a shrug. "Best get checking on those apples, I'll save you one for later?"

I recognize a brush-off; both in Grant's words and the pleading look he throws me.

"Please, I haven't had a baked apple in donkey's years. I'm beat; I think I'm going to have a nap. See you guys later." With a wave I head up to my apartment, hearing Grant's kitchen door slam shut.

I have a feeling he's finally come to the conclusion there's nothing for him behind Olaf's pretty, but coldly empty, blue eyes. I'm sad for him, for the uncomfortable confrontation he's facing, but I know he'll be up those stairs to come find me when he's done.

Funny, I was itching to get out while I was confined to Jake's house, and now that I'm out and about, I just want to go back there.

I should be happy to be surrounded by my own things, but my apartment feels empty when I walk in, despite the fact I know my junk is all over the bathroom sink and my clothes are in the closet. This space should feel familiar, like home, and I can't quite put my finger on what changed that.

In the sink are some dishes I didn't wash, so I tackle those first, hoping that doing the mundane things, falling into a regular routine, might bring back that feeling of belonging I had when I first settled in here, not that long ago. With my kitchen and living space straightened up, I head for the bedroom. My bed remains unmade, dirty laundry on the floor and a few things tossed over the chair. What can I say; housekeeping was never my strength.

I'm restless; my mind won't let me settle. Being the target of a couple of attacks, just for being in the wrong place at the wrong time, is enough to have a nervous breakdown over. But that's not even all of it. It's like my life has become stuck on a spin cycle these past few months. I feel in constant flux, where before I led a predictable, even boring existence. Right now, just keeping up is a challenge. So much has changed already. Mostly for the better, with Mom looked after, the house sold, new living quarters, but also my job a big question mark, and of course finding myself in a relationship. Ironically the last is perhaps the most unsettling, or at least the thing I'm most unsure about, that I feel most vulnerable with.

I try to shake my head clear of the runaway thoughts, and quickly collect the laundry. I pile it in the hamper, and put away the few stray clothes draped over the chair in my closet. There I go through my limited options for my date with Jake. I don't even know what to expect, although he did mention a nice meal. That would imply a nice restaurant, right? So maybe a dress? Don't own many of those, but I do have a sweet little sundress that can be dressed up or down, depending on the occasion.

A touch vintage, white background with large,

deep red exotic flowers, wide straps over the shoulder, a sweetheart neckline, and an A-line skirt that flares away from the fitted waist. It looks cute with a pair of flip-flops or white Chucks, yet becomes quite dramatic when you add a pair of heels. Benefit is that I can add a few inches to my rather short stature, but the downside is I don't always do well on heels. The struggle is real.

Judging by the clock on my nightstand, I have hours left, no need to start stressing over what to wear yet. Maybe I'll have a quick nap and give my head a break.

The moment my body hits the unmade bed, the slightly out of place feeling I've had since walking into the apartment disappears. I close my eyes and breathe in deeply, letting the lingering scent of Jake still clinging to my pillow settle me.

The moment the realization hits me; my eyes pop open. That's it—that's what's wrong. Other than the whiff of Jake I got from the bedclothes, there's no evidence of him anywhere in this place. I miss him here.

With my mind settled and a smile on my lips, I let my eyes get heavy and drift off to sleep.

At first I don't know what wakes me up.

I lift my face from the pillow I've been clutching and roll on my back, alert to my surroundings. My ears pick up a slight sound from somewhere in the apartment; like fabric brushing against a solid surface. I rise up on my elbows and keep my eyes peeled on the closed bedroom door.

Again I hear it, and I swing my legs over the side of the bed.

"Grant? Is that you?"

When there's no answer, I get up off the bed and move to the door. I reach for the knob and next thing I know, I'm flying back toward the bed, landing hard on my ass on the floor.

"Olaf?" Confused, I look up at the tall, silent figure filling the doorway. His face is impassive, devoid of any emotion, and his eyes are cold and detached. "Is everything all right? Where is Grant?"

Wordlessly he steps into the room and a cold fist tightens around my insides. I scramble back until I hit the side of my bed, as he closes the distance and crouches in front of me. He tilts his head to one side, scrutinizing me.

"I don't see it," are the first words he says.

JAKE

"Get Radar on speaker," I bark at Dimi, who is not having any success getting hold of Rosie or Grant.

I'm hitting triple digits as I weave through traffic, narrowly missing an elderly couple trying to cross the road on Horizon Drive. Normally, I have the ability to stay sharp during stressful situations, but I'm struggling to focus as panic threatens to overwhelm me.

"I need all you have and whatever you can find on Olaf Fens. Any prior brushes with the law, family history, work, relationships—any fucking thing you can get your hands on, " I rattle off the moment Radar answers the phone.

"Already on it," is his quick answer before he continues, "twenty-nine, born in Holland. No siblings. Parents were farmers and immigrated to the US in the mid-nineties when he'd just turned seven. They moved to a small farm near Pella, Iowa, and were heavily involved in the local Dutch Reformed Church community."

"Let me guess; homosexuality is a sin?"

"Bingo. Looks like our boy was cast from the flock, so to speak. The latter part of 2004, he starts popping up on police records in LA County. Soliciting, prostitution, some minor drug offenses."

"Christ, he would've been what? Sixteen?"

"About that," Radar confirms. "His parents died about a year after he settled in LA, from carbon monoxide poisoning. It was blamed on an old furnace. Then nothing until 2009, when police questioned him after a retired casting director in East Hollywood, he had been working for as a houseboy, died in a fire."

"Boy toy is more like it," I observe.

"Hmmm, yes, police records show they'd received some complaints about the old guy over the years. Inappropriate conduct with minors. I wonder if our boy was getting too old for him."

"Possible," Dimi contributes, as I navigate a sharp turn onto a side road to circumvent traffic lights on North Seventh Road. "Rejection can be a powerful motive."

"True," I add, "but how does that tie in with Rosie?"

But even as I'm saying that, I remember the glimpse I got from the surveillance camera on the hotel hot tub a while back. The blond hair flopping over a blissed out face, mouth wide open, as Steele is giving it to him from behind. Steele, who probably discarded him, just like he did with all the other fuck toys he got tired of. Steele, who seemed to have developed more than just a fleeting interest in *my* gorgeous redhead.

"I'm two blocks away," I tell Radar. "Give me more. What does he drive?"

"Probably one of the production vehicles. They left behind two GMC Acadias, black, for the remaining crew to get around in. Avis rentals."

"Get the tags and tell Bree to get on the horn with GJPD."

"She already is."

"Good, then get her those license plates stat, because I don't see the car here."

I see the backs of Grant and Rosie's cars poking out of the driveway, but no sign of an Acadia. It's not until I pull almost even with the house that an acrid smell hits me.

Smoke.

ROSIE

"Where's Grant?"

He scares me, but with my back wedged against the side of the mattress, I have no means of escape, so I try to distract him with my words. To no avail, they don't seem to register.

"I don't see the attraction," he muses, his eyes carefully taking in my features in a way that makes me sick to my stomach. Controlled and calculating. "You're too old, too fat, and too plain for the likes of him."

"Who? Jake?"

This time I get a reaction; his eyes squint in confusion at my question.

"Who is Jake?" he asks, but doesn't wait for an answer before continuing. "We had something special, he and I. He tried to deny it, but I knew. I've known all along. I wouldn't have minded waiting, but when he started fucking everything he could stick his dick into, I had to do something. I thought making him jealous would work, but he laughed at me. Said I'd been just another hole to fill, that he'd never end up with some *'Muscle Mary.'* And then he started watching you…"

"What?" I try to process what he is saying in that bland, disengaged voice, all the while keeping my eyes on the left hand he's slowly reaching behind his back. "No. That's not it, I saw—"

"I *saw* him fall under your spell," he cuts me off,

more impassioned than before and infinitely more frightening. "Watched him eyeing you—came on to you strong that night by the pool. It seemed poetic for you to have an accident right there." He shakes his head, a low growl rumbling from his chest. "*You!*" he suddenly yells, stopping my heart as spittle hits my face. But then he starts chuckling. "You're like the proverbial bad penny. Each time I think you're taken care of, you pop back up."

"I don't get it. I haven't done anything," I plead, and I hate I'm about to lose control of my bladder. I was wrong about him; this man is not fucking controlled, he's batshit crazy.

"Sure you have." He leans in and hisses, his features distorted, just inches from my face. Then he suddenly straightens up and says in that cold detached voice, "You distract him, you have to go."

"But you're wrong!" I yell, just as I see something sailing toward me. Then everything turns black.

JAKE

"*Sonofabitch!*" Dimi curses beside me as I swing the car into the driveway, partially blocking the sidewalk. I don't give a good fuck.

A dark plume leaks from a slightly opened kitchen window and a moving red glow is visible just inside. Dimi beats me out of the truck and starts running to the side door. I'm close on his heels.

"The door is warm to the touch but not hot," he

says when I reach him.

I unceremoniously shove him out of the way and kick the damn door open. Immediately the red glow flares up into a bright golden hue, as the added oxygen feeds the flames licking at the walls.

"Rosie!" I yell, but immediately dissolve into a coughing fit as the acrid smoke forces its way into my lungs.

"Here," I hear Dimi call out. I just see him duck down behind the kitchen island, right where a familiar pair of legs is just visible. "Help me."

Pulling the neck of my T-shirt over my mouth and nose, I brave the heat and the thick smoke to get to where Dimi is bending down, slipping his hands under the prone form on the floor.

"Take the legs."

Together we manage to get the body outside, away from the worst of the smoke.

"Fire department and ambulance on the way."

I look up to see the neighbor from down the street—the one who witnessed the attack on Rosie in front of his house—come running up to us. I nod in acknowledgment, before looking down at the mangled face of Grant Peabody.

"Peabody," I try, although I'm not holding out much hope, his face looks like it's been through a meat grinder. "Can you hear me, Grant?"

I'm surprised when I hear a grunt and what I wouldn't have recognized as an eye, open.

"*Olaf got to her*," he whispers, barely audible.

"We know. We're on it. Stay still, the medics will be here soon."

"*No.*" He shakes his head forcibly, flicking a spray of blood from his lips. He says something else, but I can't hear it, so I bend closer.

"Say it again?"

"*Home...Rosebud.*"

It takes a minute to sink in, but when I clue in and turn to the garage, my heart drops like a stone.

Black smoke is billowing out of the cracks of the garage door, snaking up the side of the structure and already almost obscuring the apartment above. I don't hesitate, I'm on my feet and running, taking the stairs two at a time.

I don't even hear the approaching sound of sirens.

My eyes burn from the smoke, and the heat stings my skin.

The fire is concentrated along the far wall of the apartment, with flames licking up from below. The source appears to be from the garage downstairs, but I don't have time to worry about the floor collapsing under me, I have to find Rosie.

Using furniture to guide me, it feels like hours, but is likely just seconds, when I finally spot her on the floor of the bedroom. Here too, the fire has snaked up the wall and I feel the hair on my arms singeing. There's not much time.

"Rosie—baby, we've got to get out of here," I mumble, while struggling to lift her up.

There is no reaction. Her body is like dead weight

in my arms, as I stumble blindly toward where I think the door is. I don't even know if she's still breathing. I shake my head and blink against the tears. From smoke, or fear, I don't care—I'm holding my heart in my arms, and I have never been so scared in my life.

She's alive; she fucking has to be.

A draft of cooler air hits my face and I turn in that direction, forcing my legs to carry us outside.

"I've got her," Dimi's voice greets me, even if I can't see a thing.

"No," I croak, pulling Rosie prone body even tighter to me.

"All right, Hutch. Okay."

An arm is wrapped firmly around my waist as he guides me down the stairs and away from the heat. The moment I feel soft grass under my feet, I sink down, letting my legs collapse under me, Rosie still clutched tightly to my chest.

"Sir, let me look at her."

I blink a few times to clear my eyes and can make out the firefighter crouching down in front of me. Still I won't let go.

"You got her out, now let them look after her. You've gotta let her go, Hutch." Dimi's calm voice sounds beside me.

Reluctantly I loosen my grip on her, as she is taken from me and laid flat on the grass at my knees. Her beautiful ivory skin is dull with soot, and her luxurious red hair is singed and streaked with fine black dust. A mask is pressed over my face and rather than fight it,

I give myself over to the sob ripping from my chest.

The agony at the possibility I may have lost her is a pain unlike anything I've ever experienced. My life hangs in the balance with hers; I can't remember my life before her, or imagine a life after.

Love has always been an elusive concept to me. Something frivolous people indulge in, giving them rose-colored glasses to see the world through. Sappy, saccharine, and so sweet, it made my teeth ache. I had it all wrong.

Love is equal parts bliss and torture—it's passion and fear—and once discovered, it becomes as essential as breathing.

But right now, in this moment, love is shredding me.

CHAPTER 25

ROSIE

Good Lord.

I almost sag through my knees at the sight of my beautiful friend's face. Tubes and wires appear to tether him to the hospital bed, which appears at least a size too small for his large frame.

"Hold up, chickie. Let me get you a chair," Hillary cautions from behind me, and I feel myself pushed down on a seat. "The swelling will come down over time, and aside from the large one running down his forehead, his scars will fade as well."

"It's his spirit I'm most worried about," I confess to her over my shoulder. A slight movement in the bed draws my attention, and I catch the obsidian glint of Grant's single visible eye.

"Nothing wrong with my spirit," his gravelly voice rumbles from between his wired jaw, only making my tears stream harder. "And quit your sniveling, I'm not dead yet."

Hillary snorts behind me. "As you can tell, there's

nothing wrong with his sharp tongue. He's been a handful, full of his usual beans since he woke up."

"I'd kill for some beans," he fires back. "All you guys have been feeding me is Jell-O. That stuff is only good in a blow-up pool, with a couple of juicy twinkies tangled up in it."

His off-the-wall humor is music to my ears, and for the first time since waking up in the hospital yesterday, I let relief wash over me.

I don't remember what happened, all I can recall is Olaf knocking me out with something. Jake says it was a tube sock, filled with sand, which they managed to recover from my apartment. Or what's left of it. Jake had to fill me in on all of it.

Jake—he was the first thing I saw when I opened my eyes. He looked like he just crawled out of hell against the stark white interior of the ambulance. Covered in soot, his bloodshot eyes wet, and sucking in deep breaths through the oxygen mask over his nose and mouth. Pulling the mask away, he leaned over and gently kissed my chapped lips.

"Sweetheart."

I could hear everything in that single word. His voice, raspy from smoke inhalation and pent-up emotion, betrayed it all: fear, worry, relief, and love— such incredible love.

I tried talking, but couldn't make a sound. So I

held his eyes, and with mine, tried to bare my soul to him.

He wouldn't leave my side, not even in the hospital when medical staff tried to push him out the door. He held on tight to my hand, refusing to budge until they finally gave up and worked around him.

Although the scan showed no damage to my head, they admitted me for a concussion and smoke inhalation. Jake stayed too, dozing off and on in the chair next to my bed, and bit by bit, filling me in on the events of the day. He dismissed every nurse who came in, wrinkled their nose, and offered him a chance to clean up. Through all of it, he never let go of my hand once.

But this morning, when Hillary came into the room, he had met his match. She told him, in no uncertain terms, he was stinking up the place and needed a shower. When he resisted, she turned on her heel, walked out, and returned just seconds later with both Dimas and Yanis in tow. Only under threat of severe physical harm did they finally manage to pry him off me, and took him home to shower and change.

That's when Hillary told me Grant was awake, and I made her take me to him.

"Better get you back to your room," Hillary says, helping me out of the chair, her arm supporting me in case I get wobbly again. "Almost time for rounds, and I don't want to get into trouble because you've gone AWOL."

I lean over the bed to give Grant a kiss, but there's no safe place to touch.

"This would be an excellent opportunity to have you kiss my feet," he quips. "But I can't vouch for their condition at this time."

"Always a smart-ass," I mumble through my smile, as I carefully lift his hand and press a kiss on top. Emotion laces my voice when I add, "And don't ever change."

"Couldn't if I tried."

When we walk into my room, the doctor is there, tapping a pen on the chart he's holding, and giving Hillary a death stare.

"Told you," she hisses in my ear, before trying to hustle me back in bed.

"Don't bother," he says, waving her off. "Ms. Perkins will be going home as soon as her release papers are ready. Might as well help her get ready and dressed."

His words slap a harsh reality in my face. I may not have a home to go to. I'm not sure of the extent of the damage the fire caused to Grant's house, but from what I gather, there is not much left of my apartment. I don't even know if they managed to salvage any of my things. Not that I had a lot, some old pictures with my dad, a few old diaries, just memories; snapshots of my life to date.

I'm quiet as Hillary sets me up in the shower,

while she digs up a pair of scrubs, and some paper booties.

"You okay?" she wants to know as she helps me get dried off and dressed.

"I'm sure I will be."

JAKE

"Better have news for me," I growl when the guys manhandle me into the passenger side of Yanis' ride.

"Apparently airport security had a vehicle matching the description towed from the drop-off zone, outside departures last night. The impound lot filed a report with GJPD a few hours later, but by that time he'd flown the coop," Dimas outlines. "Our boy was in a hurry and skipped town. Hopped a flight to Vegas where we lost track."

"*Fuck.*"

"Not so fast," Yanis jumps in. "We thought he was in the wind too, until about forty minutes ago when I got word he was picked up." I turn and check his stoic profile, except for a muscle flexing along his jaw.

"And?" I prompt him.

"Cops were called out on a domestic disturbance at a gated community in Hidden Hills, at four thirty this morning, and found a man curled into a ball, lying beside a lifeless body," he reports, emotionless, if not for the persistent twitch of that muscle. "The body was identified as Kyle Steele. His head was caved in with the base of a sculpture."

"Jesus…"

"Steele's suitcases were found still unopened in the bedroom. He didn't even have a fucking chance to unpack."

A niggle of guilt works its way to the surface. Since yesterday, I've discovered, aside from being a catalyst, Kyle Steele had no involvement with the attacks on Rosie, as I previously suspected, and now the man is dead.

"Fens confessed his guilt voluntarily to the arresting officers," Dimas takes over. "I'm sure we'll find out more in the next couple of days, but I'm thinking he was still high on adrenaline when he arrived in LA. Not sure how he got even got there, he must've rented or stolen a car, but it's safe to say he wasted no time. Probably his reception at Steele's place was not what he expected, or perhaps he let slip what he had done, but it's obvious his object of obsession would have nothing of it. I think we already know Olaf does not take rejection well."

It's quiet in the car the rest of the drive to my place, each of us lost in thought. I can't stop thinking how small the eye of the needle Rosie and Grant crawled through had really been. He could've easily killed them outright, but I guess he wanted it to look like an accident so he could walk away. His delusion there was still a future for him with Kyle Steele was what motivated him.

Both my truck and Rosie's new wheels are in the driveway when Yanis pulls up to the house. I throw a questioning glance over my shoulder at Dimas, who shrugs dismissively.

"Radar helped. Rosie's keys are on the kitchen counter, your keys are here."

He hands them to me and I nod my thanks at the explanation.

"Now get the hell out and get cleaned up. Dimi and I are heading back to the house to meet with Bree and the fire marshal. She's going to try and get us in to pull whatever is salvageable from the apartment. The house itself has extensive damage to the kitchen, and smoke and water damage in other parts of the house, but that should be fixable."

"Thank you," I voice to both of them. "You don't have to do that, but I appreciate it. Rosie hasn't said anything, but I'm sure the reality will hit at some point. Anything you can save for her will be welcome."

"Of course," Dimi states as a matter-of-fact. "She's yours, so she's family."

Fuck, those words mean everything. I force down the lump in my throat and reach my closed fist over my shoulder to bump his, and I do the same with Yanis, swallowing hard.

"Before things get too touchy feely in here, you should know I'm gonna dock your pay for a thorough detailing job," Yanis comments, a disgusted look on his face as he sniffs the air. "You stank up my ride. Smells like a fucking chemical fire in here."

Relieved at the levity, I grin and grab for the handle. "Yeah, whatever."

I hear Dimas chuckle as I get out.

⌒

What would normally be a three-minute shower lasts a fuck of a lot longer. The moment the hot water hits my back and shoulders, I can feel every single muscle that has been tightly coiled since yesterday. Pleasure and pain, as tension is slowly released, and with it every contained emotion I've tried to control. Like sand in an hourglass, pouring faster and faster until I'm left drained and tired to the bone.

The only thing stopping me from collapsing on my bed is the need to get back to Rosie. So I grab a pair of clean jeans and a shirt, pull on a pair of sneakers, and am tossing the dirty clothes in the washer when my phone rings. It's Hillary.

"Rosie can go home."

"What—right now?"

"Yes. I just helped her get dressed." I can hear hesitation in her voice when she continues, "Jake…I… she can stay with me if she needs a place."

"That's nice, but she has a place," I assure her. "With me."

"Phew! What a relief," Hillary exclaims, making me chuckle. "Not that I wouldn't love to have her, it'd be fun to bunk with her. It's just when I suggested it, she looked almost disappointed. I don't think I'm her first choice."

"I'll be there shortly. Let her know I'm on my way."

Her eyes are on the door when I walk in, twenty minutes later. I left the vehicle under the watchful eye of the guard, after explaining I was picking up a patient. By the way Rosie is perched on the edge of her chair, she's ready for a quick getaway.

"Your chariot awaits—that is, if you're ready to go."

"I so am," she says with a big smile, pushing herself up when I walk to her, wrapping her arms tightly around my midsection.

I put a finger under her chin, tilt her face up, and kiss her mouth short and sweet.

"Then let's go home."

Her eyes glisten as she smiles up at me and nods her assent.

We start walking to the door when Hillary comes in, pushing a wheelchair.

"Hop in," she says to Rosie, who grumbles but still sits down as instructed. "Hospital policy. Suck it up, buttercup."

Hillary insists on pushing Rosie all the way outside.

"You brought my new car." She smiles when she sees the Subaru I brought, figuring she'd be happy to see it survived the fire unscathed. "Or should I say your new car?" she adds with a sharp tone to her voice.

Ouch. Serves me right to try to pull a fast one on

her. I'm guessing she saw my transaction with Brick go down in front of his garage. I'd been in a hurry to get to the meeting and passed on Brick's suggestion to step into his office to finalize the deal.

"*Your* new car," I repeat with emphasis, putting my hand on her neck as I lean down in her field of vision. "And *my* peace of mind to have you drive around in something reliable. That's worth much more to me than a couple of bills."

A little smile is back on her lips. "Apology accepted. Just don't lie to me again."

"So noted. And in the spirit of honesty, I'll admit I wanted to test drive it, and didn't just bring it because it'll be easier for you to get in and out of than my truck," I tell her, earning a snort.

"Not like I broke my leg, honey. I'm pretty much good to drive." I simply raise an eyebrow and help her out of the chair and into the passenger seat. "Spoilsport," she mutters under her breath when I strap her in.

"I don't ever want to see you here again," Hillary says, leaning into the car to give Rosie a hug.

"Ha. Afraid that's not going to happen. I'll be back tonight to see Grant. You'll tell him, right?"

Hillary promises, and after a lengthier than necessary goodbye—including some discussion about when and where they might meet up soon, and a whole lot of waving—I resolutely pull onto the street and aim us for home.

"You don't mind, do you?" Rosie asks after a

while, and I try not to look clueless as to what she's talking about. "Grant doesn't really have many people. I'm the closest he has to family."

"Of course not." I reach over and grab her hand, lacing our fingers together. "He's part of your life, that makes him my family too." I pretty much echo Dimi's words to me from earlier. I mean every word, even though the brilliant smile she shoots me is a nice bonus.

"And maybe then we can swing by Mom's too, if we're in the neighborhood anyway," she adds cheekily.

"By all means," I agree, grinning, because I know if either Mazur brother were listening to this, they would rib me to no end.

Whipped already, but I'd be lying if I said I minded.

ROSIE

"Are you sure?"

My response to Jake's question is to pull off his shirt I'm wearing, over my head, and toss it over the side of the bed.

"Mmmmm." He knifes up, slides his hands from my ass to press lightly against my upper back, and presses his face between my breasts.

I look over his head at the approaching night outside the window. In the light of day, I can see the mountain ridges in the distance. Beautiful, just like the man who is bringing my body to life with his touch.

We spent most of the afternoon in bed: dozing, snuggling, but mostly talking. He told me Olaf was in police custody, and he likely wouldn't see the light of day for a very long time, and why.

I cried when he told me Kyle was dead, in part because it made me sad, but also because I realized how lucky I had been. Especially when he gave me some insight into Olaf's history. A sad story all around.

At around five, Jake got up to make us some grilled cheese sandwiches. Neither of us had eaten since breakfast, which in my case was a cup of yogurt and a banana. Our stomachs filled, we headed out for a few necessary groceries, and paid a quick visit to Grant and my mom.

By the time we got home, I was exhausted and crawled right into bed and promptly fell asleep.

Jake was lying beside me when I woke up just now, looking sexy and relaxed, one arm tucked behind his head, and the other protectively around me, his hand loosely resting on my butt. So tempting. I didn't last long before lifting my leg over his hips and settling my aching pussy over the ridge of his dick. That's when he woke up.

"I'm positive," I whisper as his lips tug at my nipple, and his hands slide back down and slip under my ass, fingers playing in the wet collecting at my core. "I need you inside me," I finally tell him with some urgency. "I want to feel you."

His hands lift my ass off him, and for a moment I expect him to free his cock and slide me down on it. Instead, he twists around, flips me on my back, and keeps me trapped on the mattress with his body.

"I need you to understand something," he announces seriously, his nose almost touching mine. "Growing up like I did, barely remembering my parents, other than an occasional mental snapshot, there were parts missing in my upbringing. Things I should've learned from parents or family, that I was never taught, or shown. The only loving family I was exposed to was the Mazurs, but as much as they made me feel at home, I still felt like an outsider looking in."

My hand involuntarily comes up to cup his face. "I'm sorry."

With a smile, he removes my hand and captures it in one of his above my head.

"Don't be. This is not about that. What I so inadequately am trying to tell you is it doesn't make a difference that I never really experienced it, understood it, or ever used the words. Loving you doesn't require any teaching or experience, or even understanding. It just is. I love you instinctively, because there's simply no other way."

"*Jake…*"

My chest is so full; I barely make a sound when I say his name.

"Shhh," he soothes with a finger against my lips

when I try a second time to respond. "Just let me love you."

He leans to one side and grabs my leg behind the knee, pushing it up and out, before settling into the cradle he creates. My body open in wide invitation, he slowly fills me, until there's no room for anything else but him.

Later, when we lay together, our bodies tangled, sated and spent, I press my lips against the hollow between his collarbones.

"I've lost just about everything this past year," I mutter in the dark, feeling his steady heartbeat against my skin. "But I've never felt richer than right now. I love you."

The fingers of his hand in my hair twist tightly as he tugs me closer, his lips touching the shell of my ear as he whispers.

"I know…"

CHAPTER 26

JAKE

"I'VE GOT THE cooler. Do you wanna grab the bread?"

I wait for Rosie to get the bag from the back seat before I lock the doors and follow her up the path.

"Place looks great, right?" she says over her shoulder.

It does, it looks amazing.

Grant started the work on his house the week after he got home from the hospital, well before he saw even a penny of his insurance settlement. The large garage and apartment have been replaced with a smaller one-story structure, making room for the renovations he's made to the house. The kitchen was done first, built on the footprint of the former one, but designed as per his own ideas.

The final, and most obvious change is the large wrapped porch he had built on the front, along the side and part of the back of the house. Work on that was just finished this past week. Hence the reveal party today, a warm-up to the holiday season, as Grant called it.

It's been just shy of three months since I brought Rosie home from the hospital, and during that time I've laughed more, played more, fucked more, or argued more than I have in the past thirty years. She's given me a completely new perspective on life. I now have friends, brothers, a family, and as of two weeks ago, a rescue dog. I happened to mention I'd always wanted a dog growing up, and before I knew it, a mangy looking mutt, with legs the size of a small horse's, had taken up residence in my corner of the couch.

I watch as she steps onto Grant's new porch and turns to wait for me, her nose red from the cold spell that's held us firmly for the past three days. She stops me in my tracks. God, I love that woman.

"You coming?" Her eyes dance under the hood she's pulled way down.

"Right behind you," I say, smiling back at her as I close the distance, pull her toward me, and kiss her hard on her cold lips.

"Oh for Pete's sake, you're like fucking Siamese twins. Every time I see you two, your lips are fused together. Do you have to be so disgustingly happy?"

Rosie giggles in my arms, before she twists free and throws herself in her friend's arms. "Come here, you big grump. You're just jealous because Richard is on call this weekend." He grumbles, but lets her hook his arm and drag him inside.

Ironically, a few weeks after Grant was released, he bumped into the ER doc, who'd patched up his face, in the meat department of the City Market around the corner. As the story goes, sparks were flying over the free-range pork display. Grant's doc is a good guy. A little older than Grant, but according to my woman, he's a silver fox. Whatever that means.

I grab the bread bag she dropped on the steps when I kissed her and follow along behind them.

I glance around the room and catch Hillary throwing her head back as she laughs at something Dimi says.

There are groups of people spread over the living room and new open concept kitchen. The food is amazing and plentiful, and luckily Rosie received quite a few compliments on her breads—an art she finally mastered after months of practice.

A couple of us are at the dinner table, playing a few hands of euchre. Another skill set I'm afraid Rosie needs some practice on. The whole concept of left and right bower seems to elude her, but she's a good sport and laughs at herself when she mucks up.

"I need another drink," she announces when she loses yet another hand. "This game requires a far more advanced level of inebriation."

"Beer, sweetheart?" I ask, shoving my chair back.

"Please. Thanks, honey." She blows me a kiss.

"Nauseating, isn't it?" Grant says to the small

group. I shake my head and grin as I fish one of Rosie's beers from the cooler. "They're this way all the fucking time."

"New love," Marvin, Grant's buddy, pipes up. "I vaguely remember the days, but it must've been well before kids. Those little assholes kill the romance."

"Right," his wife says. I think her name is Neeta. "It wouldn't have anything to do with the dirty socks you like to leave around the house, or the after dinner tuba concerts you try to gas me with." She turns to Rosie. "Please ignore my husband, it's clear he was raised by primates."

"No worries," she responds, smiling wide. "I'm sure you both speak from experience."

"Ahhh…" Neeta chuckles. "We have a diplomat. Let me ask you; what's your stance on kids?"

The question comes from left field and leaves Rosie instantly blushing beet red. I sit back down and cross my arms, curious to find out her answer. Kids are not a subject we've broached, but I've noticed Rosie's glances every time we pass a pregnant woman or see a family with babies or small children. She looks with longing.

Kids have never been on my radar. Not with the kind of childhood I've had. I've never harbored the illusion I would be able to offer anything to a child. But just like with everything else in my life, Rosie entering my world has me considering possibilities I never would've before.

Her eyes shoot to me, slightly panicked, and I

give her a little nod of encouragement and a wink.

ROSIE

Why me?

Is the ticking of this biological clock I started hearing a while ago that loud, people around me can hear?

I like Neeta, I do, but right now I could shove her down a canyon. Grant clearly thinks it's all quite amusing, snickering behind his hand, and Jake…well, him I can't read.

Kids. *Gah*…Cute little babies with dimpled fists and wet gummy smiles. The pregnant woman, with a protective hand so naturally resting on the child inside. A rambunctious toddler, with a shock of dark hair and gray eyes, a miniature version of his daddy, from whose shoulders he discovers the world.

I want all of it.

For years I'd harbored the dream of a family, but eventually simply gave up even hoping. My fortieth birthday had been a come-to-Jesus moment when I felt I passed that invisible barrier between; *it could still happen,* and *your ovaries now grow dust bunnies.* That's what I'd told myself; women after forty do not have babies, until a couple of months ago, Hillary told me she was so excited, because a girlfriend of hers got pregnant and asked her to be the birth coach. The friend is a single forty-five-year-old woman. Aside from thoughts around whether you should, or shouldn't, make a conscious decision to have a baby on your own at any age, let alone in your mid-forties, the story cracked the seal on what I thought were hopes long buried.

Once a thought like that is 'out there,' it doesn't leave you alone. It's like the genie that won't go back in the bottle.

And a subject I have not had the guts to broach with Jake. Avoidance sometimes seems the safer choice, because you don't give someone a chance to disappoint you. Totally self-defeating, because you will get disappointed, it just won't be right now.

Well, right now has arrived with Neeta's question.

"Love kids," I tell her honestly. "Had dreams of having my own once, and then it felt like time just ran out. You get older, life happens, I had my mom to look after, there just never seemed to be a right moment. Recently I've been wondering…"

I let my voice drift off and look surreptitiously at Jake. There's nothing surreptitious about the way he stares at me; not a hint of rejection shows, just open curiosity.

"You can always adopt if your eggs are too shriveled," Grant offers with a wave of his hand. "I told Richard just last week I want to look at adopting some rug rats. He's not getting any younger, and I always wanted a family of my own."

I slide my arm in his and put my head on his massive shoulder. "Maybe try not to refer to your future children as rug rats?" I tell him. "But I think you'd make a wonderful parent."

"And you'd make an amazing mom," my slightly inebriated friend returns.

"Thank you, but the truth is, I'm not sure how kids would work now. The shelter is taking up so much of my time, and it's not even set to open until the end of February. It'll only get busier."

I'd been surprised when I heard Guild Film Productions wanted to donate Kyle Steele's earnings from *Basics* to finance the homeless shelter. Of course, the company played it up for ratings, and made it sound like they were granting the star of their movie his final wish. It's all about the ratings, even Kyle's funeral had been a media frenzy, and although *Basics* won't be released for another six months, the hype around the movie is already high.

Drexler called me a week later, just when I was building up courage to contact him at Jake's urging. He said since I put this whole shelter thing in motion, I might as well show him what I had envisioned. With Jake and Hillary's help, and lots of research on zoning, building permits needed, government rules and regulations etcetera, I had a plan off to him the next week. I received a one-line message back within hours.

It said: ***Now make it happen.***

So I did. I made it happen, with a shitload of help. It's so far the most singularly rewarding thing I think I've ever been involved with. But aside from caring for my mother, it's also the most time consuming.

Already I sometimes feel Jake and I don't get enough time together.

Adding kids to that mix is bound to make it worse.

I had too much to drink last night.

Woke up with a steady thump in my skull and was ready to cancel all activities for the day and stay in bed, but Jake wouldn't let me. He watched me swallow down a couple of pills with the water he brought me, and then force-fed me bacon and eggs.

"See?" he said smugly, when I walked out of the bathroom after a cool shower he suggested would make me right as rain again. "Now put on your coat. You know your mom is probably already waiting by the window."

I snort, because the only reason Mom waits by the window on Sundays is that Jake comes with me. Mom's healed surprisingly well from her fall, but her mind is far gone now. She hasn't forgotten how to flirt, something she still does with Grant to this day, but her new favorite subject is Jake.

When we drive up to our regular spot underneath her second floor window, I don't see her face peeking out from the sheers.

"Mom?" I call out when we walk into the empty room, Jake following in behind me. The door to the small bathroom is open a crack and odd sounds are emerging. I carefully push the door wider and peek around the corner. "What on earth?"

My mother swings around, shock on her face, just as Jake looks over my shoulder. She is standing barefoot with her pant legs rolled up to her knees, in the middle of a substantial, and growing, puddle of water, apparently trying to shove her cane down the toilet.

"What are you doing, Mom?"

"Watcha up to, Connie?" Jake adds.

She looks from one to the other and settles on Jake. Figures.

"Cleaning up."

I'm not sure what it is she's cleaning up, but it's making a mess.

Jake moves faster than me and with a quick, somewhat disgusted peek in the bowl, puts an arm around Mom's shoulders, guiding her from the tiny bathroom. "Why don't you tell me all about it and we let Rosie clean up the mess, shall we?" he coos at her, shooting me a wink in passing.

Fucking wonderful.

It would appear my mother had an accident, and instead of calling nursing staff to help her, she tried to hide the evidence. This by flushing her soiled underwear down the toilet.

Mom will not wear Depends. She refuses adamantly. There are times the woman forgets her own name, but she does not forget her pride. Of course the toilet is plugged up, and I'm guessing from the amount of water flowing over the bowl, she's tried several times to flush.

It takes maintenance an hour to get there after I discover she's shoved her soiled underpants too far down the drain for me to retrieve, and by the time the man is gone, Jake has coaxed Mom to bed and she is peacefully sleeping. She probably won't remember a thing tomorrow.

"Thanks for your help," I snipe at Jake when we walk out.

"Figured it would be good practice for you," he tries to joke. I assume he's referring to wiping butts or whatever, a play on last night's discussion about kids, but I'm not amused and not afraid to show it.

Following me around the truck, he grabs my arm, swings me around, and pins me to the passenger door with his body.

"Bad joke," he whispers with his lips on mine, before cupping my face in his hands. "Truth is, if your mom was in full control of her mind, that situation would have been embarrassing. I was trying to preserve her dignity, distract her, pretend I was oblivious. The way she is now she may not have cared, but I do."

Just like that any irritation, any anger, is gone. I cover his hands with mine and lift my mouth for another, much better kiss.

"You're a good egg, Jacob Hutchinson. Hey!" I yelp when he pinches my butt.

"Killing my street cred, babe," he says with a smirk, as lifts me into the passenger seat.

"Whatever." I roll my eyes and look up at my mom's window as he backs out of the spot and turns onto the street.

"You would, you know?" Jake says a couple of minutes later, hands on the wheel and his eyes on the road. "You'd make a great mom."

No reference was made to the whole kids discussion from last night, until his poor attempt at a joke a few minutes ago. Nothing was mentioned and now he hits me from left field with this remark. I'm not sure whether it's anxiety that we're actually going to have this conversation, which is causing the nervous fluttering in my gut, or whether I should just stay away from Grant's spicy enchiladas. I need a second to take a deep breath before I speak.

"I'd try to be," I say softly, turning my gaze out the passenger window. "I would've liked to have that chance, but it just doesn't seem to make sense at this point; with everything going on in our lives."

Neither of us says anything else until Jake pulls into our driveway with a beautiful view of the mountains in the back.

"We could make it work," he says, after turning off the engine and shifting in his seat to face me. "If you wanted to, we could make it work. We just have to sit down and talk it through."

"You want this? Kids?"

He shrugs his shoulders and smiles as he reaches and pulls me over to his side, and takes my hands in his.

"Not kids in general maybe, but possible kids with you? Yeah, I think I do."

EPILOGUE

JAKE

"I'LL TAKE CARE of the gear and my brother. You get your ass home to Rosie. Maybe she can lift your mood."

The mood Dimi is referring to is a foul one and it's been like that for the past three weeks. Ever since the goddamn one-week assignment in Honduras turned into a month. During that time the weather in Grand Junction went from zipping up a hoodie and my down vest against the chill when I left, to sweating my balls off in this T-shirt the moment I stepped off the plane.

"No maybe about it, asshole," I grumble, snagging my duffel from the trunk. "Unless there's a tsunami coming, don't fucking expect me in tomorrow morning either. Tell Yanis I'll be by after lunch to do up my report." I start walking to my truck when Dimi calls after me.

"Give Rosie my love."

"She'll get love all right, but it won't be yours," I return over my shoulder. "Get your own woman."

Dimi is still chuckling when I pass him on my way out of the parking lot. *Asswipe*.

I'll have a lot to make up for when I get home. We'd just celebrated Rosie's birthday a few weeks before the new assignment came in and Dimi and I left for Honduras. I'd given Rosie an engagement ring on her birthday. The plan had been for us to drive to Vegas last weekend to get married. She didn't want a big wedding, mentioning things might've been different if her mom had been of sound mind, but since Connie doesn't recognize her own daughter anymore, Rosie didn't want to make too big of a deal out of it. That was just fine by me, I wasn't exactly looking forward to that dog and pony show myself.

Instead we'd go do the deed—just the two of us— and would announce it at a party we should've had this weekend. The idea was to keep it all a secret until then, which is why I didn't mention anything to Yanis or Dimi. Rosie has been very understanding when I've talked to her, but I could tell she was disappointed.

Like I said, I have a lot to make up for, and it doesn't help I'm hitting heavy Friday afternoon traffic on my way home.

I'm glad to see Rosie's Subaru in the driveway when I pull in. Before I can even turn off the engine, the front door swings open and Rosie comes flying out.

"Longest four weeks of my life," she mumbles in my neck, where she buries her face the moment I get out of the truck.

"I missed you. Love you, baby. I'm so sorry."

I make a mental note to let Yanis know I won't take any assignments longer than a week at a time. If it means adding bodies to the team, so be it. I'll take a pay cut to make that happen.

"Hush." She leans back and frames my scruffy jaw in her hands. "You're here now. That's all that matters." She rises up on tiptoes and presses her lips against mine.

Four weeks is too fucking long without touching her. The kiss gets hot and heated real quick, as she responds to my hunger for her in kind. With my hand on her lush ass and the fingers of the other tangled in her riotous hair, I swing her around and with my full body, press her to the side of my truck.

The sound of a bicycle bell has me tear my mouth from hers. Two young kids snicker as they ride their bikes down the street.

"Time to take this inside, baby" I don't give her time to answer, but put my shoulder in her stomach and lift her up to loud squeals. The moment I walk in the door and kick it shut behind me, I see the balloons. "What's this?"

"If you'd put me down, you primate, I could tell ya."

I look around as I let her slide down my body until her feet touch the ground. "Rosie, my birthday is not until October."

"Yeah," she drawls, looking around her a little uneasy. "About that." Her eyes come to me and I visibly see her steel her back. "I know we've sort of touched on the subject, and I believe you weren't entirely opposed, but it looks like you might be sharing your birthday month."

I'm tired, I want to get my woman naked, have a shower, and sleep for twenty-four hours, and I don't have enough functioning brain cells to decipher what she's telling me. "I don't get it."

She pulls from my arms and walks over to the coffee table, picking up a small box with a much too large bow.

"This is my early birthday present," she says, smiling, as she hands me the box. "Open it."

I don't hesitate. The sooner I can get this over with, the sooner I can get her undressed.

It takes me a second but the instant I recognize the item in the box, I drop to my knees and bury my face in her belly. Her hands come up to run through my hair.

"A baby?" I can't quite wrap my head around it, but there's no denying that ultrasound image.

"A boy," she whispers, tears in her eyes, and my eyes find the clusters of blue balloons. If I wasn't exhausted I would've picked up on that.

Maybe.

"How do you know?"

"Because of my age the doctor suggested I have a few tests done to screen for chromosomal abnormalities."

I get to my feet and pull her to me, firmly declaring,

"Our baby will be perfect."

"That's what it looks like," she says, smiling. "They were able to tell the gender and I thought you might want to know."

"A baby…" I cover her still flat stomach with my hand.

"The doc says my due date is October twenty-fourth."

"A week after my birthday." I grin down at her.

"Unless he's early."

We stare at each other for some time, emotions almost overwhelming, when suddenly a thought occurs to me. "We're flying to Vegas tomorrow."

I expect her to protest, but she throws her head back and bursts out laughing, tears still streaking her face.

"What's funny?"

It takes a few moments for her to collect herself, before she answers with a grin on her face.

"You. You're so predictable. I already packed us a bag."

My nose stings as I stare in her beautiful eyes before kissing her reverently soft on her lips.

"Perfect.

THE END

ABOUT THE AUTHOR

Freya Barker inspires with her stories about 'real' people, perhaps less than perfect, each struggling to find their own slice of happy, but just as deserving of romance, thrills and chills, and some hot, sizzling sex in their lives.

Recipient of the RomCon "Reader's Choice" Award for best first book, "Slim To None," Freya has hit the ground running. She loves nothing more than to meet and mingle with her readers, whether it be online or in person at one of the signings she attends.

www.ingramcontent.com/pod-product-compliance
Lightning Source LLC
Chambersburg PA
CBHW070236200726
48293CB00005B/1645